Other Books by Robin M. Ambrozic

The Gray Mage Novels
Piccolo the Gray Mage
Piccolo the Initiare: The Dark Gate
Piccolo the Initiare: The King's Gambit

Gods War Chronicles:
Dragon Half-Breed Series
Dragon Amour

The Lovers Series
Tatum's War (coming 2017)

Miscellaneous:
Choice (short story)
Piano (short story)
The Executioner (short story)
The Grape Escape (Children's story)
Wolf's Pack (short story)
Night's Knight (poetry)
The Girl next door (poetry)

Dedication

Joan Joy Ambrozic

A wonderful Mother and an amazing author.

Thank you for all of your encouragement and love.

Dragon Amour
A Dragon Half-Breed Novel

ROBIN AMBROZIC

©2016 Robin M. Ambrozic. All rights reserved. No part of this publication may be reproduced, distributed, or transmitted in any form or by any means, including photocopying, recording, or other electronic or mechanical methods, without the prior written permission of the author, except in the case of brief quotations embodied in critical reviews and certain other noncommercial uses permitted by copyright law.

ISBN: 978-1-48358-928-2 (print) • ISBN: 978-1-48358-929-9 (ebook)

Prologue

Why does *love* require blood? Shouldn't love require nothing more than just an open heart? A heart vulnerable to the possibilities of never ending dreams, beautiful sunsets, moonlit nights, and any number of fantastic adventures in the depths of the eyes of the one you love? To waste countless hours in shared moments, which can't be described but are instantly recognized by the spiritual connection between them? Two lovers so closely intertwined with a common sense of purpose that each is incomplete without the other.

Isn't *that* what people imagine when describing love?

Now, I understand that love is a thing of strong emotion; the heaven of heavens, the hell of hells and arguably the most glorious, pathetic, euphoric, and most painful thing a person can experience in their relatively short lives. I mean, civilizations have been destroyed because of love! Troy and Camelot are two that come to my tired mind, but it's more than an emotion. It's like a drug. A drug so addictive than even the most potent medications throughout history can't be compared. But it's worse than a drug; it's better than a drug. Love is deceiving that way, because it places its consumer in an altered state of morality. Love has no moral compass. It breaks down a person's moral judgement to the point that it can over write years of learned sensibilities, and make a person do things that even evolution or religion has engrained in you not to do. It is its own *Being*. A *Being* of great power. A *Being* of cruelty. A *Being* of ecstasy. A *Being* of harmony. So, after all that, I ask: Why do people crave, seek, and desire it? I'll tell you in one word: Freedom.

The freedom to delve deep into one's own heart and explore a range of emotions that is incapable by any other means. To examine the very core that makes up a person's total being, and lay open the flaws and strengths in each of us. Who would do that? What sane person would want to expose themselves like a fish being filleted for the world to see. To become so vulnerable and naked that everything a person has done is open for criticism or praise. All for an emotion that offers no guarantee that the other will feel the same way as you do…. I would.

Have you ever noticed how cold stone can get if you lie upon it for any length of time? Or how blood, as it runs down your arm, leaves warm steaming beads that rises into the cool night air, just like if you were stepping out of the hot springs at Steamboat. I miss Steamboat. I never really gave much thought to those sensations. Frankly, I never gave much thought to anything around me. I have great friends, a wondrous family, and a life that is actually really fantastic. Unfortunately, in typical teenage fashion, I hate my life, my friends are average, except my family rates a ten. All of which shows just how stupid teenagers are. Anyway, I guess it's just a curse of being young I suppose. Youth is wasted on the young, some famous actress said. But that isn't really fair. Everyone views the world differently. In fact, I myself just became aware of how large and wondrous our world is.

Ever noticed how bright the moon can be? You really have to get away from the lights of Denver and even the mountain towns to truly appreciate it. If you just go outside the city and gaze up at the moon, especially when it's full, it's like a spotlight. A spotlight on the stage of life. Beautiful.

What is that? It looks like something is moving in the forest barely hidden in the shadows of the trees. Maybe my eyes are playing tricks on me. Funny how your eyes play tricks on you in the dark, even if the moon is bright. Shadows appear to move even when there is nothing there. But there are lots of things in the night that we are not aware of. Not the normal critters that run around looking for food or those that become food, but 'things'. 'Things' live in the dark. And not your usual monster movie things either: vampires, werewolves, zombies and such, though I'm sure they are out there too. I mean, 'other' things. Things that would make a vampire shudder. Things so hideous that to look upon them is to look into the very depths…what was that? Nothing. More tricks. Despite the warm summer night, I'm so cold. My arm isn't warm from the blood running down it any longer. Wonder why? Have you noticed that blood doesn't look as red at night? Actually, nothing looks as good as it does during the day. Except him.

My Dad listens to a band, and older band an there is a poem from one of their songs that reminds me of tonight. I think it goes like this….*cold hearted orb that rules the night, removes the colors from our sight, red is gray and yellow white, but we decide which is right and which is an illusion.* Beautiful, isn't it? I wish I could write like that. Let's see… I think the band's name is *The Moody Blues*. A great band, really. I like their music. I'm so cold.

But that isn't true either. I have seen the most beautiful thing I have ever seen during the day, and probably at night too. Probably the only fixation that defies my earlier observation and sounds as sappy as it is true. Even now, I can see his face so clearly, just as if he were standing right in front of me. Golden blond hair, cut neat against his ageless face. Hazel colored eyes so wise and warm, eyes you could gaze into and forget that time continued forward. And his smell. Oh, god. I use to get as close to him as I could, even from the beginning, he just smelt so good! He smelled like…honey…and the scent of fresh caramel corn, just like my grandmother use to make before she passed when I was in elementary school. His smell is intoxicating. He…Wait, did I hear something moving? The surrounding forest is so dark, despite the full moon. It is so hard to see now. I'm growing tired. Is something moving over in the woods? Damn, I wondered when they would find me. I knew it wouldn't take them long with all the blood I left behind. But I hoped. Their devils, you know. I can't quite see them, but I can smell them. Death and decay. I wish I'd recognized it earlier when I could have done something about it. But now, I don't need to smell them, I see their red glowing eyes watching me.

"Scared, cowards!" I can't even tell if those words came out.

You might wonder who 'they' might be. Remember the 'things' I mentioned earlier? That's what's sulking in the forest out there. My mind is growing slow. I can't think. The soft beat of my heart and the soft rhythmic beating of the egg fills my ears. I can hear the rustling leaves in the wind. Have you noticed that when the wind blows through the leaves it sounds like water? I love water and ice cream. Ice cream is where I first found out. By accident of course. Isn't that how most things happen? By accident? Happy accidents, I love them. Ah, I miss him. Those red eyes are moving now. I see them, even though my vision is fuzzy. Just now, a shadow has passed in front of the moon. It looks like a plane, but with a funny tail. The sound of its engines I can't hear but it quickly becomes a shadow against the night sky. My heart races and pounds in my ears, maybe that's why I can't hear the plane. Closer now, the red eyes are…cautious. The red eyes move slowly across the ground. I am about to die. Blood. Blood and love. One and the same.

"I love him!" My voice cries out into the night.

Cruel laughter floats back from the woods, or is it the wind?

"My blood is his!" I yell to the laughter in the wind.

The wind gusts and what sounds like a helicopter's blade chopping the air echoes through the night. The red eyes disappear, looking over its back I guess at the sound, and when they turn around, I see the fear in them. Fear! Deep fear!

"Afraid!" My hoarse voice whispers.

The red eyes turn cruel. Rage, death, and a lust for blood have replaced the fear - almost.

"My friend has arrived. My best friend, Brooke!" I laugh, but it comes out more like a gurgled cough. I feel something wet run down the side of my mouth. The red eyes move faster now. They slither across the ground, wanting to kill me. Needing to kill me.

I think it will. I sigh. She won't get here in time.

Love is the greatest thing ever. It solves all the problems; it cures all the aches of the heart; it makes each day a joy to live. I'm glad I finally got to experience it before I die. I thought I had been in love before, but those were just pre-loves, better than crushes, but not as good as the real thing. More like training wheels of the heart. But of course I have my best friend Brooke to blame or thank. I think I'll thank her. She's the one that started this whole journey.

The eyes race at me now. I see the fear, hate, and cruelty in them. Everything opposite of what his eyes held for me.

I let my eyes close and hug the egg as close to me as I can; just as I didn't get to do as often as I would have liked with him. My senses have become hypersensitive as I near death. I can hear the 'thing' running across the ground now. Closer and closer it rushes while my heart slows.

My last thoughts will be of him. I will remember, from the very beginning, how I met him, came to like him, and eventually learned to love him.

As I think of him, I cough a laugh. His real name I can't even pronounce. Never could. No matter how many times I practiced it, I just couldn't.

I hear the 'thing' leap into the air. Its mouth opening. In my mind's eye, I see its four large fangs dripping with saliva in anticipation of its meal.

But I only think of his name.

The one I came to love.

The fangs dig deep into my side.

I scream one word in pain – "Gabriel!"

Chapter One

Apollo Academy

Brooke reached across the aisle and handed me a note. My eyes shifted up nervously to Dr. Daugherty writing on the smart board with his finger; most of the other teachers use the pen, but Dr. Daugherty told us he thought it was cool to just use his finger. Magic he called it.

I crumpled the note in my hand and shook my head, no. Brooke nodded for me to open it, her blue colored hair, (the color of blue berry cinnamon flavored snow cone syrup, which no one could replicate), emphasized my compliance.

"No." I mouthed.

"Chicken." She mouthed back.

I knew she's was baiting me and *she* also knew my curiosity would eventually get me. With forty minutes left in Dr. Daugherty's

English class, the note was like a cookie in front of the Cookie Monster. My eyes fixed her with a steely gaze of death, but she covered her mouth and giggled.

I rolled my eyes. You might be wondering why I hesitated in opening the note. For one thing, it's going to be some dumb drawing, and despite Brooke's excellent art work, it will be a little on the raunchy side. Then I'll laugh, causing everyone to look at me, and I hate being the center of attention. The other reason was, as soon as I start to open it, no matter how quiet I think I'm being, Dr. Daugherty will hear me. Even though his back was towards us, he'll embarrass us both, which is why I think Brooke does it. She liked the attention.

As Dr. Daugherty began to lecture about the nuances of rhythmic poetry and finished writing the day's assignment on the board, my hand clenched tighter around the note. Dr. Daugherty's calm rhythmic speaking voice did nothing to curb my growing curiosity. I looked back at Brooke and she didn't meet my eyes. This made me believe that Dr. Daugherty had already deduced my transgression even before I had begun. I turned to look; he still had his back to us. Several muffled giggles reached my burning ears, but none more loudly than Brooke's. Knowing I should just give in, I resisted my urges for a few more agonizing minutes before running out of willpower and gave up. Keeping a close eye on his back, I pain staking, ever so slowly open the note, and without turning around or missing a beat, Dr. Daugherty's voice reverberated like a church bell through the room.

"Ms. Ritter, unless you want to share with the class the drawing of what Ms. Wasabi and yourself will be doing this Christmas break,

I humbly suggest that you put said note into your backpack and wait until lunch, which is only a small amount of time away."

My face flushed as everyone turned towards me. Brooke absorbed the attention as her blue eyes sparkled with mischief.

"I think you should make them show us anyway, Dr. Daugherty." Robby Fredricson announced.

"What they do on their time is their business, Mr. Fredricson." He said. "No need to embarrass them. Correct, Ms. Wasabi?"

Brooke smiled. "I appreciate your understanding of the situation, Dr. Daugherty. A woman's affairs are *not* for public scrutiny. Her time is her own."

I laughed as did others. Even Dr. Daugherty's shoulder's moved up and down with mirth. Brooke was indeed one of his favorites and it's because they banter with each other as if they were both from the 18th century.

"Agreed," he concurred.

I placed the note in my bag. "How did you know?"

He pointed to the back of his head with his left hand. "I have a third eye."

The class laughed.

Then he held up his right hand and wiggled his index finger. "Magic."

The class laughed again.

After the earlier incident, the end of class came pretty quickly.

"Okay, make sure you finish the poems by Cole, and I want a three page analysis of Random Matthew's poem, *Knights Night,* and Alexa Gharster's poem, *Loves Lost Labors.*

An audible grown issued from the class.

"But it's Christmas break, Dr. Daugherty." Nancy Ettle whined.

"The world still turns, Ms. Ettle." Dr. Daugherty whined back, closing his books. "People still work, the weather still comes and goes and the universe continues on. Times stops for no person. Three pages and I don't want to see double spacing between each word, clear Mr. Jones?"

Carl Jones, our star wrestler, nodded sourly.

Mona Fritz raised her hand. "Why did Random Matthew kill himself?"

Dr. Daugherty sighed. "A poet's life, I guess. Poets probe the darkest and brightest reaches of society and their own mind. They push for understanding at the very edge of metaphors, life's questions and how everything fits or doesn't fit. They remind us of what it is to be human; a monster, a lover, and everything in between. Some can come to grips with what they reveal and others can't. Sylva Plath and others are great examples of being haunted by their own demons and being unable to cope with them. I guess he was the same way."

Brooke raised her hand.

"Yes, Ms. Wasabi?"

"What are you doing over break?"

Dr. Daugherty's eyes lit up. "I'll be in England for two weeks rummaging through every out of the way book store I can find." He rubbed his hands together.

"That sounds fun." Carl smirked.

The bell rang.

"It is." Dr. Daugherty smiled. "Be safe out there, and love as much as you can."

I smiled. He says the same thing every day at the end of class. He's one of my favorite teachers too, even if he is the head regent of Apollo Academy.

The lunch cafeteria was crowded, which it always was. Even though the campus is open for juniors and seniors, the principle, Mr. Resler and the regents, have the local culinary school come in and prepare meals every day for the students. The food is usually so good and the cost so cheap, that everyone just stays. Which is the way the regents want it, I think. Each lower grade has an upper buddy grade that comes to lunch with them, so the meals are very diverse. Luckily, seniors can opt out if they choose. Brooke and I won't be buddies next semester, but we'll still help with the afternoon daycare for the kindergarten through second grade, so we'll see plenty of the kids we worked with at lunch.

Brooke and I wondered through the long tables that separate each grade. It didn't take long to find the senior table and I waved to Taylor at the kindergarten table; she's lives down the block and is a junior. She waved back, just as her kindergarten buddy tossed salad onto her nice sun dress. Taylor sighed and then a voice rang out over the din.

"Nick Carter!"

Taylor's kindergarten buddy buried his head under her arm.

Mrs. Shoen stormed over to the table and addressed him. "Is that appropriate behavior?"

Mrs. Shoen's lean six foot frame was very intimidating if you didn't know her. One of the nicest teachers on campus, she was an avid volleyball player and workout freakaholic. The prevailing theory was that she could take Mr. Winkler, the gym teacher and an Iron Man champion, in an MMA fight.

Nick looked sheepishly up at her. "No, Mrs. Shoen."

"What do I expect?" her voice rang out clearly.

"To treat people with respect, so I can get respect." He said.

Mrs. Shoen nodded. She patted him on the head, "Now, do you have something to say to Taylor?"

"I'm sorry Taylor." His voice very low. "Are you still my friend?"

Taylor's green eyes became teary as she hugged him, "Of course, Nick."

Mrs. Shoen nodded, winked at us and we moved on. She instituted the buddy program when the school opened. She was also the behavior specialist for the school, if you hadn't figured that out, but what sets her mostly apart from the rest of the teachers are her flip flops. It could be snowing, raining or a beautiful day, and she will always have her flip flops on. I'm surprised she hasn't lost any of her toes.

We found some open seats, nodded to the other seniors sitting there, and Brooke looked around.

"Who you looking for?" I put my backpack down, fished out the note and opened it. "Seriously?" I flipped the note at her. "A flower?"

Brooke winked. "I just wanted to see if I could make you look. Mission accomplished."

"You are such a bitch." I crumpled the note and looked at the menu on the table.

Each day the menu was completely different. Since today was our holiday lunch, the school went all out: turkey, stuffing, glazed ham, which was more expensive, and all the trimmings. My stomach growled.

"Christian."

"Christian Cameron?"

"Of course, who else." Brooke's head moved like it was on a swivel.

Christian was one of the nicest and albeit more attractive senior boys, but shy beyond belief. "Probably sitting by himself." I said. "Look over by the second grade table, he has a buddy."

"I know!" Brooke stood up and peered over that way and then waved vigorously. I couldn't see, but I'm sure he blushed. Brooke sat back down. "We'll be going to prom together."

"He won't ask you." I laughed.

"He won't need to, I've got it all figured out." Brooke's blue eyes clouded over again with mischievousness. "That girl, his second grade buddy…"

I nodded.

"… well that is Anne Thomas's little cousin, Catherine. She is going to be my go between. He's been tutoring her in math, and I've already talked to her mom, and when he goes over to tutor her, I'm going to have a meal all planned out. I'll wear my most seductive dress, showing ample cleavage, my wondrous blue hair all girlied up and when I come out of the kitchen, he'll…"

"Screech hideously and run from the house." A voice behind her said.

Standing behind Brooke were the rainbow twins: Jill Hotchkins and Katie Brown.

"Nice dream, Brooky Blue, but you have no chance." Jill swung her overpriced, fake Gucci bag over her shoulder. She was dressed in a very tight shirt that emphasized her very small chest and a mini skirt that barely was within the dress code. Her clothes hung on an anorexic frame, and did little to flatter her chicken legs. She pouted her too thin lips into a bitchy grin.

"He'll be going with me."

Katie nodded in agreement. Her dark hair and mixed racial features made her face plump, her overlarge chest jiggle with her nod, and her clothes were more down to earth. Alone, she wasn't that bad, but around Jill…major bitch.

Brooke laughed, which drew the attention of the senior table and most of the junior table. "With as many dicks that your mouth have been around, one - he'd catch something, two - he's way too classy for a bitch like you, and three - your stuffing is sticking out the side of your shirt."

I covered my mouth and several moans issued from the table. The reason they are called the rainbow twins was because of a little thing that happened at parties. Girls will put different colored lip stick on and give head to the boys, leaving the color around their dicks. There used to be four of them, but two were expelled from school, when they were caught giving head to two of the baseball players in the baseball dugout. Needless to say, the boys were expelled too, seeing as Mr. Resler doesn't tolerate any breaking of the school's rules. One of the boy's parents tried to sue the school, but they lost, and then the regents sued the boy's parents for defamation of character on the school and won. The money went into the general school fund. Neither the regents, nor Mr. Resler were afraid of parents. Guess that's why the school had a ten year wait list.

"You blue haired bitch!" Jill fumed and stormed off while fiddling with her shirt.

Several of the seniors nodded to Brooke who returned them. You don't mess with Brooke, she'll tell it like it is and it usually isn't very kind.

"Anyway, where was I… oh…"

"Ms. Wasabi?" Mr. Resler's voice boomed.

Brooked closed her eyes. She drew a deep breath and then opened them as wide as they would go, making her look like some Manga character. "Yes, Mr. Resler?" she turned to him.

Mr. Resler walked up to our table. He had short, dark brown hair, cropped close to his scalp and a slight balding area showed through his brown hair. He had on a bright red tie, blue shirt and black pants. "Did I hear foul language coming from this table?"

"Why, no, Mr. Resler?" Brooke said shaking her head. "I was just elaborating on Jill's inability to catch balls with anything other than her chin or forehead." She explained in earnest. "I told her she might want to use her hands?" Brooke raised her hands in the act of catching a ball that one of the other seniors pretended to throw.

More stifled laughs echoed around the table.

"Uh, huh." Mr. Resler narrowed his eyes. "And did you mention that she should wear a facemask, so they don't leave marks?"

The table erupted in laughter.

My eyes grew so big, I thought they might pop out of my head.

"No, Mr. Resler, but I will mention it to her, if it comes up."

More laughter.

"Please do that, outside of school time. We do have young children eating with us." He inclined his head and sauntered off toward the buddy tables, but stopped and turned to us.

Brooke shook her head.

"Got lucky on that one, Brooke," I told her. "He…"

"Ms. Wasabi, see Coach Winckler. Five laps for using the b-word."

"I spoke to soon."

"And try not to knock Ms. Hotchkins down this time, for she will be joining you." He turned and then busied himself with the third grade buddy table.

Brooke sighed, but nodded. "Oh, she'll see the dirt plenty." We laughed and ate our lunch.

The rest of the day went pretty easily. After the lunch room fiasco, which went around the school in record time, I wondered off to the first and second grade hall for the after school program. Brooke went to see Coach Winkler to run her laps, as the bell rang for the 5th through Kindergarten classes to end. That was one of the cool things about Apollo Academy; the little kids go early and the middle and high school kids come late. All the classes after lunch were electives for the high school, while all the main core class were early. This worked well, because of sports and jobs. Since the school doesn't charge tuition like many of the other Colorado charter schools, the administration tried to work with students as best they could. We have one of the best graduation rates in the country.

I walked into Mrs. Law's class and sat down. Her second grade class was just finishing up and as she let them go, several of the children ran over and hugged me. Those who were staying, started to push the desks back, as Mrs. Law helped the others with their coats and lined them up.

"Watch'em till I get back." She said to me.

"Sure thing." I told her as I started to pull out the games.

"One, two, three!" She commanded.

"All eyes on me!" The line replied.

"Everyone have a good holiday, and wish Ms. JJ a happy Christmas."

"Happy Christmas, Ms. JJ." The line chanted.

I waved and smiled. "You too guys."

"Okay, hands to yourselves and let's go."

The children marched out of the room.

I turned to the rest of them. "What are we playing?" I asked.

"UNO!" They yelled.

"Fine." The marathon Uno game commenced.

It was well past six o'clock when Brooke came in. She also helped with the after school kids, but mostly with the kindergarteners. As usual she looked beat. Compliments abounded anytime Brooke was around the little ones, and most of the comments are about how she becomes one of them.

"Tired?" I said as she slumped down into one of the little chairs and plopped her blue haired head down on the table.

"Why am I cursed?" she whined.

"Cursed?" Mrs. Law said. She was just cleaning up. The last of her second graders had been picked up by a mom who had a late meeting and finished writing the next day's plans on the smart board for after break. "Those kids love you!"

"That's why I'm cursed!" she moaned into the table.

I laughed. "Well, guess you will make a great mom someday."

Her head popped up. "No way. Best form of birth control out there. Babysitting." She took a deep breath and her blue eyes lightened. "Coming tonight?"

I scrunched my nose. "Where?"

"The game of course. You haven't been to one all season." Brooke looked up at the clock. "Crap!" Jumping up, she rushed to the door. "Hades ice, seven, see you there. Go Valkyries!"

I nodded as she sprinted from the room. Brooke was the goalie for the boys' ice hockey team. That is a story in itself, which I'll get into later, but let's just say, Brooke isn't afraid of anything. Not even the regents. Brooke was a natural though. She seemed to be talented at everything she tried. I often wished I had that kind of talent.

"Why do they have a game on the night before Christmas break?" Mrs. Law said shaking her head.

I shrugged. "I don't know. Well, have a great holiday break."

Mrs. Law nodded and waved. "You to, JJ. Have fun."

I waved and walked toward Apollo Hall. The sun had long set and I could see little snow devils blowing around outside from the hallway lights. I wondered how Brooke's run outside went. Guess it wasn't too bad, but I bet Jill froze.

As I turned out of the second grade hall and entered the main hallway that connected the front offices to the rest of the school, something in the corner caught my eye. I stopped and stared. The corner was dark. It struck me as strange at first, for the lighting in the school was usually very good. Mr. Resler believed it should be as bright inside as it was outside. But the longer I stared, the more unnerved I became. I couldn't put my finger on it though. I guess

I thought the shadow in the corner seemed different. It wasn't like the light from the ceiling couldn't penetrate the shadow. But more like the shadow was trying to hide in a shadow that wasn't there to begin with.

Then something appeared to move and the hair on the back of my neck rose up. Two red eyes suddenly materialized within the shadow. I stepped back involuntarily as Ms. Pendragon came rushing down the stairs at the end of the hallway from the upper classrooms. The red eyes flashed with what appeared to be fear before disappearing like smoke on the wind. Upon seeing me, she stopped. In the hallway lights, her gray bangs stood out even more against her velvet black hair, and they seemed to glow. Looking back, the shadow was gone. The after image of the red eyes lingered, like a flash going off in your face. Light collected into the corner to illuminate it just as the architect had designed it to. Baffled, the hair on my neck remained at attention and I began to doubt I saw anything.

Ms. Pendragon slowly stalked over toward me. Her eyes shifted around the hall like a predator searching for the smallest movement of its prey. Her muscular frame moved easily along the hall. A feline gate that had made her the fantasy of many adolescent males and females who had her for class or saw her running on the Trail of Tears.

Her dark blue eyes lingered on the corner where I had imagined seeing the red eyes. As soon as she was within arm reach, her eyes turned from concern to interest and her beautiful smile graced her thin lips. She had on a modest gold turtle neck sweater that came to her elbows. The sweater's sleeves didn't cover the slight off color of her left arm that had a gray ash tint to it compared to her golden tanned skin. This gave her an even more exotic look that didn't deter most of the boys from puffing their chests. To complete her outfit, she had on a pair of nice blue jeans and a pair of *Wallace* running shoes. She had been known to go running anytime the mood would take her and that included taking her classes with her. Everyone knew to wear running shoes to class, and it didn't matter if you were in a dress or nice clothes; if she wanted to run, you ran. One of the many quirky teachers we have here.

"Are you okay, JJ?" she asked. Her voice was a little rough, not like Miley Cyrus rough, but more refined, like a soft trombone playing the blues.

"Yes, Ms. Pendragon." Though the feeling of uneasiness still lingered.

"Where are you going?"

I forced a smile. "I was headed to my locker, then over to Hades Ice for the game. And you? I thought most of the teachers were long gone."

A knowing look came into her eyes. "Is Brooke in goal?"

"Of course. Coach Winckler wouldn't have anyone else in goal. Not against Valor High School." I laughed. "He's not going to let them beat us."

Ms. Pendragon nodded in agreement. "Very true. I'm headed to Apollo Hall, need some company?"

I blinked back my surprise. "Sure," looking back at the corner. I still felt a little uneasy, and I'm not usually uncomfortable about things, but for some reason I didn't want to walk the hallways alone. Ms. Pendragon made one final glance back at the corner and then we turned and walked away.

Apollo Hall was on the far side of the second grade hall. The school was shaped like a seven story pentacle. Each side housed a different grade. If you were to stand the pentacle up on one end, the two lower triangles would make its legs. The elementary school would be the two lower triangles, with the middle school being the two outer triangles; seven and eighth grade on the left side and ninth housed on the right. The high school filled out the top triangle with tenth through twelfth. An outer ring encompassed the pentacle allowing you to walk all the way around to reach each of the areas. The outer ring held the elective classes and the administration. The only open portion of the school was the middle. This held the playground for the elementary kids, and the amphitheater for performances and graduation. The kids use the amphitheater as a gathering place for each grade. The amphitheater held nine rings of seating. The bottom ring and floor were reserved for seniors only. Anyone foolish enough to venture down to the bottom rings were met with open ridicule and hostile threats. Even the boyfriends or girlfriends of the seniors, who were underclassmen, ventured there with caution. The eighth and seventh rings were for the juniors; sixth and fifth rings for the sophomores; forth and third rings for the freshman; second ring for the eighth graders, and the first ring for the seventh graders. Each grade had a sphere of influence that was respected by all the other classes and none ventured into each other's territory.

Ms. Pendragon and I walked along the outer ring towards the back of the school, while the athletic complex came into view. Unlike the school, the sports complex harkened back to ancient Rome, and could have easily been mistaken for a Roman town. The football stadium was like a miniature coliseum upon entering. The ice rink's façade was designed with columns running its length, a cobble stone path paralleled the columns, which led you to the tennis courts that were on the north side with the lacrosse and practice fields. On the south side was the baseball field that was also used as the little kids' soccer field much to the annoyance of the baseball coaches.

Despite its ancient look and feel, the athletic complex was a state of the art money making machine. Two full rinks with exceptional seating was the bread and butter of the school and the envy of the state. They were in use twenty hours a day every day except on Sundays, when maintenance was completed. State of the art solar and wind turbines provided the electricity for the ball fields, the twelve tennis courts, natatorium, the ice rinks and the small restaurant that was the centerpiece of the complex.

Plenty of parking separated the main school from the sports complex, which was why most of the state tournaments were held here. The front gate that led you off of Broadway Ave., had a little guard station to check incoming visitors known as the West Bunker. Every upper classmen had to work one semester in the morning, afternoon or evening; it was part of their community service hours for the school. When the main gate was closed after hours, there was a gate on the south side with a guard shack, known as the South Bunker, to let people into the sports complex off of Dry Creek Rd. Since Apollo Academy didn't charge its students, the revenue generated by the ice rinks and the natatorium kept the school in the black, along with generous contributions from Sean Donahue, CEO and Co-founder of Alien Inscriptions Technologies. Because of that, those monies made the school independent of donors and the assumed obligations that came with those donations. This made the school a place of learning instead of politics.

As we passed one of the many open spaces in the outer ring, a couple was canoodling on one of the couches. We stopped.

"If you are going to the game," Ms. Pendragon's voice boomed, "you are not going to find a ticket up her shirt!"

Matt's hand quickly shot away from where it was headed and Sarah looked up mortified. Matt's dark skin darkened even more at the embarrassment of being caught and Sarah quickly covered her reddening cheeks.

"Yes, Ms. Pendragon." Matt stammered. They grabbed their backpacks and quickly scampered down the hall.

"Don't let me catch you in the school!" She lifted her left arm and the gray skin on her arm shimmered in the hallway light. She huffed. "I miss those days."

I laughed. As she dropped her arm to her side, my eyes couldn't help but stare. She noticed.

"Happened when I was young." She said.

At having being caught, I flushed and looked away. "I'm sorry, I didn't mean to stare." I stammered.

She laughed, which was musical, but touched with a deep sadness. "Don't be embarrassed, you're not the first. I got very sick one time, almost died," she started. "I was about your age, living in Germany in a small village high up in the mountains. My grandfather was a simple man, grew grapes for a very expensive winery. I slipped and my left arm got drenched in some chemical pesticides that the winery had sent to my grandfather to use." She chuckled. "He never used pesticides in his life and was furious, sued them."

"What happened?"

A broad smile came to her lips, "Now he owns the winery."

"Is that where your parents are?" I asked as we resumed our journey.

"No, they passed away when I was still young."

I immediately regretted my question. "I'm so sorry, Ms. Pendragon."

She waved aside the sympathy. "No need to be sorry. Random things happen."

We walked on in silence. I didn't know why, but I felt a sense of honor come over me that she would share that with me. Not much was known about Ms. Pendragon. She rarely talked about herself and if anyone asked her a question, she would quickly turn it around to where you were talking about yourself again. I vowed to keep her secret to myself.

"Well, here you go, JJ." We stopped. "I have to go see Professor Eitle. Enjoy the game." She waved and continued around the ring.

"Bye, Ms. Pendragon. Have a great break."

She waved back and disappeared. I hurried to my locker, gathered what I needed and headed off towards the game.

Chapter Two

Christmas Jitters

I waited inside the Edesia at the bar for Brooke. Named after the Roman Goddess of feasting, the food was really good and it was a favorite spot for Dr. Marcus, the econ teacher to hold classes. The game had ended with an overtime 1-0 win for the Valkyries. It was Brooke's ninth shutout of the season much to Valor's goalie Marco Falkenstein's dismay. He was rated number two behind Brooke in the state. I waved to Connor behind the bar and he nodded and began to make me another virgin margarita. Connor had graduated three years ago and worked part time during his off time from college for extra cash. He had been a star diver his senior year at Apollo Academy, which would have been my freshman year. He was quiet and shy, but had a quiet humor that was really funny if you could catch the side comments under his breath. He dropped it off, smiled and walked back to the counter to continue washing the glasses as the restaurant was beginning to close. My eyes lingered on one of the many T.V.'s on the wall while I waited for her. Since Brooke was the only girl on the team, she got the girl's locker room to herself and always tried to run the hot water out.

Coach Winckler was grinning and extremely pleased as he came out of the locker room hallway. The restaurant was mostly empty with some of the parents and boys from the team finishing up their meals. Coach Winckler nodded to several players and came over to me and pulled up a stool. He was a large muscular man, with a black goatee speckled with gray and a bald head. His smile was broad and his laugh full and deep. He reminded me of a Viking warrior.

"Hi, JJ." His deep voice boomed.

"Congrats on the win, Coach Winckler." My voice cracked as I pressed my forehead from the brain freeze.

He laughed. "Might want to drink that slower. Thank you. Brooke played well out there. She is a fiery beast in goal."

My eyes began to water as the brain freeze slowly receded. "I know. I love how she just sits in goal like a wall, even when the opposing team is coming at her, then 'wham' she juts out and makes the save or block. I think it really frustrates the other players."

"Ah," he moaned. "Don't remind me. It drives me nuts! It's almost like she is asleep in goal. Makes my heart skip beats. That girl is going to give me a heart attack."

"Not before we win the state title." Brooke's voice floated over his back.

She walked in, dumped her stuff on the ground at the table near the bar and sat down. "Connor, could you get me a diet Dr. Pepper please?"

"Sure thing, Cinnamon." Connor said. "Do you want anything to eat? I don't think the micro wave has been cleaned yet?"

Brooke shook her head. "No, JJ and I are going out to get something to eat, but thank you." She huffed. "Man, I am tired!"

"You wouldn't be if you would stay in goal when we are on power plays." Coach Winckler gripped.

"Then we'd lose precious time. You like it when I go out, it creates more opportunities for our team if the opposing team has less time to change lines." She winked at him. "Besides. The puck never gets by me? So why worry?"

"Because," He boomed. "That isn't what goalies do!"

Brooke waved her hand at him. "Being in goal all the time is boring. I need some spice!"

Coach Winckler shook his head and got up. "I'm not going to argue with you…" He started.

"Only because you know you would lose." She smiled.

"… No, I'm not going to let you raise my blood pressure any more than you already do."

"You are a wise man, sensei." She put her hands together and bowed.

Coach Winckler rolled his eyes and left.

I chuckled. "You are crazy."

"It's the blue hair."

Connor brought Brooke her usual drink, we talked about the game, finished our drinks and left. I climbed into my candy apple red

CJ Jeep and followed Brooke in her Accord to our favorite place; the Cyber Dragon Café.

On the way I called my Dad to let him know where we would be going and when I would be home. He told me to be careful in the snow that he loved me, and we'd talk when I got home. I told him I loved him too and knew he'd be awake when I got home. See, my dad was an animation graphic artist for video games. He worked on lots of games and was really good. Since my mom passed away from breast cancer, when I was ten, he never remarried. Being an only child, we had become more close than most other families, I supposed. Even though he was my dad, he was also my best friend and I his. It was kind of weird I guess, but it worked for us.

We pulled into the Cyber Dragon Café off of Littleton Blvd and parked. The red dragon holding a laptop and looking confused, burned brightly in the night. I pulled my coat tighter around my body and waited for Brooke as she fumbled with some quick lipstick. My fist pounded on the car window, "Let's go!"

She ignored me and fumbled with her blue hair in the mirror. Most of the time she never bothered with makeup, she was beautiful without it, like most athletes were. But unlike most athletes who tried to wear makeup, she actually knew how to put it on. And when she did, she was even more beautiful.

I pounded again. "I'm going!" The snow crunched under my heavy steps away from her car. The sound of the car door opening and closing, plus her hurried footsteps crunching in the snow made me brace for the hug I'd receive when she caught up to me.

Grabbing me with her arm, her breath rose into the air. "I have to look good if Cameron is here."

"He won't be. He's hardly ever here."

"But he might be," she said as she hurried on.

A noise caught my attention and my eyes looked up at the roof. A shadow moved. I froze. I noticed that branches were moving in the wind creating shadows from the parking lot light pole. My breath slowly escaped my lips and I quickly followed Brooke.

The place was bustling with activity. As we looked for a seat, we spotted Kaylene behind the counter and waved. Kaylene was a senior, who had aspirations of being an actress. She was a great singer and got the lead rolls in most of the plays. In fact, she got the lead role of Lady Macbeth in *Othello* for the spring play. She pointed to a table in the corner and we marched on over and sat down. We shook out our jackets, placed them on our chair and looked around.

"Great game, Cinnamon." Several classmates called out.

Brooke waved, "Couldn't have done it without my teammates. I'm not much good out on the ice alone."

Always gracious.

Kaylene came over. "Usual?"

I nodded, "Yes please."

"And you, Brooke?"

"Me too." She said looking around.

Kaylene smiled. "If you're looking for Cam, you just missed him."

Brooke's face fell. "In that case, add a strawberry shake to those nachos."

"Drowning your sorrows." I chided her.

She nodded, then, "He didn't leave with that whore Jill did he?"

Kaylene laughed. "She tried, almost raped him in the booth, but I overheard him tell her he had to go help his mom and dad pack for their cruise."

Brooke's eyes widened. "How adorable." She turned to me. "I'm going to marry him."

"You and everyone else." I said.

It wasn't long before our food arrived and we devoured it. I sipped on my Dr. Pepper as Brooke worked on her second malt.

"Feeling better? Might want to slow down, you do have to drive home, you know."

"Ha, ha. You just don't understand what it means to be in love." She sighed dramatically.

I rolled my eyes. "And neither do you. He'll be old news after break and someone else will take his place." She hit me on the shoulder. "Ow. Bitch."

"He will not!" She huffed. Then she smiled. "Okay, you're right. My beauty can't be confined to one man."

"Aw, you are insufferable."

"I know. Are you and your dad still coming over for Christmas Dinner?"

I nodded. "Your parents are great for having us." Since my mom had died, we usually spent Christmas with Brooke and her parents. It was nice to have some company. Up until Brooke and I had become friends our freshman year, holidays were usually very somber and short. My dad's grandparents had died early in my parents' marriage before I was born and my mom's parents had died shortly after mom. Since she was their only child, I guess they didn't have much to live for after that. Even though my dad told me they loved me, I didn't really believe him. Wasn't I good enough to live for?

"No trouble." Brooke said. "My mom appreciates it. That way she doesn't have to listen to my dad talk about his video gaming. Your dad usually wears him out for a whole year." We both laughed.

"By the way, guess what?"

"What."

"I need you to come with me to the airport on New Year's Eve."

I frowned. "Why?" DIA was so far away.

"My cousin from Japan is coming to stay with us until summer. Mr. Resler already approved him for school." She said in between slurps.

"I didn't know you had a cousin? Are you from Japan?" I said.

"I was born there, but moved here when I was a hatch…baby." She quickly corrected herself.

I frowned again. *She never mentioned this before?* I chuckled. It was funny how she slipped like that. Sometimes I think she was a bird. "Is he cute?"

She nodded. "Not Cam-aliscious cute, but yeah. I haven't seen him for a really long time, but I think he'll meet your standards."

My eyes popped open. "What is that supposed to mean?"

"Psht. Really? Tanner? Are you telling me you forgot about him?" She waved her arms in the air as she spoke, "Mr. Prince Charming, the love of your life?"

I blushed. "That was freshman year. Besides he moved away."

"There have been others." She pointed at me and mouthed the words really slow. "Pooooorrrrrr, tttaaaasssttttteeeee."

"Shut up." I said burying myself in my drink.

We finished up around eleven o'clock, walked out, hugged, told her I'd call her tomorrow and drove home. I pulled into the driveway and the lights were still on in Dad's study. The jeep door swung open and I gingerly stepped out onto the slick driveway. With my backpack around my shoulder, I slowly made my way to the front door. Going inside, my golden retriever, Cooper, greeted me by jumping up on me and tried to lick my face. I rubbed his ears and kissed him on his forehead. I heard Dad's chair move across the floor and the door open. He stretched as he came down the stairs. Cooper immediately ran to him and almost tripped him; he had to catch himself on the banister. Dad grumbled, but it was hard to get upset at Cooper, he was just so happy. Placing my backpack down on the ground, I wiped my feet and received my Dad's hug and kiss on the cheek as we both walked towards the kitchen. He filled the teapot, pulled out our favorite mugs, and filled his with instant hot chocolate and mine with sleepy-weepy tea. It was a ritual we did every Friday night, no matter the time.

"How was the game?" Dad asked.

"Good," I sat down at the island counter. I leaned across the island and pulled a cinnamon-raisin muffin from the breadbox, tore it into four pieces and placed two next to my Dad's chair. "Brooke had another shut out, ninth of the season."

He whistled. "That's great. Maybe she'll be recruited by a college as a goalie."

"Maybe."

The teapot whistled. He poured our drinks and placed them on the island.

"How was your day?" He said burning his lip.

I chuckled, "When are you not going to do that?" Cooper nudged his nose up under my hand. "Good. Dr. Daugherty is going to London for break."

"More books?" Dad blew gently on his hot chocolate.

I nodded and popped a piece of the muffin in my mouth. "Yep."

"That man must have a plethora of books at his house." Dad broke off a piece of the muffin and fed it to Cooper. "Hope he doesn't die at his home. They'll never find him."

"What a horrible thing to say." I said.

Dad shrugged his shoulders. "I've seen worse on *YouTube*."

"Shouldn't you be working and not browsing?" I chided him.

"Can't work all the time." He laughed.

"Brooke asked if we are coming over for Christmas. I told her we were, is that still happening?" I ate the last piece.

Dad sighed. "If that is okay. I love Mrs. Wasabi's cooking."

I agreed. "I don't have any problem with it. But you just like Mr. Wasabi's sake, the food is just a bonus. How was your day?"

"You know me too well. Good. Did some more work on that new video game for Archan Don. Other than that, nothing too interesting. Took Cooper for a few walks."

"Nice and chilly." My face smiled.

"Not for him. Isn't that right, puppy." Cooper had his head on Dad's leg, staring up at him.

"Dad?" I started but stopped. I debated about telling him about what I saw in the hallway at school.

He looked up at me, "What?"

I decided against it. Since I wasn't sure what I saw, I didn't what to bother him. "Brooke asked me to go to the airport to pick up her cousin with her on New Year's Eve."

Dad's eyes lit up. "Is he single?"

My eyes rolled. "Seriously, Dad."

"Hey, just looking out for my little girl." He smiled. "That's not a problem. I was invited to go to a party at the gaming company, but I'll probably stay home."

"That isn't good. You should go out. You are cooped up in this house all day."

"Eh, I just don't feel like it."

I knew why, and I knew he knew, I knew why he didn't go out, but I wasn't going to bring it up. "Maybe we can do something."

Dad scoffed. "You'll be with Brooke and her cousin. Wink, wink." He laughed.

"Stop. Brooke told me I have poor taste in guys."

"Really."

"Yeah, she keeps bringing up Tanner."

"He moved and it was your freshman year."

"I know. That's what I told her."

"She's just jealous." He patted my hand.

A broad smile appeared on my face. We talked for about another hour about nothing in particular, then I went to bed.

The weeks went by well enough. I finished what homework I had, so I could enjoy the rest of break. The morning before Christmas the smell of fresh baked bread filled the house. I finished putting the last ingredients in the pumpkin pie for tomorrow and popped it in the refrigerator. Brooke and I hadn't seen each other over the past week. We never do before Christmas it seemed. I've even stopped by their house, but no one is ever home. When I bring it up, she just tells me that I just missed her.

Dad was busy putting the final touches on two pieces of salmon, before putting them in the oven to bake. Cooper followed him like a faithful servant, cleaning up any messes that Dad happened to let fall to the floor, which seemed to happen quite frequently. Snow was falling outside. They forecasted a slight chance of snow for Christmas, but as everyone knows who has lived in Colorado, white Christmases were a hit or miss proposition.

The oven door closed and Dad clapped his hands. "Well, what should we do until dinner?"

"Well," I slid a box across the island to him.

His eyes widened in surprise. "I thought we were going to wait until tomorrow."

I shrugged. "Daughter's prerogative."

He picked up the card. "Would you go and get my reading glasses from the stand, please."

"Sure." I got up and headed into the living room. As I approached his reading chair, a small wrapped box with my name in gold lettering sat under his reading glasses. I felt his hand on my shoulder.

"Merry Christmas." He whispered.

"I thought we were waiting."

"Dad's prerogative."

I handed him his glasses and opened the small box. Inside was a beautiful gold necklace with a small red teardrop ruby attached to it. I immediately recognized it and turned to him. "This is mom's." My voice was barely above a whisper.

"It's been sitting inside that jewelry box for too long. I know she would want you to have it. It belonged to your great-great-grandmother." He took it from my hand and put it around my neck. It was beautiful.

"Are you sure this is okay? I don't want to ruin it." A tear fell down my cheek.

"Your mother wasn't one for much jewelry. But this was her favorite. And if you ruin it, it doesn't diminish the love that goes with the giving. You are your mother's daughter and you deserve to wear it when you like. I love you honey." He then wrapped me up in his strong arms as I cried.

I wore it for the rest of the day.

That night Cooper laid on my bed asleep as I sat in my window sill looking out over the moon filled night in my night gown. The necklace sat on my night stand, next to a picture of Dad, and a picture of Brooke and I at Dave & Busters.

The night looked so serene. The snow had stopped and the wind blew gently in the leafless trees. The light from the moon made the snow sparkle like diamonds and brought a smile to my face.

Suddenly, a shadow moved across the white snow. I watched it sulk from shadow to shadow. At first I thought it was a fox, a long tail moved back and forth along the ground as the black dog body deftly leaped from spot to spot. My gaze followed it and the same feeling from the school began to intrude upon my thoughts.

"Ah!" Cooper had jammed his nose under my hand. My heart raced. Cooper jumped up on the window sill and looked down at the backyard. I rubbed his chest while trying to calm my heart. The black dog thing had disappeared. *No doubt scared off by my scream.* I thought. As I continued to rub Cooper's chest, a low rumble sprang into it. His eyes were darting around the yard, trying to track something, but it was obviously moving too fast. I watched, but couldn't see anything.

"What ya see, boy?" I continued to watch the backyard. "A rabbit?"

Cooper's head moved about then slowed, and his tongue came out panting. He licked my face, and bound off the sill and back onto the bed. I made one last look, took a deep breath, and got up. I shoved Cooper to the side, crawled under the covers and tried to fall asleep.

I tossed fitfully around in my bed. When I peered at the clock, it read 2:30 am. *Jeez, only an hour.* I rolled over, put my arm around Cooper and pulled him in close. I closed my eyes and listened to Cooper's soft breathing.

Tap.

I snuggled up closer to Cooper.

Tap.

My eyes popped open.

Tap.

I tried to lift my head, but it wouldn't move.

Tap.

My eyes tried to look over Cooper's head, which was lying in front of me, but I couldn't see where I thought the sound was coming from.

Tap, click, scraaaape.

My heart raced. I began to panic when my body wouldn't move. My hand shook Cooper, trying to wake him, but he just continued to snore. My eyes strained to see. A black shape came into view and moved just out of my vision before I could get a clear image of it. I felt it move around my bed. I tried to turn my head to see, but couldn't. Goose bumps sprang to life, my heart beat faster. I was having trouble breathing. A hand moved next to my ear and it tingled. My hair moved back away from my ear; my body completely froze as did the scream on my lips. Finally, my head slowly began to roll over as if an unseen hand was gently pulling my chin, then red eyes gradually started to come into view like an eclipse finishing its run. Horrified, I . . . sat up and screamed!

Cooper jumped off the bed and began barking wildly. I quickly looked around and saw nothing. My window was closed, then my door burst open and my Dad in his Pj's rushed in.

"You okay!?" he asked with concern.

I tried to calm my breathing as my Dad came over, sat on my bed and rubbed my shoulders. Cooper had calmed down and pranced anxiously in front of my bed.

I nodded. "Just a dream."

Dad wiped my brow with the sleeve of his jammies. "That leaves you sweating? I hope he was cute?"

I chuckled. "Bad dream, Dad."

"Oh, of course. You okay?"

I nodded. "Yes, Cooper chased him away."

Cooper jumped up on the bed and nuzzled my face.

"He's a good watch dog." Dad rose. "I hope your dreams are better." He said squeezing my shoulder before leaving and shutting the door.

"I hope I don't dream." And continued to pet Cooper in the dark.

Christmas day came late. I had trouble falling back to sleep and it wasn't until ten in the morning when the aroma of fresh bread woke me up. Cooper had long ago abandoned his guard duties and I'm sure he was down stairs with dad. I walked over to my dresser, looked at my disheveled blond hair in the mirror and then absently checked my neck. When nothing appeared, I laughed to myself, pulled my blond hair into a ponytail, threw on my robe, and went downstairs.

Dad was at the kitchen table reading his paper, steaming coffee by his side, and an empty cup next to his. He motioned to the counter where the coffee machine burped with ready coffee. A loaf of fresh bread sat next to the coffee machine. I cut two slices, grabbed the apple butter from the fridge, poured a small amount of coffee for myself and sat down.

"Sleep any better?" Dad asked taking the offered slice of bread and generously smothering it with apple butter.

"Yes." I lied.

"Good." He flipped the paper. "We'll head over to the Wasabi's around four." He pulled another package from under the table, "Merry Christmas."

"Dad," I lamented as I took the multi colored wrapped paper. "Yesterday was good enough."

He shrugged. "Dad's prerogative to spoil his only kid."

"Thank you." The wrapping came off quickly and in my hand were two tickets to Europe. I stared at them.

"Just don't get picked up for the sex slave trade. Okay?" Dad said seriously.

"We won't even talk to anyone." I threw my arms around him and hugged him.

"Everyone should get to backpack around Europe. You mother and I did it for two months. That's when I knew who I was going to spend the rest of my life with..." He choked up on the last.

I rubbed his hand.

"I hope you find someone to love that much, JJ. It's worth all the pain." He wiped his eyes.

"I do too, Dad." I lied again. I'll never fall in love. Too much pain comes from it. If it weren't for me and Cooper, I think my dad would have withered away and died shortly after my mom.

We finished up breakfast and busied ourselves throughout the day until it was time to go over to the Wasabi's. I wrapped the ticket again and placed it with the other gifts for Brooke and the Wasabi's. Dad had gotten Mr. Wasabi a nice bamboo fly fishing rod; they always go during the summer, and for Mrs. Wasabi, a decorative planter for her roses. Mrs. Wasabi was an expert at growing them, she had won several local contests with her roses, and several of the local flower shops used them in their arrangements. Brooke and I usually got each other gag gifts. Last year she got me a rainbow assortment of lipstick. I almost punched her. But this year, I decided to give her a real gift. We had gone to the renaissance festival last summer in Larkspur, something Brooke always likes to do. While there, I had one of the vendors, who specialized in charcoal portraits, draw one of the two of us. Brooke had been against it, but I forced her, knowing what I wanted it for.

"Ready?" Dad called up.

"Coming." I grabbed the presents and headed down stairs.

Dad tossed me my keys to the Jeep. "You drive. It's sake time!" Dad was usually a very light drinker. I think the only time he really every drank a lot was with Mr. Wasabi, and I knew it was because Mr. Wasabi made his own sake.

"I'm not carrying you into the house." I told him.

He came over and gave me a hug, "You wouldn't leave your poor old dad out in the cold?"

"I'll leave Cooper with you."

Cooper barked.

The ride to Brooke's house wasn't very far. Since I lived in Littleton it was a short jaunt up Santa Fe drive to Sedalia and they lived right off the highway towards Deckers. They owned about five acres of land nestled up next to the hills. Forty minutes later, we pulled into the drive in front of their oversized ranch style house. The house had a British Tudor look, with a distinct Asian landscape that you might not have thought would have worked, but it actually worked really well. It was a beautiful house and I sometimes got jealous.

Dad sighed. "Maybe I'll buy a house in the mountains, when you are away at college."

"Then you would be a recluse. You'll end up like Hemingway."

Dad shook his head. "Nope, I don't like opium." We laughed and walked up to the front door.

The door popped open and Mr. Wasabi greeted us with a bow. "Come in, my friends."

Cooper shot past and barking echoed through the door. The Wasabis' had a white Terrier named Ajax, and soon Mrs. Wasabi was yelling at the dogs in Japanese. Mr. Wasabi smiled as he hugged me.

"Sorry about, Cooper." I apologized.

"No, no. Good to spice things up." Mr. Wasabi said in perfect English. He ushered us in, we wiped our feet and took off our shoes. Dad had on his winter wool socks, his feet always got cold.

I heard Mrs. Wasabi shoo the dogs outside and slide the back door shut. Brooke came sprinting around the corner from the kitchen. If I didn't mention it before, and if you hadn't guessed by now, Brooke was adopted. Standing next to her father, her white Eastern European features contrasted sharply with those of her parents' Japanese heritage. Mrs. Wasabi shuffled in, a stained apron covering her clothes, and hugged us warmly. She smelled of spices and roses. In fact the house smelled of contrasting floral and cooking spices that always filled me with warmth.

"Hang your coats, and come in. Toyo, get some drinks for our guests." Mrs. Wasabi scolded her husband.

Mr. Wasabi rubbed his hands. "Sake coming up." Dad followed him halfheartedly complaining it was still too early for Sake.

"Come on." Brooke grabbed my hand and led me upstairs to her room.

Just like her hair, her room was a multitude of differing blues. I always felt like I was walking into an underground glass cave surrounded by water. She had little on the walls, a few posters of teen celebrities, but they always seemed as an afterthought, like she didn't really care about them. In fact, her room was really kind of sparse, but the few things she did have, were very shiny and bright.

"Here." Brooke pulled a package from under her bed.

"What is it this year?" I asked, handing her the gifts.

"No, you are going to like this." She ripped open the wrapping on the tickets. Brooke squeaked with pleasure. "Europe!"

Smiling, I opened the package, and another package was inside. So I opened it and another smaller package was inside of that. Brooke laughed as I continued through six more boxes in descending size until I came upon the last box and opened it. A blue coin was cut in two and connected to two gold necklaces. The broken friendship coin sparkled as I pulled them from the box. Brooke grabbed mine and placed it around my neck. It was cool against my skin. I in turn put Brooke's on and then we hugged.

"Friends for life." She said.

"For life." I agreed.

Brooke opened the picture I had made and hugged it to her. She got up, unceremoniously tore the Jonas Brothers poster down above her bed, and hung our picture there.

While she busied herself with her project, I noticed a new picture on her dresser. I wonder over to it and as I approached a new scent tickled my nose. The picture was of two boys and Brooke.

"When did you take this?" I said as I drew the picture to me and sniffed it.

"What?" She said.

"This picture, and who are these young men." My hand smelled, but I couldn't put my finger on the scent.

"Oh, that's my two cousins. Gabriel and Set. And it was taken last summer silly, when I went on vacation. Gabriel sent it to me. It came yesterday. Don't you remember anything?" She laughed.

"Guess not. Who names their kid Set?"

"It's short for Seth."

I still frowned. Gabriel and Set's features were hard to distinguish in the photo. Their faces were slightly off, almost as if the camera couldn't quite focus on them, but had no difficulty on the surrounding countryside.

The smell from the frame became overpowering. I turned around to make sure Brooke was busy, she was fiddling with the picture, and I put the frame to my nose and took in a deep smell.

Caramel corn. I snarled. "Okay, where you hiding it?"

"What?" Brooke turned to look at me surprised.

I raised my hand. "The caramel corn. I can smell it all over this picture frame." I tapped my foot, suddenly feeling foolish. "Not that I was smelling this frame or anything. You know I love caramel corn. So where is it?"

Brooke looked at me and her face drained of color. "What did you say?"

"Don't give me that? I smell caramel corn coming from this picture. Where are you hiding it?" I put the picture down and began rummaging through her room.

Now, Brooke isn't one given to emotional responses. I think I've only seen her cry twice in the four years we have known each other, so I was a little surprised when tears began running down her face as she sat down on her bed.

"What are you doing? It's just caramel corn." I stared at her. "It's not that big a deal. Well, it's a big deal to me, because I love the stuff, but no need to cry. That is unless you ATE all of it!" I lunged at her, knocking her onto her back and crawled on top of her.

Brooke turned her head and tears ran down her face.

Surprised, I got off her. "What's wrong? I couldn't have hurt you."

"Nothing," she said in between sobs.

I pulled her up and hugged her. "Then why are you crying? I've never seen you cry." I wiped away her tears. They looked blue on my hand.

"Jennifer," she began – she never calls me by my proper name – "I want you to know that you have been the best friend I've ever had. And I will do anything to protect you."

I laughed. "Protect me from what? I don't even have a boyfriend." I rubbed her back.

She laughed, and wiped her nose. "Just know I will be there for you. I'm sorry."

"Nothing to be sorry about, okay?" I stood. "Let's go find our dads', they are probably already halfway to la la land and you better not have eaten all the caramel corn."

Brooke smiled.

The rest of the day was perfect. Mrs. Wasabi made a great stir fried meal that I couldn't eat enough of and Mr. Wasabi and Dad were in happy land. We sat in front of the fire place. Brooke and I ate the pumpkin pie smothered in heavy whipped cream while we listened to Dad and Mr. Wasabi try and sing Christmas songs. The dogs howled. Mrs. Wasabi paid no attention to her husband or Dad, and talked with Brooke and I about how she was going to incorporate the new planter into the yard.

Later that evening, around one thirty in the morning, we said our goodbyes and I helped Dad into the jeep. He flopped in, while Cooper jumped in back, and smacked Dad in the face with his tail. He didn't notice, and Dad began snoring in earnest.

"You going to be alright?" Brooke asked.

"Yeah, he'll be okay by the time we get home. If not I'll leave Cooper with him to keep him warm." I shut the door. "Are you okay?"

A sad look came to her eyes, but she smiled. "Yes. Don't forget about New Year's Eve. My cousin's plane comes in that afternoon, so we can still go downtown." Brooke said.

"Sounds great. Thank you for the gift."

Brooke squeezed my hand. "Best friends."

"Best friends." I started the jeep and drove off.

The road was clear and I only passed one car before turning onto Santa Fe Drive. I shook my head at Brooke's sudden break down and wondered what that was about. I lifted my hand and the faint smell of caramel corn still remained. It smelled so good. But Brooke never did reveal her secret stash. Immersed in my thoughts of caramel corn, a whiteout suddenly started in front of me. I felt the force of the wind against the jeep, pushing it to the side. I slowed and turned on the overhead lights and the snow lit up. I leaned forward to try and get a better view, but it was useless, the whiteout was complete. The jeep crept along and I hoped that I didn't get rear ended. Coloradoans were a strange bunch, despite living with the snow, you'd think they never seen it before with the way they drive from year to year. I strained to see any red lights, when Cooper started to move back and forth in the back seat. He began to whimper as he tried to force his nose out the side windows.

"Cooper, settle down." I told him.

Then as the wind rattled the soft top of my jeep, Cooper's whimpering grew in volume. A deep chopping sound of the air reached my ears and I strained to see out the front window. The sound reminded me of a helicopter rotor chopping the air, but not with the same steady tempo. I slowed the jeep even more, just in case there was an accident ahead of me.

Suddenly, a figure appeared on the road in front of my jeep. I slammed on the breaks and the jeep started to slide. I turned the wheel and the jeep began its three hundred and sixty degree dance around the figure. Time slowed to a crawl. Fixated on the figure in front of me, my mind couldn't wrap itself around the image of the red eyes staring back at me through my front windshield. When the lights of the jeep reached nighty degrees from the figure in the road, lightning lit up the whiteout and briefly illuminated a large shape. Then everything was loss to the darkness as my jeep finished its three hundred and sixty degree turn and slid to a halt.

My heart pounded. I whipped my head around and watched as the whiteout dissipated to nothingness in the bright lights and nothing was on the road. Cooper barked until I placed my hand on his head and he quieted. Dad slept. The wind calmed. I got out of the Jeep; the skid marks of my three sixty stood out on the road and glistened in the moon light. Looking around, the sky was clear, and the night was crisp. I heard the jeep door open and my Dad stumbled out.

"Everything ok?" he slurred.

I walked over to him and ushered him back into the car. "Yes, go back to sleep."

"Okay." He crawled back in.

I gave one glance back to the road, and drove home.

Chapter Three

Gabriel

New Year's Eve came quickly following the Christmas night incident. Dad asked me the following day how he got the large bump on his head. I exaggerated and told him he had hit his head getting out of the jeep. He had nodded, which made him grimace and then went back to bed. I didn't even tell Brooke about it, the whole thing was so bizarre that I'm not even sure how the events had transpired.

Brooke picked me up around eleven thirty that morning and we traveled along I-225 until we got to I-70 and then the off ramp to Pena Blvd. The drive was quiet, which was a first for both of us when we got together. Brooke seemed uncharacteristically withdrawn. I didn't mind though, the Christmas night fiasco was still bothering me and I appreciated the thinking time. But even as I watched the countryside go by, my consciousness couldn't shake the creepy feeling the red eyes had left upon me. They had disappeared almost as quickly as they had appeared. Their unmistakable color reminded me of the experience at the school in the hallway when Ms. Pendragon had arrived, but those had vanished in the blink of an eye just as these had. And then there was the noise of the helicopter. An unforgettable sound, but not quite like any I had heard before. But as I searched the sky after the whiteout for any indication that it had flown by or landed, there was none. There weren't any cars around for the figure I saw, either. Maybe the light from the headlights could have made their eyes look red, just like in a picture, but didn't explain why nobody was around. I just didn't get it.

"There's something for you in the glovebox." Brooke said breaking me out of my reflection.

We had just passed 58th Ave. and the white peaks of the terminal were just on the horizon. I popped open the glovebox and a bag of caramel corn rolled out into my hand. I squeaked with pleasure.

"Since you thought I was holding out on you at Christmas." Brooke smiled.

"You were." I tore open the bag and presented it to her. She wrinkled her nose and shook her head. "No, thanks."

"Good. More for me, since you hogged the pumpkin pie at Christmas." I popped several into my mouth and savored the taste.

"I didn't." She snarled.

"Whatever." And we lapsed back into our respective silences as the blue demon horse sculpture came into view. I was thankful we were here during the day so the freaky red eyes didn't give me the shivers.

It wasn't long before we parked in the west garage and walked toward the terminal. Gabriel was coming in on British Airways and we'd meet him where they exited the tram. As we walked toward the tram exit, I remembered my Dad telling me stories about a time when you could greet people as they exited the plane. He explained how people would propose to their loved one or how families would be reunited. He said it always felt like a family gathering with people cheering and not caring if you were a part of their family or not. At that moment, everyone was connected. It sounded very romantic. He had met Mom there from a trip with flowers one time. He said the concourse erupted in cheers, just as if they all knew one another. He also mentioned the tearful departures of couples young and old, each saying their heartfelt goodbyes.

Now with the restriction since 9-11, the terminal just didn't have the same homey feeling as the concourse did. I wouldn't know, since I never knew any different. But since I watched a lot of old movies with Dad, I kind of got the feeling he was right. How great would it be to walk out of the plane tunnel and be looking for someone you cared for, not seeing them and then the crowd parting and there they would be; your world, the absolute love of your life, holding flowers, a sign, a ring, or just their smile that you missed terribly. How great would that be to know that kind of feeling. *Someday. Maybe.* I laughed to myself.

Brooke scanned the arrival's board. "Looks like he's delayed." She looked at her phone. "Let's go grab a good spot."

We meandered through the terminal until we came to the entrance. The water feature was running and we made our way over to the spot that gave us a good view of the exit. We sat on the wall.

"I'm going to get a drink. Want anything?"

I fished in my pocket for money. "DP."

She waved my money away. "I'll get it." And headed off into the crowd.

I sat dangling my feet, absently eating the caramel corn as I watched the people go by. The airport is the best place to watch people. So many different walks of life. It's just fascinating to try and think of where they are going, or coming from, or what experiences they have had up to this point in their life by the way they dressed or acted. I think an airport would be a great place to do research for your PhD if you were a sociologist. I loved it.

I was watching a particular Latino couple busily arguing when someone touched my shoulder and almost made me fall back into the fountain.

"Whoa, sorry JJ." Christian steadied me with his hand.

My heart raced. "Don't sneak up on me!" I punched his shoulder.

Christian smiled his perfectly white disarming smile, which in turn made me smile. "I'll remember that."

"Good." I offered him some caramel corn.

He shook his head and stepped back. "No, thank you." He said with some distaste.

"What are you doing here?"

"Picking up a friend of mine, she's staying for the semester." Christian looked around.

"Wow, not a girlfriend?" I asked. Brooke wouldn't be very happy at that notion.

He laughed, which was light and deep. "Oh, no. Just a family friend."

"That's good."

"What are you doing here, and where is Blue?"

My eyes widened. Brooke has many nicknames, well one really, just Cinnamon, and she hated it when people called her Blue. I don't even call her that unless I'm annoyed at her. Usually that nickname is reserved for very special people who she really, really likes, and that would be reserved for her family only. So, to hear Christian use it didn't bode well for him.

"Uhm, I wouldn't . . ." I started when he spoke.

"Hey, Blue." Christian called out.

I turned and the look on Brooke's face was precious. You'd think someone had placed a puppy in her lap, with the way her blue eyes were all wide with adoration. Her steps slowed, and the drinks in her hands trembled as her face flushed a little. Appalling.

"Christian." She finally forced out.

Quickly handing me my drink she hugged him, which he returned warmly. I blinked back more surprise. An unpleasant smell wafted briefly over my nose. Someone must not have showered for it smelled of rotten eggs. With all the passengers and people in the terminal, I couldn't place it.

Christian wasn't known for his overtness, and the way the hug lingered, you'd think they were best of friends. I got a little jealous.

"Don't mind me." I grumbled sipping on my drink.

"What are you doing here?" she asked with a nauseating giggle after it.

More white smile. "I was just telling JJ, how I was picking up a friend . . ."

"A girlfriend." I interjected maliciously and got the desired response. Suspicion leaped into Brooke's eyes.

Christian caught it too. "Just a family friend," he said looking at me.

I mock smiled.

Brooke's eyes relaxed. "Oh, good. We're just waiting on my cousin. Is she coming up through here?"

"Oh, no. She's just getting her luggage. I just happened to see JJ, and thought I would say hello." He hugged her again. "Well, I should be going."

"Bye." I waved to him.

"Bye." Brooke said.

"See ya Blue; enjoy the rest of your break." Then he was lost to the crowd.

Brooke grabbed my arm. "Come on."

"No." And held my ground. "Why?"

"I want to see if she is pretty or not." She tugged even harder. People were starting to appear from the tram exit.

"No. She's probably beautiful and you are ugly."

She turned on me. "You're such a bitch. Take that back. No one is prettier than me." She flopped her blue hair.

"Everyone is prettier than you and I'm certainly not going with you now that you called me a bitch." I hunkered down on the wall. "Go by yourself, if you are that insecure." I waved her away with the caramel corn bag.

Her eyes narrowed, then she looked at her phone. I knew she was calculating how much time she had before her cousin might show up.

"Fine." She turned and walked quickly towards the baggage claim.

"Take a picture, ugly." I yelled to her.

She was soon lost to the crowd. I went back to watching the people as they began greeting loved ones or friends as they came through the tram exit. More people gathered, and soon there was a large group between me and the exit door. I sipped, munched, and waited. I couldn't remember very much detail from the picture, but as more and more people were coming out the exit, I began to worry as Brooke failed to come back. I stood up on the fountain wall and was quickly told to get down by a security guard. Frustrated, I continued to watch the exiting people, but no one even came close to matching the faint description I vaguely remembered.

Finally, I closed my eyes and took in a deep breath. I did that several times, and on the last deep breath, the aroma of caramel corn tickled my nose. I quickly exhaled and breathed in again and the aroma was stronger. My body felt suddenly warm and sleepy, just like you are after eating a good Thanksgiving dinner. I tried to open my eyes, but my eyelids were heavy with sleep, and a warm contentment coursed through my body.

"JJ?"

An unfamiliar voice spoke to me. For a moment, I couldn't be sure if I was dreaming or not. The voice was soft, deep, and strong. It reminded me of a wise sage from the Kung Fu movies my Dad made me watch when I was a kid. Fluttering my eyes opened, I gazed into the most beautiful eyes I had ever seen. Warm hues of golden hazel peered at me with soft centers of black that seemed oval in their appearance. One pupil was slightly larger than the other, but both held a deep fountain of understanding and peacefulness. For a moment I was lost upon a golden field of wheat. As I blinked, the handsome face came into focus and a small gasp escaped my lips. Perfect colors of golden brown skin, white teeth, harvest wheat colored hair, and a strong jaw completed the statuesque figure before me.

"JJ?" he asked again.

My head bobbed awkwardly in acknowledgement and I accidentally dropped my drink, which he caught in one catlike motion.

He handed it back to me with a smile, "Might want to be more careful." His musical voice said.

The caramel scent didn't last and I found myself on the verge of hyperventilation. Then, "Gabe!"

He turned as he welcomed Brooke into his arms. "Blue!"

With the spell broken, I slid off the wall and found myself breathing in large gulps of air. *What just happened?* I watched them for a moment as the drink and caramel corn bag shook in my hands. My knees felt weak and pit had opened in my stomach.

"Oh, it's so good to see you!" Brooke hugged him again. "You look great, you old man."

Gabe laughed. As I peered up, he had on a white cotton long sleeve shirt, brown cargo pants and brown leather shoes. As people walked by, the loose fitting shirt rustled revealing the taunt body underneath, and I sucked in my breath again.

"You might want to wipe the drool off your chin." Brooke mocked me.

My face flushed as I involuntarily wiped my chin, which was dry. Scowling at Brooke, who laughed at my discomfort, I regained my composure.

"I'm Gabriel." Gabe offered me his hand.

While I fumbled to shake his hand, another voice spoke. "Do I get a hug, Cousin?"

Turning, a separate Adonis stood next to Gabriel; but if Gabe was the day, then this young man was the night. Midnight hair framed a perfect face. Dark brown eyes that were almost black, gazed out coldly, and a mischievous grin couldn't mask the cruelness that was harbored at the corners of the grin.

Brooke looked angry and confused. "Why is Set here?"

"The change was last minute." Gabriel quickly answered, stepping in front of me as if to protect me from any harm.

The aroma again threatened to wash over me and carry me away.

"Do I get a hug, Cousin?" Set said again.

Brooke eyed him, then stepped up and quickly embraced him, which was short and unaffectionate.

"Has something changed?" Brooke asked.

Set nodded. "Yes."

Concern flared in Brooke's eyes, and she nodded curtly. I stepped away to catch my breath.

"Who is this, morsel?" Set offered his hand. His dark brown eyes surveyed me.

"JJ, this is my cousin Seth." Brooke said.

"Nice to meet you." His grip was strong, like Gabriel's, but where his was gentle, Set's was more like a vice. He lifted my hand and kissed the top of it. It was cold, sending shivers up my arm and neck.

"Set." Brooke warned.

Set laughed darkly as he released my hand. "Nice to make your acquaintance." He turned to Brooke. "I'm sure there are *other* delicacies you are acquainted with?"

Brooke punched him in the arm, hard. I've seen her punch other guys with less force and the bruises they leave, but Set turned angry eyes upon her like the punch was more of an annoyance than anything else. He delivered a punch just as hard. She didn't flinch. *I'd hate to see the bruise that punch was going to leave.* Gabe quickly stepped in and defused the situation. "This isn't going to help. May we go?"

Brooke turned on her heals and nodded with her head for them to follow.

As I fell into line, I noticed we passed the baggage claim. "Don't you have luggage?"

Gabe turned to me and I melted into his hazel eyes again. "Should be delivered tomorrow. We had to send it, cheaper than paying the baggage fair."

I nodded, thinking it was strange to mail your clothes, but as I gazed into his eyes, anything seemed possible.

The ride home was quiet. I was told to ride in the back with Set, as Gabe protested that I should be allowed to sit in front. Brooke shook her head. I said I didn't mind sitting in back, even though Set made me uneasy. After getting in, I knew I'd have a perfect side view of Gabe's face and that was the only reason I wasn't upset. Set appeared uninterested in my company and he quickly shut his eyes. His breathing eased, making it seem he had fallen asleep.

Brooke turned up the music, which was a little too loud, but shouldn't have kept me from hearing whatever conversation the two were having, though it did. Watching his lips move, they talked the entire way back to my house, but I couldn't hear a thing. Several times, Gabe caught me watching him and each time my face grew hot as I tried to busy myself with something outside the window. Also, Set would grunt a laugh during points in their conversation and each time Brooke would gift him with a hard stare through the rearview mirror.

We pulled into the driveway in front of my house, Brooke parked the car and everyone got out except Set.

"Thanks for going with me, we still on for tonight?" Brooke hugged me.

"We don't have to, if you want to spend time with your cousins." I said, trying not to stare at Gabe.

Brooke shook her head. "No way. Should be fun watching all the drunks downtown. I'll come get you around nine, and we'll ride the train down."

"Okay." I turned to Gabe and held out my hand. "Nice to meet you."

He took it in his warm hand. "My pleasure."

We held hands for the briefest, longest, moment then he gently pulled his free of mine. I felt as if a part of me was being taken away. I smiled awkwardly again and retreated to my front porch.

"Dress warm." Brooke yelled as they pulled out of the drive. I waved to them. Standing there, I felt warm, while I watched the car disappear down the street.

"I don't have the money for the wedding that your imagination is conjuring right now." My Dad said startling me.

Blushing, I punched him in the arm. "I don't know what you are talking about." I entered the house, a warm feeling began to spread throughout my body. I hung my coat on the coat rack, meandered over to the couch and plopped down. Cooper sprinted from the kitchen, half jumped into my lap and I rubbed his ears. "Beautiful."

My Dad laughed. "The dog or the young man?"

"Dad!" I acted shocked at his statement, but I knew he wouldn't buy it.

"Handsome guy." Dad smiled. "Who is he?"

"Brooke's cousin." I kissed Cooper on the nose. "He's here from Japan visiting for the semester. I told you this already."

"Not that he was staying." Dad leaned forward. "Lucky for you."

"I don't know what you mean." I ignored him.

"Now I won't have to call an escort service to get you a prom date." He laughed.

Mortified, I stared at him. "Am I that ugly?"

"No, you are that *picky*." He got up, came over and kissed me on my head. "Try not to grope him tonight. Try and wait until the second date." He walked off to the kitchen.

"He's not even going tonight!" I yelled at him. "I'm not a slut, you know."

"Never said you were, honey." He yelled back, "But the last time I saw that look in your eye, you came home crying because he wouldn't kiss you!"

"That was fifth grade, Dad!" I screamed.

A muffled 'uhuh' issued from the kitchen followed by fake crying noises. Scowling, I rubbed Cooper's ears again and kissed him on his forehead and pushed him off me. Walking upstairs, the warm feeling had finished coursing through my body and the biggest smile was on my face. One I haven't seen in a long time on the hallway mirror. *I've got to wear the perfect outfit.*

I went into my room, looked at my closet and knew that it wasn't there.

Chapter Four

A Hero Arrives

The hands on the grandfather clock creeped along as if time had abandoned me. Even waiting for Christmas Eve as a kid didn't take as long as it did for clock hands to reach nine o'clock.

After showering, I spent the rest of the evening trying on seven or eight different outfits, and combinations, and I hated them all. I finally settled on a cute blue sweater, that complimented my Mom's necklace and the friendship necklace Brooke had given me. Dark brown jeans, and light brown fake fur rimmed boots finished the outfit. Dad complimented me on my cuteness. I stared at him mortified, before running back upstairs and changing three more times before returning to my original outfit. He kept silent this time when I came downstairs, except for a few teasing remarks about how somewhat attractive I was when I tried.

I stared at the clock with its hands move with agonizingly slowness towards nine, and wondered if he would be coming. *He should be tired from his trip? I wouldn't go if I were him.*

"Could you stop your leg from bouncing? It's annoying." Dad commented from his reading chair.

My hand pushed on my leg to keep it from bouncing, a nervous habit I've always had, and gifted him with a snarl.

"Cooper, go keep her company." Dad told him. "She's obviously lonely. Prince Charming isn't here yet."

Cooper obediently got up from in front of the fireplace and came over to me. His side was super warm from the fire as I rubbed it. The warmth reminded me of Gabe's eyes and the nervous butterflies sprang into my belly. I heard my Dad laugh.

"Oh, young love." He chuckled again. "I can't believe someone actually could make you look like this."

Startled, I jumped up, "Like what?" I moved to the mirror by the door. It wasn't until I saw nothing wrong that my Dad's laughter grew in my consciousness. I turned on him and gave him the evil eye, which he immediately made the sign of the leprechaun; a quick shamrock followed by both hands coming together in a circle.

I waved him away.

"This is going to be so much fun." He turned and set his paper down. "You know this right?"

"Ha, ha. It's nothing. I won't give you the pleasure of teasing me, cause there isn't anything to tease me about." I turned my head to look out the window hoping Brooke's car had arrived. It hadn't.

He clapped his hands together and rubbed them. "Oh, this is going to be good."

Just then, Brooke arrived. I noted that Gabriel wasn't in the car. My heart sank, but I put on a big smile. "See, he isn't even in the car. You lose, old man." Quickly checking myself in the mirror one more time - god my hair needs to be cut - and skipped out the door with my Dad's words floating after me, "Don't kiss him on the first date!"

I jumped in Brooke's car and waved to my Dad, who stood in the window, waving and making kissy faces.

"What's he doing?" Brooke waved to him and he waved back.

"He thinks he's being funny." I turned my head away from him and his continuing antics in the window.

"But he is funny." Brooke remarked before driving away.

Music blared from the speakers as we headed up Broadway toward Mineral Ave. and down to the light rail station at Santa Fe.

Brooke bopped back and forth to the music and she seemed in a much better mood than earlier and I commented on it.

"Oh, that? Set is just a jerk sometimes." She said. "He likes to push things all the time. He knows what buttons to press to get me upset. He's just a jerk like that."

"Oh. How did Gabe recognize me? How's your arm? He punched you pretty hard." I was trying to get around to asking if we were going to meet up with them, well Gabriel, without actually asking.

She waved her hand at me. "I sent him a picture of us back in ninth grade. He has a really good memory for unremarkable things." She snorted at her joke.

"I really hate you sometimes." And turned to look out the window.

"No you don't. And Set hits like a girl."

Only Brooke would say something like that. Cause most girls don't hit like she does. "Are we meeting anyone?"

She frowned. "Like who?"

I played it off. "Oh, I don't know? Did anyone call you?"

"No, did anyone call you?"

"No. I was just curious. I thought maybe Christian had called."

She laughed. "Christian doesn't call anyone."

"I don't know. He seemed awfully happy to see you at the airport today."

Brooke pushed me, but I could tell her brain was racing. "I didn't find him, so he's probably holed up with his friend he picked up."

Perfect, my opening. "And what about your cousins? Are they staying in?"

She nodded. "I believe so. Set went straight to bed after we got home and Gabe was talking to my parents when I left."

I nodded trying to look happy. "Good, girls' night out." Though deep down I was really disappointed. I'm not sure why I was, I only just met him today. But there was just something about him. I filled my lungs with a deep breath, trying to smell the caramel corn, but nothing surfaced and I let it out as a long sigh.

"Sad?"

"Nope. Just gearing up for the celebration." I gave her a high five.

The trip downtown was uneventful. The train was packed. People were already heavily intoxicated, and it was almost as much fun watching these drunkards as it was watching people at the airport. At each stop we stuffed more people in and soon, the stink of heavy perfume, booze, and just body odor was starting to overwhelm me. I edged closer to the door to try and catch as much fresh air when the doors opened as I could. We had just stopped at the Mile High Station, I moved to get out of the way of several revelers stumbling out of the door, when someone grabbed me from behind making me yell out in surprise.

Several people looked my way, when Alexa, Carly, Kennah and Laura came around front. Kennah had been the one to grab me. They laughed.

"Scared of something?" Laura asked.

I hugged them. "No, you just startled me. What are you guys doing down here?"

Alexa pushed me back onto the train as the conductor's voice announce the train was moving. "Kennah's boyfriend's dad has a loft down on the mall. We're heading there to watch the fireworks."

Kennah's boyfriend went to Valor, something that caused quite a ruckus among the other cheerleaders on the squad. But Kennah did whatever Kennah wanted. They greeted Brooke who returned the greetings.

"What about you two?" Carly asked, shuffling herself into an open area.

"Just going to watch the fireworks and the drunks." Brooke told her.

"You should come with us?" Laura piped in. "Should be really good viewing."

I shrugged. "I'll call you if we do." Brooke didn't like any of the Valor crowd, and so it was best to keep her away from them.

"Ah, they aren't that bad." Kennah's nasally voice rose above the din in the train. It was like she was always in cheerleader mode and her voice boomed.

Brooke scowled. "Maybe not your boyfriend, Kennah, but as a whole they suck."

Kennah rolled her eyes and found something interesting to watch out the window. Soon we were at Union Station and the multitudes exited the train. We waved goodbye to them while we walked toward Wynkoop Street and then toward 16th Street. We laughed and joked about the different costumes of the people we saw and meandered up the street. Well-dressed couples walked towards their destinations and I found myself watching them with a certain amount of envy. I couldn't help but imagine myself and Gabe being one of those couples, going to some high class party put on by our friends or our work. How romantic.

Brooke looped her arm in mine and we continued our exploration of downtown. I loved downtown. The lights, the tall buildings, and the cool shops made downtown Denver great. We strolled in and out of shops, and bought some trinkets for New Years. Brooke bought a blinking tiara that made her blue hair even bluer in the lights of downtown. I purchased some wide brimmed glasses that had rotating lights around the rims and we both got some clackers. Several roving gangs of boys tried to engage us and we were invited to several parties, but we would just laugh, act like we were clueless, and moved on. It was really fun playing stupid.

As midnight approached, we wondered over to the 16th Street Mall and began our search for a good spot to watch the fireworks. In truth, there wasn't really a bad spot, since they had fireworks at both ends of the mall. Brooke dragged me along behind her while she shoved her way through the crowd unceremoniously. My eyes continued to survey the crowds when I caught sight of him. My heart jumped. Gabe was on the other side of the street, heading in a determined manner back the way we had come. I tapped Brooke on the shoulder, "Over there." I broke free of her grasp and pushed my way through the crowd towards the direction Gabe was going. Brooke's protests were lost in the roar of the crowd while I ran across the street and jumped up and down to see where he had gone. I traveled along the street searching but couldn't see him. I merged with the crowd again and made my way through until I came out near an alley. People were sitting on either side of the opening, drinking steaming hot chocolate, seemingly unaware of anything around them. Curious, I approached a couple on the left side of the alley opening and to my surprise they appeared frozen. Each appeared to have been stopped in mid-sentence and their eyes were glazed over. A man and his son on the other side of the alley were affected the same way. A tingling sensation started moving all over my body like ants. I took off my blinking glasses and peered down the alley. Two people were standing at the far end. In the dark, I couldn't see if one was Gabe or not, though the build of one of them looked familiar. Swallowing my heart back down into my chest, I entered the alley and the noise from the street suddenly stopped. The stench of something really gross assaulted my nose. It didn't smell like sewage or the sick horrible rotten egg smell of natural gas. I don't know what a decomposing dead body smelt like, but this had to be pretty close.

    I pressed my back against the alley wall and my breathing sounded very loud in my ears. Walking as slowly and as carefully as I could, I headed for a dumpster, until coming within hearing of the two.

At first, I couldn't hear anything, but when I crouched behind the dumpster, an odd sound began filtering towards me. Soft squeaks and clicking sounds, like dolphins chattering reached my ears. I put my back to the dumpster and tried to hear better. As the sounds continued, my body pressed harder against the dumpster in an effort to hear more, when the dumpster gave way. I slipped and the squeal of the wheels echoed down the quiet alleyway.

The clicking and squeaks stopped.

Holding my breath, I scrambled to the wall, pulled my knees up to my chest and tried to press myself into the alley's wall. Moments passed. My eyes looked back down the alleyway to the entrance and as people walked by without looking down, I wondered how fast I could run to the end.

Just as I was about to make my move, the sound of something sniffing around began to grow in volume. I watched the edge of the dumpster with growing fear, until the tiniest finger reach around the edge of the dumpster. As my heart stopped and my body felt as weak as any nightmare I have ever experienced, the finger wasn't actually a finger but grew into a flat flipper. It inched its way around the dumpster until the paddle shaped appendage moved along towards me. Frozen, my eyes stared at it and then a snout slowly appeared that grew into a black skeletal dog shaped head. Soft growls, like rocks being rubbed together, issued out of the sharp white toothed mouth. The head slowly turned towards me and I stared full faced into a beast from hell. Glowing green eyes pierced my brain, as another tentacle moved around from the side; its paddle shaped end suddenly sprouted thorns along its entire surface and looked like a cactus leaf.

The other paddle sprouted thorns also and the high pitched scraping along the dumpster was worse than any fingernails on a chalkboard.

Horrified, my scream caught in my throat as fear; fear like I have never known, began shutting down my consciousness and my body tried to revert back to is primordial instinct of flight. My arms and legs pushed my body away from the wall with the intent of running towards the alley entrance, and with what little consciousness that remained, it began registering the pain traveling up my leg. The paddle shaped appendage had torn into my leg, spinning me into the alley and down on my back. Scrambling backwards, I caught a glimpse of the thing. A tiger's body, black as night, stood in the alley with a dog's face. Two tentacles sprouted from its back and whipped around in the air, like squid tentacles. Suddenly, each tentacle flared upwards and then shot towards me with blinding speed. I scrambled backwards while the two people who I had originally seen, watched the bizarre proceeding with glowing red eyes.

Before the last vestiges of consciousness forced me to flee, I began crab crawling backwards as fast as I could. But the flat paddles were almost upon me, ready to rip into my body, when somewhere from above, a giant alligator looking creature with wings landed and crushed the tiger creature in a gooey mess. The creature didn't look back at me before charging the two people. I ran from the alley.

When I crossed the threshold of silence into the din of the crowded street, my scream finally found purchase and rang forth with the clarity of a church bell ringing on a Sunday morning.

And then he was there.

Chapter Five

What was I thinking?

Gabriel grabbed me with strong arms and pulled me into his rock hard chest. His chest consumed my scream that moments ago would have brought any would be rescuer to my side. But since everyone could see I had found my hero, no one took noticed and continued on with their celebrations.

"Shhh." His strong soft voice cooed, as my arms clung onto him as if he were the last person on the earth. I closed my eyes.

My heart thundered in my chest. His soft heartbeat through sheer force of will corralled my runaway heart and brought it under his control until they both beat in perfect harmony. His peculiar, distinctive scent penetrated the fear that had placed my body in a hypersensitive state and my mind began to slowly calm down. I pressed my head further into his chest until I could hear his blood flowing through his veins and the quiet, rhythmic inhaling and exhaling of his breath. His skin, through his cotton shirt, was smooth like a statue in the park.

"Is she okay?" Brooke's concerned voice came from behind me.

I felt his head nod in answer to her question and then a peculiar thing happened. As my mind continued to come down off the adrenaline and the pain in my leg began to seep up to my brain, I felt small vibrations emanating from his chest. Pressing my head harder into his chest, the sound became more distinct as if he were making the sound deep within, like a cat purring, but more like the deep rumbling of a whale in the ocean. I had felt this one time before, when a friend of ours had placed some sub-woofers in his ride. You couldn't actually hear the deep booming sound, but you could feel them as they pulsed through your body and that's kind of what was happening. They penetrated my body, then stopped. Then again, and stopped. It felt like he was having a conversation with himself, but he wasn't speaking. As the conversation continued, pain was becoming more and more prevalent until I couldn't stand it any longer and cried out into his chest.

"She's bleeding." Brooke said.

Gabe whisked me effortlessly up into his arms and started to carry me off to an open area in Writer's Corner, like a bride through a doorway. His strength made me feel secure and before I knew it he was placing me down onto a bench. Disappointed the trip didn't last any longer, Gabe lifted my bad leg and was examining the wound. In the light of the street lamps, his warm brown skin seemed to radiate heat in the cold night air, and like a mirage upon a desert plain, his body shimmered with heat.

Gabe turned his hazel eyes to Brooke. "Call Set, we need a first aid worker and some of the dust."

Brooke nodded and walk off a short distance. She pulled out her cell phone, and placed it to her ear. I frowned.

"Hey, JJ."

I looked down into his hazel eyes and felt myself being pulled into them again. He smiled and his white teeth shown in the light.

I nodded, transfixed by his beauty.

"You shouldn't go stumbling around in dark alleys. You managed to cut yourself on a trash dumpster. You'll have a nasty scrape."

"You'll fix it." I heard myself say. I'm not sure why I had said it, but I felt it was true.

His smile grew and deeper I fell into his eyes. "Sure I will."

"Brooke said you weren't coming?" I whispered.

"Changed my mind." His smile momentarily made me forget the pain.

"You okay?"

I involuntarily reached up and placed my hand on his face. It was warm, smooth, and incredibly strong. "I am now."

Suddenly, pain shot up my leg, through my side, and lodged deep in my brain and stars filled my vision. I cried out in pain and when I reopened my eyes the ugliest woman had taken his place. Her bright colored safety jacket assaulted my eyes, her black hair looked like snakes in the grass and she smelt of beer and sweat. I wanted to retch to the side, but I kept the contents of my stomach down. Looking around, Gabe and Brooke were standing off to the side, watching.

"Nasty scrape you got there." The First Aid Lady chuckled. "What did you do?"

Again pain shot through my leg and body. "Ow! What the hell are you doing, cutting it off?"

"Iodine, sweetie. Gotta make sure you don't get any nasty infections. This is going to hurt again, try not to cry." She laughed as she applied more of the stuff and I bit back my scream.

"She stumbled into a dumpster as we were looking for a good place to watch the fireworks." Brooke explained.

"Did she also get poked with needles?" The First Aid Lady asked. "There are several punctures. They're not very deep, but it looks like fish hooks punctures."

"Bad razor shave?" Brook offered.

The First Aid Lady smirked. "Whatever." She closed her bag. "I'd take her to the doctor to get a tetanus shot. Those dumpsters *are* very rusty. She should be able to keep the leg though." She walked off as her radio blared with a new casualty of the night.

I reached down to rub my throbbing leg, and a part of my jeans were gone. "She cut my jeans!"

"Price of being stupid and getting hurt." Brooke walked over and looked at me. Her blue eyes glared into my own, they were ablaze with anger. "Don't wander off again!"

I swallowed down my own angry retort. "I saw Gabe." Was all I got out as the familiar laughing of the Rainbow Twins intruded the night.

Set walked up with arms around each one as they held onto him as if he were a prize they had won. In his left hand was a red pouch that dangled next to Jill's gaudy earring. He tossed the pouch at Brooke and she snatched it out of the air like a cat grabbing a bird.

"Hi, Brooky Blue." Jill laughed.

It was clear they were drunk.

"Did you find them?" Brooke hissed between her taunt lips.

"Oh, I found them alright." Set greedily eyed his meals and then kissed them on their heads as if he were giving them his blessing.

"Set." Gabe said.

Set nodded. "Red did. Now my cousins, I bid you farewell"

"You're Brooky Blue's cousin." Katie slurred. They both laughed as the three of them reentered the streaming throng of people.

Gabe walked over to Brooke and took the pouch from her trembling hand. He knelt down again and began to unwrap the bandage around my leg. "I'm going to kill him." Brooke hissed.

Gabe laughed. The sound was like chimes in the night. "You say that all the time." He looked up at me and I quickly put my hand down. I was about to touch his face again.

"Deep down, she likes him." He smiled.

I smiled back, unable to keep the smile from going from ear to ear.

"No I don't." Brooke fumed. "He's an arrogant, self-centered, ego maniac!" The last finished on a higher note than the first. Gabe just chuckled and I couldn't help but chuckle at Brooke's tirade also.

He had finished taking the bandage off, and I could see that the wound wasn't very big, but it was really red. He looked at it with some concern. He opened the pouched and poured some dust into his hand. It sparkled like diamonds in the light.

"What's that?" I asked.

"It's a powder that helps stop the swelling and keeps it from getting polluted." He explained. "It's used a lot in the village we come from in Japan."

"Polluted?" I asked.

Gabe looked embarrassed and my heart skipped a beat. "Uhm, infected I guess is a better word." Then he looked earnestly into my eyes. "I won't lie to you, JJ. This isn't very pleasant. It's going to hurt, a lot." Then, "Trust me?"

Fireworks began to explode in the sky above us, illuminating the area even more. As the sparkles of fireworks reflected in his perfect, glassy eyes, I caught my breath as I nodded and the butterflies reawakened in my stomach. His smile reassured me that everything would be okay and then as the fireworks continued, out of the corner of my eye, I saw his hand toss the power onto my leg and the night went black.

My head bounced against the tram window and it shook me awake. Groggily, I placed my hand on my aching head, and Brooke slowly came into focus in the seat across from me.

"Hey, sleepy head." Her smile mocked me.

"Where are we?" My body ached. I peered around for Gabe, but only unfamiliar faces gazed back at me from the seats and aisle around us. "Where's Gabe?"

"On his way home, just like us. Weren't the fireworks great?" She sighed contently.

"Fireworks? I don't remember seeing them."

Brooke nodded sadly and gestured to those around us that I had been drinking.

"I didn't drink anything." I angrily whispered at her, which made my head hurt.

Brooke nodded again. "I know." She patted my leg.

I shoved her hand away. "Fuck off."

She laughed.

Folding my arms across my chest, I watched the lights go by through the window. We didn't speak the rest of the way, though she chatted with those around us, which annoyed me. We walked to the car in silence and the drive home was the same way.

I got out, slammed the door and limped up to the house. The living room light was on, something my Dad always does for me.

"Hey, I'm going to be gone until semester starts." Brooke yelled to me. "I'll call you when I get back in town."

Even though I was angry at her, I didn't want her to be gone for a week and a half. "Where you going?"

"Vaca with the parents. Going back to Japan to see some relatives." Brooke said.

"Are your cousins going too?"

She nodded. "Take care of that leg, and come up with a better story for your dad. Not that he wouldn't believe that you ran into a dumpster, but at least make it more exciting."

I snarled. "Ha, ha."

She laughed, waved and drove away.

While I watched her go, and as she came to the end of the block, her brake lights came on. I shuddered as they reminded me of the glowing red eyes of the people in the alley. "It wasn't a dumpster." I whispered to the cold air, before entering the house to a dog happy to see me.

Going to my room, I peeled off my clothes, but not before I gave them a deep inhale. I immediately threw them into the corner; they smelled of alcohol, smoke, and stink. Not what I was hoping for. Disgusted, I limped to the bathroom, washed my face, put on my night shirt and climbed into bed. Cooper jumped up on the bed, turned around several times before settling at the foot. I put my hands behind my head and stared up at the ceiling. As I turned over the nights events in my head, my leg throbbed.

"I know it wasn't a dumpster." The night heard me say. "Dumpster's don't have glowing green eyes and tentacles with spiky cactus pads on them. And what about those two people I saw? They had red glowing eyes? Was it just a trick of the light? People don't have glowing red eyes, except in pictures." I sighed. My eyes widened. "Vampires?" A cold chill went through my body. "I can't imagine falling in love with someone who could never see the light of day or touch a body with the temperature of an ice cube. Much better to have the warmth of the sun, than cold of the night." Again I sighed. "This is ridiculous. Why would Brooke think I ran into a dumpster? Then again, I don't remember telling her what happened. Not even during the ride home. It was just too bizarre. Anyway, I…" the knock at my door startled me.

"Anyone in there I should be concerned about?" My Dad's voice asked.

"Just a beautiful, golden haired, four legged man of my dreams." On cue, Cooper barked.

He laughed. "People are going to talk if you keep sleeping with that dog, not that I mind."

I smiled. "He loves me unconditionally, I'll never find that in a boy."

My Dad sighed through the door. "Someday honey. Anyway, glad you made it home safely. Want to go to breakfast?"

Mostly safe, I thought. "Sure," I started, then, "can we go downtown for lunch instead?"

There was a hesitation behind the closed door. Dad doesn't like to go downtown. The crowds bother him. Not that my Dad is a recluse, he doesn't mind small functions, especially the ones at school. He loves going to those, but the idea of mingling in large crowds never set well with him. I remember Mom having to hold his hand like a small child anytime we went Christmas shopping or anytime we went on vacation to Disney Land or Eliches.

As the silence stretched on, I started to regret asking, when, "Sure, honey." His voice was tight.

"We don't have to, Dad. I know how you hate the crowds."

"No, no, it will be good to get out. Stretch the legs see how the populace lives. Any place in particular?"

I nodded my head, and was glad he couldn't see me do it. "No, just someplace on 16th Street."

His response was very controlled. "Eleven Thirty?"

"Great. Love you Dad."

"Love you too, JJ."

I heard his footsteps retreat down the hall and his door close. My leg continued to throb lightly and when the ceiling finally fell out of focus, the rhythmic beating of a helicopter's blades gently lulled me to sleep.

The next morning came too early, even though the knock at my door sounded at Ten Thirty. Groggily I rolled over and Cooper stared at me expectantly by the door. A small whimper escaped his lips.

"Oh snap." I jumped out of bed and opened the door. My Dad was about to knock again as Cooper shot passed him like a lightning bolt with me behind him. Down the stairs and through the kitchen, Cooper raced and slid to a halt in front of the sliding doors. My fingers fumbled with the latch, Cooper whimpered again, and when I got it open, Cooper dashed out into the yard, found his spot and peed.

"Sorry, Cooper." I apologized from the door.

Cooper turned his head towards me, the relief clearly visible on his face. I left the door open and turned to my smiling Dad.

"That was close." He went over to the table and sat down.

"Yep. Guess I was really tired." I sat down at the table and picked a piece from his cinnamon roll.

"What did you do to your leg?" He asked.

I quickly reached down and covered the bandage with my hand. My leg had stopped throbbing and when I pushed on it, it didn't hurt. Embarrassed, I tried to think of something. "I . . . I got a tattoo."

"Really." He said over his hot chocolate cup. "Can I see it?"

My face flush. He knew I would never get a tattoo, I abhor them, but wasn't ready to tell him what happened until I got to see the dumpster. Therefore, "You got me. I stumbled into a dumpster as we were looking for a place to watch the fireworks."

Merriment sprang into his eyes and I steeled myself for the abuse that was about to begin for being clumsy.

But instead, "Do we need to go and see the doctor?" he asked concerned.

I stared at him. "What?"

Even though the merriment in his eyes never drained away, he placed his hand on mine. "Do we need to see about it? I don't want you to get blood poisoning or anything?"

I shook my head. "No. Nothing funny to say?"

He stood. "JJ, as your father, I'm concerned when you get hurt. Besides, I'm sure Brooke had plenty to say."

"She did. Thank you, Dad."

"No problem." He left the kitchen and then he called from the stairs. "Honey?"

"Yes." I answered back.

"Should we order a robot boyfriend for you from Japan?" His laughter continued through his shower.

He was still chuckling at his joke the entire drive downtown. I wouldn't have minded so much, but every time he answered a question or pointed something out, he would use this obnoxiously bad robot voice. And then when I would make a lane change or anything he thought might be even remotely wrong while we drove, he would blurt out, "Danger, Will Robinson, danger!" Then continued laughing. While we parked, signs of the fireworks were still visible on the street. Trash collectors were busily cleaning up and the little street sweepers cruised along picking up stuff in the gutters. A smattering of people walked the mall, enjoying the bright sunny day. I took my Dad's arm and walked together down the mall. We chatted about nothing in particular as I carefully steered us towards the alleyway across from Writer's Corner. When we approached the alleyway, my stomach tightened and I gripped his arm tighter.

"Ow!" He complained.

I nervously laughed. "Just sneaking in a shot for all the abuse I've been taking."

He laughed back. "If I wasn't picking on you, you'd think I didn't care."

"Uh, huh. How many times have I heard that one?"

He squeezed my arm. "More than you probably care."

I nodded and continued to steer him towards the alleyway.

"How about the *Breckenridge Brewery*?" Dad suggested.

"Ah, no. You don't drink and I don't like their food. How about…" Then I stopped. "Oh, snap. I just remembered that I lost my lipstick in that alley last night. It's just over here."

I pulled him along as he protested. "When have you started wearing lipstick?"

"Dad, I had to look good last night, what if I met someone?" My apprehension grew as we closed in on the front of the alley and my resolve was starting to erode. My knees were getting a little weak and my body began to tingle.

"Oh, of course. In case Brooke's cousin was there. Got ya." He nudged me as if he understood.

"Right." I answered as I involuntarily began to slow.

"Couldn't you just buy a new one? Downtown alleys give me the creeps. Too many monster shows when I was a kid."

I completely understood that sentiment. "No, it was one of my favorites. Want me to explain about a girl and her lipstick?"

"No."

Girly stuff was the easiest way to get him to change subjects. We stopped in front of the alleyway and my body shivered. Dad hugged me closer thinking it was from the cold, but it was because of last night's events rushing upon me. In my mind's eye, I could clearly see the two people with their red eyes down by the dumpster, which would have been about halfway down the alley. I involuntarily reached down and rubbed my leg. The image of the creature thing's eyes staring at me after it flipped me on my back dominated my consciousness. I looked up at the buildings that made up the alleyway, and I marveled at how big that crocodile winged creature must have been to fly in from above me. Those buildings were really high. Dad squeezed me.

"We going in or have you come to your senses and realized it would be easier to buy a new one?"

I shook my head, took a deep breath and plunged forward. I expected things to repeat themselves, but the sound of the people walking by and the street sweepers continued to filter down the alleyway. Slightly disappointed and relieved at the same time, I half-heartedly searched the ground as I kept an eye on the blue dumpster that neared. Like walking up to someone you don't want to talk to, the blue dumpster waited patiently for me to approach.

"Honey, seriously. This is a waste of time. And what were you doing down here anyway?" Dad complained from the other side.

"I have to have it." I replied, ignoring the second part of his question.

His muffled grunt of resignation was combined with the occasional can being kicked.

When I approached the dumpster, my heart began to beat faster. Black filth marred the side of it and the black lids had long since been ripped away. The putrid smell of trash wafted up and out of the dumpster causing me to hold my breath or gag. I slowly knelt down next to it and the long gashes appeared in the black goop and blue paint. Ten in all traveled in a straight line towards where my back had been against the wall. The hair on the back of my neck stood up and sweat broke out on my forehead. My hand shook as I reached out to run my fingers along the scratches. Scared deeply into the metal, the edges were smooth, as if something ultra-sharp had cut through the metal like it was butter. I leaned in to look at it better when I felt something slowly moving up my left shoulder blade and firmly grab my neck…I screamed out!

"Holy crap!" Dad cried as he jumped back. Panting, he grabbed his chest as I spun to place my back against the wall. I put my hand over my mouth to stifle the next scream.

"Dad!" Breath came in a ragged explosion from my chest as my heart beat a thousand beats a minute. "You trying to give me a heart attack!?"

"What are *you* talking about?!" He bent over to catch his breath. "I'm the one having a coronary." He took several deep breaths. "Jesus." He straightened up and walked around a bit.

I tried to slow my breath, but as I watched the edge of the dumpster, the high pitched scratching pierced my brain and I froze once again. With my Dad out of view, the black tiger's green eyes seemed to appear and coldness seeped into my body. I desperately tried to move, but the fear of last night was taking a hold of my body again and a whimper escaped my lips. The illusionary green eyes crept toward me and I couldn't break away from them. Anger, seething anger and hatred, peered out from the eyes and I felt my will being drawn out my body like smoke into a filter. But unlike a filter that cleans the air and makes it pure once again, this fed upon my will corrupting and twisting it.

Suddenly a voice called to me. The voice was so faint that I could barely register it through my unconscious induced fear that I wasn't even sure I had heard anything. The only thing my mind could focus on was the green eyes and the scratching that threatened to shut down my consciousness. Then a face appeared behind the green eyes. A shadowy silhouette that twisted and distorted into grotesque caricatures of a man I knew. Then as the face evolved from nightmare hideousness to sanely familiar, green eyes dissolved into brown eyes and I finally stared into my Dad's very concerned face.

"Jennifer Julienne Ritter look at me!"

He grabbed my shoulders and shook me.

With the illusion broken, I shook my head, peered around and flung my arms around his shoulders and buried my head. His strong arms enclosed around me like a wall that would keep the nightmares at bay. My breaths came in heavy gulps, while I held back any tears that wanted to spring up and just let myself be comforted by his presence.

"Shh, it's okay." He told me.

We stayed there for a moment before we both rose and his height made it awkward to maintain my arms around his neck. I regained my breathing and my body stopped shaking, but the cold despair still lingered.

I looked up into his concerned face and brokered my best smile. "I'm okay."

He wiped away the one escaping tear that had made its way out of the prison of my eye and ran down my cheek. "You must have really liked that lipstick."

I barked a laugh as he took my hand. "Let's go eat."

He nodded while hazarding one more glance back at the dead dumpster and shivered.

Dad pulled my hand to help me along and before I retreat back inside the walls of his protective arms, the sun reflected off something high on one of the buildings. I noticed a new set of gashes in the alley wall across from the dumpster. New goosebumps sprang alive, because these gashes looked like they had been made by a dinosaur.

Chapter Six

Disquiet at the Apollo

Lunch began quietly. My mind couldn't shake the vision from the alley and sensing my anxiety, Dad chatted on about this and that. He talked mostly about the stellar new graphics he was putting together for the video game he was currently working on, but most of it was lost to my inner thoughts. I was just happy to listen to the reassuring sound of his voice. So, I nodded when I needed too, asked questions in the right spots, and tried to safely remember what had just happened in the alley, without having a complete meltdown in front of him. The creepiness of the whole thing still bothered me, and every time I went to those memories of the red eyes or the black tiger thing, my vision would suddenly blur. Then I'd have to shake my head and focus on his voice to bring me back. After a few times of almost slipping back, I stopped all together and really concentrated on my Dad.

"Thanks for coming back!" he took a bite of his burger.

I raised my eyebrows in surprise. "What? I've been listening."

He nodded sarcastically as he chewed. "Yeah."

"I have!"

"Maybe some of the time, but where were you when your eyes suddenly glazed over in thought?" He asked.

I could feel the heat rise in my cheeks.

"I know I might not be the greatest father in the world, but, are you doing drugs?" He laid his burger down and stared at me.

His tone told me this wasn't one of his normal joking around times. His eyes were too intense and the concern on his face was genuine. The funny thing about my Dad was, he really had a hands off approach a lot of the time. I appreciated that most of the time, and hated it some of the times, but he would never fail to ask the hard question or inquire when he thought it was in my best interest. Sometimes it would cause me to yell at him, hate him, and even despise him, but in his defense he never got mad or used it against me. Something I couldn't do, and in the end he just expected me to make the right decision. Sometimes it worked out and other times it didn't, but he was always there to mop things up or congratulate me. I wasn't the best child either, therefore, I looked him strait in the eyes, "No."

He stared at me for a moment and nodded. "Okay. Care to tell me about what happened last night?"

I didn't want to answer, not because I didn't want to tell him, but because I didn't know *how* to tell him. So I stayed quiet.

"Fine." His voice was neutral.

I could tell he was upset, but not disappointed. He rarely got disappointed at me, but when he did it always crushed me.

He smiled. "When you are ready, you know where to find me." He laughed at his joke.

He is such a dork. Then I laughed with him.

We finished lunch and I talked him into walking around. The sun was brilliantly bright in the sky, and the air was crisp. One of those quirky days in Colorado where if you stayed in the shade, you froze and if you were in the sun you were on fire. So, as I dragged him window shopping, we meandered in and out of the sun and shade. We stopped in front of a clothing store that had a gorgeous strapless dress in the window. The dress was silky red, had a long flowing hem that elegantly touched the mannequin's golden tan feet, and a pair of mid-high heel shoes the color of the dress. The reflection in the window said my Dad liked it too.

"Got a date?"

"What?"

"Not a hard question. Do you have a date for the back to school dance?"

Even in the reflection of the window, the mischievousness in his eyes was running rampant. I needed to be careful not to step on any verbal landmines that would blow up in my face.

"You doubt my attractiveness?" I offhandedly remarked.

"No, I doubt young boys' assertiveness."

Stepped over one landmine.

"Then you greatly underestimate the boys at the school. They don't lack in confidence."

"Difference in confidence and ignorance…maybe you shouldn't be so mean?"

Another landmine. "What?" I acted all hurt. "I'm not mean. I'm the nicest person on the planet."

His eyes grew even more mischievous. "Mean doesn't always mean cruel, maybe you act aloof? Guys think you're unattainable."

I turned around to him. "Really? You are going to insinuate that I'm a snob?" Folding my arms across my chest, I waited. His face wavered between concern that maybe he had overstepped our game, and whether I had placed my own landmine out there, which I had.

He narrowed his eyes. "Just saying, if you act uninterested, then you appear to be better than everyone else."

Got him. "When I'm interested in the right guy, that guy will understand that I'm unique. Not that I'm somehow better than everyone else, but special for him, and he'll see that life has just gotten more amazing because of the emotional connection we share."

His face deflated. "When did you get good at this?"

Walking by him, I tapped his shoulder. "I had a very good teacher." We finished our day with smoothies and headed home.

All the way home, I pondered how I was going to get Gabe to ask me to the dance. Normally, I would have asked Brooke for help. He wouldn't have stood a chance then, because when we get together and decided to do something, nothing gets in our way. But this was different. Since she was his cousin, and my gut kinda told me that she wouldn't really approve, especially after the weird incident before New Year's Eve, I couldn't ask Brooke. Therefore, I needed to get him to ask me in such a way that Brooke would believe he did it of his own volition. Hence the problem at hand. As I gazed out the window, since I made Dad drive home, the solution began to mold itself into an idea. By the time we drove into the driveway and parked the car, I knew the plan needed an expert in manipulation and who better than a thespian.

Kelli Searle was a master manipulator, but in a good way. Filled with a ridiculous amount of confidence for a teenage girl, she had a knack of getting into conversations and maneuvering them in the direction she wanted them to go. I've seen her turn a conversation about a girl a guy didn't like, into making it seem it was his fault for not liking her. And if he didn't ask her out it would be the biggest mistake of his life. So, I knew she would be the one to ask for help. We met the next day at the Cyber Dragon Café for lunch. I got there early, ordered my usual tea, sat at our table and waited. Kelli was always late, no matter what the occasion. Luckily Kaylene was working and it wasn't too busy, so she popped over now and then and kept me company. I also got online and tried to find any information about that tiger creature or people with glowing red eyes. The search engine didn't really come up with much. I tried: black tigers, black tigers with tentacles, black tentacles, fantasy cats with tentacles, but nothing really came up. Then as I was scrolling down to the last pages of the search, an entry for a black feline cat that had tentacles called a Coeurl appeared. I scrolled further along and discovered that this was a fantasy creature created by fictional author A. E. van Vogt in the short story *Black Destroyer*. The blurb described a large cat that had longer front legs then back ones, and tentacles that ended in suction cups. I leaned back. I wondered if Mr. Van Vogt might have had a similar encounter with such a creature, but the description though similar was very different too. As I read, the article said that he had passed away in January of 2000. Frustrated, nothing more came up about the creature except for the interpretations of other authors and gamers that evolved the creature to fit their worlds. As for the glowing red eye people, there was plenty of stuff on that. Anything from red eyes from a photo flash to shapeshifters and demons. Not being one to believe in such things it must have been the light from the streetlamp when I entered the alley. But that does bring up the thing I saw at school before break. Anyway, when Kelly shouted her hello from the door, and approached, my fingers pressed the off switch. I certainly had more important things to discuss than strange creatures and weird eyes.

Tuesday of the new semester hadn't come fast enough. Not only was it the last semester of high school, but I was anxious to see Brooke and Gabe again. Brooke called late Monday night before school to let me know she was back and that she would pick me up at our regular time. I woke up very early, certainly earlier than normal, took my shower, got dressed, and waited down stairs. Dad was already up, had his run, and was hard at work on his video project. Cooper kept me company until Brooke honked. My heart immediately dropped and my mood darkened to see only her in the car. Stomping to the car, I climbed in, exchanged hugs and drove to school. We talked about what each of us did over break, though Brooke was very vague about her time in Japan, just as she always was when she got back from vacation. We approached the entrance to the school on the west side. Two juniors sat in the West Bunker that guarded the entrance. All juniors were required to spend time in the bunkers as sentries for added security during school hours. We waved to them and drove in. Parking in the student lot, many of our friends were arriving also. We greeted them and headed off to class.

I only had one and half classes with Brooke this semester; Dr. Marcus's Econ class, after lunch and Dr. Daugherty's class on every other Tuesday and Thursday. We shared quick hugs and walked off with the others classmates. I entered the foyer of the school and bowed to the statue of Apollo. It wasn't required but customary for the seniors to do, since he was the patron god of education. Several other statues of gods or goddess also adorned the foyer all having to do with education in their respective religions. The sounds of students greeting their friends echoed down the hallway along with the ruckus of the lower grades changing classrooms. I found my locker up in Zeus Hall, threw my books in my backpack, grabbed my English binder and headed off to Dr. Daugherty's class.

Dr. Daugherty sat at his desk busily writing in a binder and waved absently to the hello's from the entering students. I found my usual desk, sat down, and looked bored at the clock. The bell rang.

Dr. Daugherty stood, turned on the smart board and addressed us.

"Hi everyone."

"Hello, Dr. Daugherty." We all responded in unison.

He blushed and looked askew at us. "Let's not start that nonsense. This isn't Dr. Kodis's philosophy class. Civility is nice, not conformists. Got me?"

"Yes Dr. Daugherty." We said in unison again.

He groaned and we laughed.

"Okay, fine. Please pass up your comparative essays I asked you to do over break."

Our groans accompanied the sound of folders being opened and the ruffling of papers. The door squeaked open and close as Dr. Daugherty greeted someone. I found my paper and then looked up; my heart stopped, and jealousy ripped through my body as gasps escaped from the other girls in the class.

Gabriel stood talking to Dr. Daugherty and shaking his hand. I felt my face flush and quickly covered my mouth with my hand.

Dr. Daugherty turned to us. "Class, we have a new student. Let me introduce Gabriel Kikashi Kirohoshiabya." He scrunched his nose. "Did I butcher that?"

Gabriel smiled and several girls behind me sighed, "No that was pretty good."

"Japanese name, got it. Gabriel…"

"Just Gabe is fine." He interrupted Dr. Daugherty.

"You mean, Babe." Janis said behind and to my left.

The urge to turn and around and gift her with an evil eye stare was almost overpowering, but instead, my eyes stayed on Gabe. I drew in a deep breath, but the smell of caramel corn didn't come around. Then several more deep breaths in rapid secession when…

"Are you hyperventilating Ms. Ritter?" Dr. Daugherty asked concern.

My eyes widened, and the embarrassment made my face flush even a deeper red. I quickly ducked my head as I shook it.

"Whew, I didn't want to have Mr. Kirohoshiabya have to perform CPR on you!"

The class laughed, and my face felt even hotter as I fervently wished to fade into nothingness.

"My apologies, Ms. Ritter, I couldn't resist. Take a seat Mr. Kirohoshiabya. Now who would like to go first?"

"Where is Brooke?" Carl asked.

"She'll only be here every other week this semester. She is helping with another class." He answered.

That's where Brooke went before class instead of our locker. Mrs. Tomlinson's third grade class needed an extra hand. Since it was a heavily girl populated class, she had asked for her specifically.

Gabe brush by me on his way to the back of the class. Several 'sit here' rang out as I tried to calm myself. I couldn't understand why his distinct caramel corn odor, which had been so prominent New Year's Eve, didn't envelope me, which made me start to wonder if it wasn't just my own imagination. Slowly, the heat of my embarrassment faded away and I hazarded a glance back to see where he was sitting and caught his eye. His hazel eyes brightened up as he looked at me and I flushed again and turned my head.

"No volunteers?" Dr. Daugherty announced, "Okay then Ms. Ritter, would you grace us with your unique insight, please."

The groan that escaped my lips would have made a zombie jealous. I slid out of my desk and started the longest walk to the front and began the worst ten minutes of my life.

Lunch couldn't have come quick enough that day. In fact, if a meteorite had plummeted down and destroyed downtown Denver, it wouldn't have been as bad as the ten minutes I stood up in front of Dr. Daugherty's class and made a fool of myself. I plopped down at the senior table and placed my head down. Kaylene, Somer, and Kennah continued to munch on their lunches as a resigned sigh of despair escaped my lips.

"That could only be a guy sigh." Somer said.

"I agree." Kennah laughed. "I've used it to many times to not recognize it."

"You both are wrong," Kaylene announced. "When was the last time you heard anything like that out of JJ? She's in love." They giggled and laughed.

"Ha, ha." My head came off the table. "Love is for losers, and I'm not a loser." I pulled my hair back and put it in a ponytail.

"First sign, denial." Kaylene said between mouthfuls of her salad.

"No, there isn't anyone here I could possibly find interesting."

"That might have been true before," Somer stated, "but news of Brooke's cousin has spread fast. Fresh meat and all."

"Yep. Heard he is a really hot guy." Kennah said. "Not as good looking as my boyfriend, but I've heard he's not bad."

Kaylene's eyes popped open. "Have you seen him!?"

"No." Kennah said off handedly. "But he can't be that good looking."

Kaylene and Somer looked at each other knowingly. "He puts your boyfriend to shame, Kennah."

Kennah eyes narrowed. "I don't think so. Cheers don't date ugly boys."

I shook my head. "Can we stop talking about this, please."

"Just wait till you see him."

About this time Brooke came walking up to us with her lunch and sat down. She appeared a little out of sorts.

"Something wrong?" I asked.

Brooke thought for a moment. "Something weird is going on."

"Like what?"

She shook her head. "I'm not sure. But have you guys noticed anything strange going on?"

The others shook their heads.

"No." Kaylene said. "Nothing seems out of the ordinary, except we have fourteen weeks of school left!"

Cheers went up from the senior table.

Brooke smiled. "I guess."

"Maybe it's the commotion your cousin is causing? How come you didn't tell us about him earlier?" Somer asked.

Brooke brushed aside the comment. "It's not that important. He's just my cousin."

"Is Set going here as well?" I looked around the lunch room and didn't notice anything out of sorts.

Brooke shook her head. "No, he's over at Valor."

"You have two?" Somer said. "Is he just as gorgeous as Gabriel?" She turned to Kennah. "Text your boyfriend and see if there is as much commotion there as there is here."

"He isn't gorgeous and there isn't any commotion, girls." Brooke answered annoyed.

"What…" Somer started but stopped. She was looking at something behind me and when I turned, Gabriel was entering the lunch room. Just like in those commercials where time slows to a crawl, the model's hair is blowing in the wind, and everyone in the room turns to admire him, well, the lunchroom was quiet and everyone was looking at the new guy. For Gabriel's part, he appeared not to notice what was going on around him and looked in our direction, and headed our way. Quickly turning back around, my face felt hot, my breathing shortened, and I frantically played with my hair. Even the buddy tables were all watching him. That's when I noticed something strange.

The faces on the younger kids appeared to be in various degrees of being frightened depending on the age. The Kindergarten table was empty, but the 1st grade table was full and the kids' faces appeared frightened. Not like all out scared, but more as if they were uncertain or not sure what they were looking at and that made them afraid. Their buddies appeared to not notice. The 3rd grade table appeared less frightened and more curious, as if they were looking at something only their imaginations had seen before. The 5th grade table didn't appear to be frightened at all, but puzzled, like they were looking at something that didn't quite make sense. The 7th grade table appeared to be unaffected like the rest of us except for the girls that were openly staring at him, much like the rest of the lunch room. The other side of the table stares told me when he was standing behind me and then next to me.

"Hi." He said.

"Musical." Kaylene whispered as those around her nodded.

Brooke snarled. "Pathetic. Hey Gabe, how's the first day going?" Brooke scooted down, pushing the others away, much to their dismay. Gabe came around the table and sat across from me. "Hi JJ."

"Hey Gabe."

"Great job in Dr. Daugherty's class. Your presentation was spot on in my opinion."

My face flushed again and I placed my hand over the side of my face to hide some of the color. "Thank you." My eyes shifted around the room to keep from looking into his.

Kaylene did a not too subtle cough and elbowed Brooke.

"Gabe, this is Kaylene..."

"My pleasure." Kaylene extended her hand and Gabe shook it.

"Somer"

Somer nodded, red creeping down her neck.

"And Kennah."

Kennah was staring openly at him and Gabe seemed a little embarrassed by the attention.

"Geez, you guys suck." Brooke's face scrunched up in disgust.

Gabe turned back to me and out of the corner of my eye I saw Kennah pull out her cell phone and immediately begin texting.

"So, whose class do you have next?" I asked.

He smiled. "Ms. Pendragon's."

"Do you have running shoes?" Somer asked, concern clouding her eyes.

Gabe looked confused.

"Ms. Pendragon has a tendency to take her classes on runs as she teaches. Always good to go to her class with running shoes on." Somer explained.

Gabe laughed and more sighs issued around me. "I don't."

Somer, Kaylene and several other girls jumped up from the table, "Mr. Winckler always has extras, come with me I'll show you." Somer enthusiastically took Gabe's arm.

"We'll show you." Kaylene corrected her.

Gabe let himself be guided away from the table. "See you later, JJ, Brooke."

I waved to him and fumed under my embarrassment for not thinking of that first.

"Pathetic!" Brooke yelled at them. "That's my cousin…. you whores!"

The girls laughed and waved as they exited the lunch room.

Brooke shook her head. "I knew this would be a bad idea."

"What?"

"Letting him come here. Should have sent him off to Valor too."

Deep down I didn't agree, but on the surface I nodded. "Yeah. He might disrupt things around here and you know how Mr. Resler loves order."

Brooke agreed. "Valor is a little stricter. Less chance for him to get into trouble, not that Gabe makes trouble. He's probably the gentlest soul I know, but trouble seems to find him." She smiled.

"Is Set your other cousin." Kennah asked looking up from her cell phone.

"Yes, why?"

"He punched some kid at Valor."

Brooke's face grew angry.

Chapter Seven

An Egg?

I've seen Brooke get really mad maybe a handful of times in the four years I've known her. She's usually very cool and doesn't let much get under her skin, though, on occasion just her 'angry' look will send most people scurrying away from her in fear. But this time, her eyes grew a deeper shade of blue, her neck strained just a little, and her breathing slowed. She was majorly pissed. Brooke grabbed her cell phone and immediately began texting.

"Who are you texting?" I stared around the table gauging the different expression of the few that were listening.

Kennah was texting so fast that it was hard to see her fingers.

"My Mom. When I get my hands on him." She mumbled as her fingers flew too.

I couldn't help but wonder why Set would punch someone in the face, but having just been around him a few days or so, I'd have to say it didn't surprise me. He seemed a little too aggressive. But on the other hand, Brooke appeared to be able to handle him, so just to say he did it on purpose wouldn't be fair. I'm sure the person he punched, probably deserved it. Though you can never tell.

Brooke slammed her phone down. Her eyes narrowed and her breathing became even softer.

"You okay?" I asked uncertain. She looked ready to punch something.

She locked on me with her blue eyes, "Idiot!"

"Me?" My eyes grew larger in surprise.

She shook her head. "No, of course not. Set. This is not a low profile."

"What?"

Low profile, what is that?

She waved away my question. "It's nothing. I should have expected it. Should have kept him here and sent Gabe to Valor. Cripes."

I thank you for not doing that. "Is he always getting into trouble? Set that is."

"No, actually, he's usually so cocky that he never needs to prove himself, but usually some idiot thinks he can handle him or thinks that he is too cocky and tries to start some shit." Brooke laughed. "They quickly find out they picked the wrong guy."

Evidently.

"Well, what now?"

"Nothing, Mom will take care of it and I'll take care of him when I get home." She turned to Kennah. "Anything about the fight?"

"Plenty," she said.

Kennah looked almost awe struck.

"Tommy, my boyfriend, said that Garret, you kn…"

"I know Garret," Brooke interrupted her.

"Well, anyway, he was like, 'your cousin is a guy'. And Set was, 'more of man than you', then Garret was like, 'she's a dude, dude, and Set was like 'dude, take your skirt off and quit crying to me if you can't score on her', then Garret was like 'every guy scores on her, then Set was like, 'then ask them what it's like, since you can't' and then . . ."

"Oh my god, will you just tell us?" I said.

"But . . ."

"Shut up and tell us. Why did Set punch him?!" Sometimes it was hard to take Kennah's incessant rambling, she's like an ad for Glee or something.

Hurt, Kennah pouted her lips, which she was known for, but it quickly vanished when Brooke gave her the evil blue eyes.

"Well, fine," she pouted. "Garret threw a shoulder at him, missed but somehow he touched Set's hair, and Set put him on the ground with one punch." Kennah giggled uncontrollably.

I stared at her. "His hair?" Really? Touched his hair and he punches a guy for it. Didn't really expect that, I turned to Brooke who had a knowing smile on her face.

"Seriously? Garrett all but calls you a whore and Set punches him because he touched his hair?"

Brooke nodded her head while shrugging her shoulders. "That would sound about right."

I looked disbelievingly at her. "His hair."

She shrugged. "To each their own. Set could care less what people think of us, but when it comes to vanity, he's right at the top." Brooke leaned back and smirked. "I am so going to cross check Garret at the next playoff game."

I stood up. "Damn I can't believe you?! All you can think about is getting even with that guy? Set is going to get kicked out of school!"

Brooke looked at me as if I was going crazy. "Don't worry about it. Set isn't going to get kicked out of anything. Relax."

I was mad. Not exactly sure why, but there it was. "Whatever, I'm going to class!" I snatched my books off the table and stomped off to my next class with Dr. Zang.

Storming my way through the hallways I fumed. My mind couldn't decide if I was madder because of the comments made by others, or if I was madder that my *friends* had taken Gabe with them. Several people said hi on my way to class and I remember giving brief hellos to them. My determined feet walked into class and Dr. Zang wasn't there. Slamming my books down on my desk, I wandered over to the window and looked out at the mountains. They were snow covered and beautiful; I couldn't really enjoy them though. Looking down, the snow upon the ground was tinged with dirt, and covered with foot prints. *Why am I so mad?* I know Brooke is like that, and it's never bothered me before, but just the way those girls just hovered over Gabe, like some trophy to be won, just really pissed me off. *Ah, what is going on?!*

"Hey, JJ." Dr. Zang said walking in.

Startled, I waved to her. Dr. Zang was one of my favorite teachers. Actually, she was one of the few teachers all the students liked. She had a vicious liberal streak that she wasn't shy about sharing, but she also listened to other views before countering and getting her point across anyway. Her black frizzy hair bounced around her head; she shoved it back and sighed. Dr. Zang placed her books down on her cluttered desk then plopped down into her chair. She turned a knowing smile to me.

"Boy troubles?" Her low voice asked.

Shocked, I blushed, then regained my composer. "Tsk, when do I ever have boy troubles?"

"That's why it's so clearly etched on your face." She winked.

My face flush deeper. I went and sat down at my desk.

She opened her lesson plan and started to write in it. That was one of the cool things about Dr. Zang, she could read a person like a book. The silence stretched on, but it wasn't an uncomfortable one.

"What are we doing today?" I dug out my Latin book.

Without looking up, "I think we'll translate Ovid, might give you some advice."

I hung my head, though a smile appeared. "What do I need advice for? Revenge isn't something I condone."

"Revenge?" Dr. Zang looked up.

I told her about Brooke and Set.

"Ah, well, she is a fiery one. Almost like a harpy or dragon out of mythology." She tapped her chin, "I wouldn't worry about it, hockey is a violent sport, too violent in my opinion, and Brooke will calm down. She's also one of the most rational people I have met."

"Yeah, but it just pissed me off so much that she didn't care what those guys were saying about her."

"Really? Why should you care? You can't change someone's thoughts. Just shows their insecurities. Or is it that because Set didn't come to her defense? Or because Brooke didn't care?"

"Both!" I yelled. "Set's her cousin, he should have done something!"

"Out of honor?" Dr. Zang smiled knowingly.

"What?"

Gabe walked in, nodded to Dr. Zang, who raised an eyebrow, and placed a bag of caramel corn on my desk with a smile. His borrowed sneakers squeaked on the floor.

"This is your favorite, right?"

My gaze lingered on his eyes and slowly nodded. I wouldn't take credit for getting these snacks in our vending machines, since Mr. Resler is very conscious of providing nutritious snacks for the school, but I did make a very good argument about the popcorn, even if it did have caramel on it.

"Sorry those guys took me away, see you at practice?" His smile was like a sun.

I stared, and nodded dumbly. My body lit on fire when he touched my hand.

He winked, bowed to Dr. Zang and left the room. I watched him go and my heart thudded heavy in my chest.

"Ah, now the plot thickens." Dr. Zang laughed.

Later, my tired feet carried me across the parking lot in the snow. Once again, the forecasters said it wouldn't snow until tomorrow, and they got it wrong. Typical Colorado weather. I pulled my jacket closer to me and walked towards the ice rink. Dr. Zang probably had the most enjoyable class time she's ever had. As we translated *Ovid's Book 1 Elegy 2, Love's Victim*, she continually made off handed references that were meant to reference what Gabe had done. And just on cue, each reference would make me blush and she would laugh and the other students would look around confused. This made me blush even more, because they would eventually end up looking at me, and that just made it worse.

I smiled. That was super awesome that he brought me the snack though, which just goes to show that chivalry is not dead.

The wind picked up, and something caught my eye. Up on the roof, the snow continued to blow fiercely and from the flood lights that tried to brighten the mascot of the Valkyrie, a shadow appeared in an area that it shouldn't have. Just like with the hallway, the flood lights clearly lit the area, and the heavy snow in front of them made flickering shadows, but this shadow appeared to be outside the other shadows which again made it look out of place. Stopping, I squinted against the blowing snow and tried to figure out how the shadow could appear there, and then someone bumped into me almost knocking me to the ground.

"Sorry, JJ." One said out of the group of underclassmen that were running towards the restaurant.

Perturbed, I waved, looked up and the shadow was gone. I moved back to my original spot and still didn't see anything that would have made the shadow disappear or for that matter appear. Blinking, I shrugged and headed inside. The restaurant was busy as it always was after school. Just as with the common areas, each grade had a section it gravitated towards, and no one crossed into each other's territory, although, it wasn't nearly as defined as the amphitheater. I waved to a few hellos, greeted some others as I made my way up to the bar where Connor greeted me.

"Hey, JJ. Usual?" His smile was always on display.

"No, thanks. Any hot chocolate ready?"

He winked. "I saved you some. The middle schoolers drank most of it." He walked back into the kitchen. I pulled my coat around me, the two ice rinks always made the restaurant cold. Connor placed the steaming mug of hot chocolate down in front of me.

"Whipped cream?"

"Please."

He swirled a good helping of cream on top and then placed a cherry in the center. My smile went from ear to ear at his generosity. Placing my gloves in my coat pocket, the wrapper of the caramel corn crunched adding to the huge smile already on my face. My body began to warm, and as I reached out for the warm mug, thinking it was Gabe's face, and how soft and . . .

"Need help popping that cherry?" A cold wind blew in from behind me.

Shattering my vision, I didn't need to turn around to know who it was. "Don't you need to fix your hair or something?" The mug felt lifeless and dead in my hand.

Set leaned his body up against the bar, oozing arrogance. "There are just somethings you don't touch." Then his bimbos appeared next to him. I didn't recognize either of the two blonds, but they had to be from Valor.

"Fan club?"

He looked at the two. "Spoils to the victor."

"Aren't the twins going to be jealous?"

"They will join us later." The girls giggled.

Disgusted, I shifted away.

He leaned in. "Maybe you should too?" he cooed.

His black/brown eyes were a bottomless pit that threatened to pull you down like a whirlpool. I fought to pull my gaze away, but his eyes just kept sucking me in.

Then his head slammed down onto the bar, breaking the spell, and I blinked furiously.

"Hey, dumb ass. Don't do that again." Brooke's blue hair draped over Set's black hair as she whispered in his ear.

Connor stared, unsure what to do, as others began to look our way. Set's smashed face smiled. He easily lifted his head off the bar, as the girls he was with stared in awe and adoration.

"Take care, Blue," Set's eyes grew darker. "You may be the favorite, but I won't always be easy on you." He slapped away her hand.

Brooke stared hard at him. "As long as I'm responsible, you will listen." She stepped up and got in his face. "Understand?"

The authority and threatening tone made me even want to take a step back. Set laughed at the threat, brushed by her, picked up his bimbos, and exited the restaurant. People watched him go and then slowly turned back to a fuming Brooke.

"What happened to not worrying about it?" I said.

She slowly turned her darker blue eyes at me and they held an anger that I'd never seen before. "Don't start with me." She slung her hockey bag over her shoulder and stomped off to the locker room.

The restaurant was abnormally quiet. Even I was in shock. *Wow, never seen her like that before, and I thought I've seen all her moods. What was that about? Maybe she does care that he didn't do anything.*

That did make me feel better. I finished up my hot chocolate, paid, and went to sit in the stands to do homework.

My homework got done pretty fast, since I wanted to have as much free time to talk to Gabe when he came in, but the jerk hadn't shown yet. Inside the rink, the stands were pretty much empty. Those on the ice kept a fair distance away from Brooke in goal, especially after one of her teammates made the mistake of coming into close and jokingly sprayed her with ice. She checked him to the ground. Coach Winckler stormed off the bench and lit her up for the check, and now she was doing latter sprints for her transgression. Bored, my gaze slowly roved the stand looking for him when a golden retriever sprinted out of the tunnel onto the ice. Unable to keep its balance, he slid across the ice and skidded to a halt in the middle.

"Cooper!" Gabe's voice boomed out of the tunnel and then he appeared. My heart caught in my throat. As the commotion continued on the ice as Cooper slipped and slid around, I made my way down to the glass.

"Cooper!" I yelled pounding on the glass.

Cooper's head came up and he skidded and slid his way over to me until Brooke came in like a predatory animal and scooped him off the ice. She skated over to Gabe, handed him off, said a few curt words, and then continued her sprints. Gabe disappeared back into the tunnel and I raced back into the restaurant. Cooper sprinted out of the locker room hallway and into my arms.

"What are you doing?" Cooper jumped and licked my face.

An exhausted Gabe came running out of the hallway and stopped before me. "Sorry about that." His musical voice chimed.

His golden eyes had a deep merriment in them at the fiasco that had taken place, my heart lightened.

"What are you doing with him?" Several of the remaining underclassmen were beginning to make their way over to pet Cooper. He ate the attention up.

"Your dad left him at our house, said he had a late last minute meeting to go to. That's why I'm late, sorry." He bent down and took my hand and lifted me up. His hand was warm and it began to spread through my arm into my body. "Hungry?"

My head nodded absently as I continued to lose myself in his eyes.

He walked me over to a table.

"Hey JJ? Cooper isn't supposed to be in here, health code, so take one of the tables by the door, please." Connor stepped away from where he was petting Cooper and washed his hands.

"Okay. Cooper, come." Cooper followed us over to a table that was next to the exit and we sat down. "Lay down." He obediently laid under the table.

"We'll just grab a snack, Mrs. Wasabi is having orange chicken and noodles for dinner, wanna eat at our house?" He asked.

Of course I did, but I had to play it off. "That's really nice, but I'm sure Dad will be hungry when he comes home after his meeting, I should go home."

He smiled, "No worries, he's coming to our house after his meeting, so there you go, settled." He reached under the table and petted Cooper.

"Well, put that way." The giggle that escaped my lips sounded stupid in my ears and my face flushed.

"What'll you guys have?" Connor asked when he approached the table.

"Just some fries, ranch and water." Gabe ordered.

"Got it."

We sat in silence and it was golden. I've never been with someone where you could just sit and enjoy their company without speaking, but I had to control myself and not just stare at him the whole time. Shortly, Connor brought our fries, ranch and water and we dined. We chit chatted about this and that as he secretly fed Cooper fries under the table. I asked him about how he liked school so far and other things, he politely answered, but I have to confess I didn't hear many of his answers. My eyes lingered on his face absorbing every detail; the perfect way his eyebrows laid again his brow, the flawlessness of his marble smooth skin, the rich fullness of his hair and the depths of wisdom and kindness in his eyes to get much out of the conversation. But, during one stretch, I got caught not listening when he asked me a question about something and I nodded. His facial expression told me that my action didn't fit what he was asking, but then he laughed and it made the awkwardness all better, since his laughter made me laugh.

Then the moment was broken by the sudden appearance of a duffle bag being thrown onto the table. Gabe just managed to get the fries and ranch out of the way.

Brooke plopped down into the empty chair, I scowled at her.

"Can I have some of those?" She reached for the basket of fries, but Gabe held them at bay and looked at me. I shrugged and he handed them over to her. She quickly devoured them.

"Ah, am I tired." She stretched.

"Did you send Dean to the hospital?" That was the boy she checked during practice.

She actually looked a little embarrassed. "No, but I did apologize to him afterwards."

"What?" Gabe asked and she told him about what happened today with Set.

Gabe shook his head. "Why do you let him bother you? You know he does stuff like that to provoke you. That's what they do."

They?

"I know, but it's still pretty inconsiderate, we are supposed to be keeping a low profile." She said.

He smiled. "This *is* a low profile for him. You ready?"

Brooke nodded and grabbed her stuff.

"JJ's coming over to eat."

Brooke's face lightened, "Great."

We got up and left.

He walked me to my car, explaining that my Dad had dropped it off before coming to their house with Cooper, and then he followed Brooke to hers. Not too happy that Gabe decided to go with Brooke, though they probably wanted to talk family business, my mind raced with excitement of getting to spend more time with him. Cooper sat obediently next to me in the jeep with his modified harness for the seatbelt. His breath steamed up the windows while the smell of fries drifted from his side. I wondered why Gabe used the word 'they' to describe Set.

We pulled into Brooke's driveway about an hour later. The snow had let up from earlier in the day, but the roads were still very slick. I got out, Cooper bounded passed me to explore the same areas he always explores, while we made our way to the house. Brooke went in and Gabe waited patiently for me and held the door open, which was super nice.

"Thank you."

His smile made me feel warm. I kicked off my shoes at the door, and used the towel given to me by Brooke to wipe Cooper's feet off. He bounded off to the kitchen as Mrs. Wasabi's happy voice greeted him in Japanese along with' Ajax's bark.

"Come on." Brooke grabbed my hand and led me upstairs. Gabe waved and went to the kitchen.

"Shouldn't we stay down stairs?" I said in protest.

"You can ogle my cousin later; I want to show you something."

Surprised, "I'm not ogling anything, how dare you say that?"

"Tsk, please, you'd jump him right now if he'd let you."

"Whatever, bitch."

Brooke laughed and continued dragging me to her room. We entered and she shoved me towards the bed and shut the door. "Here, now close your eyes."

I closed my eyes, "Don't make me lick your finger or anything?"

"We're not freshman, jeez."

The sound of rustling floated to me as I began to imagine sitting next to Gabe for dinner and not having to stare at him across the table. The thought of getting to enjoy his company and maybe brush up against him a few times made my skin goose pimple. *Joyous!*

She sat down beside me and her breathing was heavy. "Okay, look."

The object she held in her hand was wondrous. The first thing you noticed was the dark jade color of it. Brilliant greens moved and flowed inside the jelly bean shaped stone that was the size of a honeydew melon. Jetting greens exploded against the surface then cascaded down like fireworks on a warm summer's eve. Over and over these explosions happened, mesmerizing the watcher as the greens began to pull you into them.

"What is that?" I breathed with awe.

"Beautiful isn't it?" Brooke whispered.

I nodded, speechless.

"It's an egg."

"Egg?"

Brooke laughed. "More commonly known as a dragon's egg."

"What?" My hand reached out and touched it. Warmth radiated from it like a sock direct from the dryer. "Wow."

"Here."

She held it out to me.

At first I didn't want to take it. Something about it made me feel it was too fragile to handle, but once I took it, the outer surface felt like a really smooth rock picked up from a river or stream bed. The warmth intensified and began to pulse like a heartbeat making the colors move inside. My eyes watched it and I began to imagine that the plumes of color were pulsating like blood flowing through arteries.

Warmth seeped into my hands and began to warm my entire body. A deep sense of calm and tranquility enveloped me like a blanket and all my troubles drained from my body. I pulled it up to my breast and closed my eyes.

Thump….thump….thump.

I couldn't tell if it was my heart or coming from inside the egg.

"How did they make this?" my whisper sounded unusually loud.

Brooke giggled. "Don't you remember how one is made from ninth grade?"

Normally, I would have had a retort for her, but the calm going through my body wouldn't allow me to. My eyes sleepily opened. "Ha, ha. There are no dragons, so tell me?"

A knowing smile appeared on her face. "So sure are you?"

"Just tell me?"

"We need to have that discussion sometime, since you are in love with my cousin."

"Tsk, whatever."

Brooke laughed. "Do you know what a lava lamp is?"

"Yes."

"Just a more sophisticated one." She stood and took it from me. I reluctantly gave it up.

My body continued to feel warm, though the feeling of tranquility began to slowly leave my body. I sighed contently.

Brooke placed it on a pedestal on her dresser. I was surprised I didn't see it when I entered the room, but when she placed it down, my eyes had trouble focusing on it. Frowning, Brooke took my hand and led me from the room.

Dinner was ready and it smelled wonderful. Mr. Wasabi greeted me warmly, and led me to a seat next to him. As everyone else began to sit down, Set walked in with all his arrogance and purposely sat next to Brooke. She gifted him with a hard stare that produced a smile from him.

"Still bitter?" Set asked smugly.

Brooke ignored him and asked for the rice bowl.

"No arguing at this table, Set." Mrs. Wasabi told him.

Set bowed his head in acknowledgement of her authority.

"Is my Dad joining us?" I asked Mr. Wasabi as he passed the rice bowl to me.

"Yes, he should be here shortly. Lobster?"

"Please," I took the lobster dish from him and scooped a portion of the casserole onto the brown fried rice. Normally, I don't eat a lot of fish, in fact there were a lot of things I didn't like to eat, until I started coming to the Wasabi's house.

Gabe came out of the kitchen carrying a large bowl of steaming soup. He placed it on the table and sat down next to me. Brooke winked at me, I flushed, and stared hard at her – begging for her silence.

"Would you like some?" Gabe asked me.

"Please."

He scooped some into a bowl and passed it to me.

"What's the fallout from today?" Brooke asked Set.

Set placed his steak down, which was extremely rare, wiped his mouth and answered.

"Nothing, since Garrett started the incident. The principal was very understanding when Mrs. Wasabi and I argued our case." Set's eyes seemed to grow a little darker brown. "He needed a little persuading to allow me to stay."

Set's smug expression rubbed me the wrong way.

"What does that mean?" I asked.

Set's eyes grew narrow, "Means we won't be having any other problems at Valor." He leaned back and ravished his steak again.

Brooke rolled her eyes, and shook her head at me. "Just ignore him."

Set smiled, blood ran down the side of his mouth. He wiped it away with his finger then succulently sucked it. "Nice." He moaned. "This should interest you, Blue."

Brooke bristled but didn't say anything.

"I'll be seeing you in the playoffs."

Her eyes grew wide. "What?"

He leaned back, "Guess word got out about my awesome right cross on Garrett and the hockey coach came to talk to me as I waited to talk to the principal."

"It's too late in the season, CHSAA won't let you." Brooke informed him.

He shrugged, "Guess the president of Valor is in pretty tight with the CHSAA president."

"Dad? This isn't fair. That is an unfair advantage." She complained.

Set laughed and it was hardy and deep. "And you aren't?"

"Not like you!"

"Afraid I'm going to make you look bad? Dispel the aura of the only female goalie in the state that can't be scored on?" Set rubbed his eyes and made crying noises.

"Set." Mr. Wasabi cautioned.

Set stopped. "It's not that big of a deal. With our prized possession on loan, I'll be too occupied to really help. But if we do see each other." He ran his thumb across his neck.

I stopped. The sweet tasting lobster dripping with butter that sparkled in the table light on the fork mere inches from my mouth, lost its appeal. "Kill?"

"Set." Mrs. Wasabi warned. The authority held in that one word made the hair on my neck stand up.

Set scrunched his face, but said nothing in retort and returned to his steak.

Mr. Wasabi patted my shoulder. "No worries, dear. Set is over exaggerating his assessment of the situation, don't trouble yourself."

I looked at Gabe, he smiled and nodded, but Brooke had a troubled look in her eyes. I couldn't tell if it was because Set was on the hockey team or because he threatened her.

Suddenly, my Dad came walking into the room.

"Dad." I got up and hugged him. He kissed me on the forehead then hugged me back. Cooper weaved in and out of his legs until he petted him.

"Hey boy."

Ajax whimpered from the side until Dad pet him too. Ajax ran off upstairs followed by Cooper.

"Hello, Mr. Ritter," Mr. Wasabi warmly stood and shook his hand. My Dad returned it warmly, then embraced Mrs. Wasabi who fussed him into a chair and began to dish food onto his plate.

"Thank you, Mrs. Wasabi."

She continued to dish food, "You eat dear."

Dad nodded and took a fork full and ate it. She smiled and disappeared into the kitchen.

"How did your meeting go, Mr. Ritter?" Gabe asked.

Dad finished chewing, took a drink from his beer that had suddenly appeared when Mrs. Wasabi came back from the kitchen, wiped his mouth and spoke, "I hate meetings."

We laughed.

"It wouldn't be so bad, but they argue over little stuff that doesn't have anything to do with what I'm doing. Oh, well, it's a paycheck."

Everyone laughed again and the night continued pleasantly.

Chapter Eight

How to Get Asked to the Big Dance (and not make a fool of yourself)

W e'd been back at school for about two weeks and Friday's classes were abuzz with talk about the Welcome Back Dance. The Faculty and student body were in full decoration mode. Everyone knew the dance doubled as a fundraiser for the school, therefore, students took extra care in making sure everything was perfect per the instructions of the student body government. The student government, known as The Council of Twelve, were the ones tasked with making sure everything about the dance went off without any problems.

The Council of Twelve are a very dedicated group of students that really care about the academy, though sometimes they had a tendency to be a little over zealous on things. But to their credit, those that make their way onto the Council of Twelve, usually ended up in politics.

Mr. Resler did a great job of keeping them in-line, though he always allowed them to express their ideas for the dance. The dance also acted as a fundraiser to help on school trips, students that have trouble paying for uniforms, or any number of community outreach programs or charities.

A huge sponsor was Alien Inscriptions Technologies. A Colorado based think tank and technologies company that was pretty amazing. The founder and current CEO, Sean Donahue, was an original Apollo Academy graduate when it first opened, and rumored to be a recluse. It was said that he only came out to this event, though he was known to be quite amiable towards his employees. Alien Inscriptions Technologies sounded like a great place to work too. It had its own golf course to entertain guests, mostly entrepreneurs from Japan and China, a full restaurant for the employees, and a nine hour, four day work week with a paid lunch. Mr. Donahue was always friendly at the dance and he was known to dance a mean salsa. Unfortunately, it was a chore for his personal security to keep the reporters out. He doesn't like the media.

While I sat in one of the lounge chairs in the sleep room before my Latin class with Dr. Zang, I reflected about the dreams I'd been having since Brooke had shown me her plasma egg. They'd been very strange. Most of the dreams were about deep lush fields of grass or rice, forests of bamboo, and some of the most beautiful oriental architecture that I'd ever seen in pictures or in movies. But the most disturbing or exhilarating thing was how real everything felt. The wind blowing on my face, the warmth of the sun, the feel of the rice on my hands made me believe that I had visited those places at some time in my life, but I never had. The sheer vividness and brilliance of detail left me breathless as I awoke each morning. Those dreams made me feel alive, in-touch with my thoughts and feelings, and I felt more at peace than I had before my mom's death. I pulled my jacket up around my shoulders. But there were also the nightmares. Horrific images of things indescribable by vernacular or pictures, would from time to time consume the tranquil scenery and blot out the light with wholesale destruction that would leave the land in ruin. Often in these dreams I would be standing on a mountain or a ledge. I'd watch a blackness race from the horizon across the land, like locust on a crazy eating frenzy, and begin rending the flesh from every living thing. Then upon consuming everything in sight, the swarm would turn and race towards my bastion of hope. At these times I would stand, fear freezing my body in place, and stare in horror as the mass of black would surround me like sharks circling their prey. That's when the red eyes would appear in the maelstrom. Horrific points of light as bright as any molten lava spewing forth from a volcano; angry, filled with hatred, bent on destruction; a visage of death.

 I would try and force my gaze away, but the sheer ghoulish nature made it always impossible to look anywhere but at the red eyes. Like the target of light you stare at when the ophthalmologist checked the pressure in your eye, the red eyes would take over your vision. Consuming everything you had been thinking or wanting to think and leave you empty. Afterwards, I'd drift in a sea of red lava, my body slowly swirling around until being consumed. Finally, I would sink down below the lava and wake up screaming in imaginary pain.

At these times I'd have sweat drenched sheets and Cooper looking anxiously from the foot of my bed. These would be my only indication that I had woken up in reality.

My body shivered and I tried not to close my eyes as the TV droned on in the lounge. I wasn't sure why these dreams would creep up from time to time and very glad that the nightmares were infrequent at best. The bell rang and everyone began to leave for class. Grabbing my backpack I followed the masses to class.

After class I made my way down to the lunch room. Dr. Zang had us watch the crappy Hollywood version of Troy and pointed out all the inconsistencies between the text and the movie, though she mentioned several times about how fitting Brad Pitt was as Achilles. In the lunchroom the elementary classes and their buddies were already there eating. Several of my friends waved to me. Christian and Catherine waved also as they sat down to eat. I noticed that Catherine had on a very nice dress and couldn't stop watching the door to the lunch room. Several people walked in, her face rose in excitement and then fell as if the right person hadn't shown yet. Smiling, I sat in my usual spot, gave Brooke a wave as she entered, where I noticed Catherine's face brighten immediately and began fidgeting in her seat. Christian smiled, spoke softly to her, and tried to calm her down. Brooke came over and sat down, soon followed by Kaylene, Alexa, and Carly.

"Hi JJ." Alexa said in her usual upbeat way.

"Hey, Alexa. How are you?"

Alexa cocked her head to the side, "Good. Find a date to the Welcome Back dance?"

"Psh, haven't wasted my time on that dance in four years, not planning on it now." I turned away looking bored, though the plan that Kelli had come up with was a little beyond my comfort level of seduction skills.

"Other words, no." Brooke said. "She's a loser."

"Speaking of which, do you have one? No? Guess you are a loser too."

Brooke smiled her disarming smile, the one that says 'you are a bitch, so shut the hell up'. I smiled my own version back.

"I'll find one before you." Brooke informed me.

"That's because I'm not looking and you desperately are."

Carly giggled. "I love when they argue." The others agreed.

"That's what single people say, when they are alone. Especially…"

"Ms. Brooke?" Catherine had come over during our friendly argument unaware.

Brooke smiled at her.

Catherine's blue eyes had excitement dancing in them unchecked, but tempered with a deep single-minded purpose that only an eight year old could have.

I looked around for Mrs. Shoen, since it was odd that one of the elementary buddies would come without their upper-classman buddy. Mrs. Shoen was talking to Christian, who seemed to be smoothing things out. With a wide smile, Mrs. Shoen patted his shoulder. She nodded her head while looking our way and with a knowing motherly smile, walked away. Christian waved away my questioning look and went and sat down at another table.

"…I'm good, thank you for asking. How are you Catherine?"

Catherine bobbed her head. "Really good, Ms. Brooke. How…" Catherine's face scrunched up as if she was trying to remember something she was supposed to say. "…I really like your blue hair."

Brooke laughed, "Thank you."

"I asked my mom to let me make my hair blue, but she wouldn't let me." Her face fell.

Brooke ruffled her black hair, "You have beautiful hair. This isn't for everyone."

"God, isn't that the truth." Kaylene commented.

Kaylene had tried to dye her hair blue, actually several girls had and all with disastrous results. No one seemed to get the illustrious blue shine that looked so natural on Brooke and of course she never told anyone about how she did it either. Considering 'all' of her hair was blue it almost made you believe that she was born with it blue.

"I guess." Catherine said. She fidgeted and looked passed Brooke's shoulder. "Don't look." She said suddenly as Brooke had started to turn around.

"I was just wondering where your buddy was." Brooke answered.

"He's not doing anything. I wanted to talk to you, he didn't send me over here or anything. Okay?"

Brooke laughed. "Okay, but I don't want you to get into trouble with Mrs. Shoen."

"No, Mr. Christian talked to her already…" She stopped and covered her mouth like she had said too much.

"What are you doing?" Brooke grabbed her sides and began tickling her. Catherine began laughing, which made everyone look over at us. I glanced back over at where Christian had sat down. Three boys rose from the table and started to walk over towards us.

The Henderson triplets were well known around the state for two reasons. First and foremost, they were an excellent singing trio. They have sung the national anthem at the Nuggets games, Bronco games and numerous other sporting events around the state. They'd won numerous singing awards and were going to be on *America Get Your Sing On* TV show next fall. They are truly amazing to listen to. The second thing, which is the most tragic, they were originally quadruplets but lost their sister to a drunk driver when they were nine years old. A sad tale, but a tale that had inspired them to become singers to honor their sister's memory. Each of them had dark brown eyes, a medium build, kind faces and were as adorable as a kitten. If it wasn't for their different styles of hair, you wouldn't have been able to tell any of them apart. Garrett, the oldest by ten minutes had long, thick hair; Josh the second oldest, by seven minutes had cropped short hair like a drill sergeants; Gene the youngest, after their sister Emma, had the style right out of the teen magazines. Each was as different as they were the same and all of them were true gentlemen through and through.

They stopped behind Brooke, who didn't notice as she continued to tickle Catherine. I glanced back at the table where Christian had been sitting and he'd disappeared. Not thinking much about it, my attention returned to the brothers as Garrett pulled out a Pentatonic Tuning whistle and blew on it. The soft multi cord sound reverberated around us and they hummed in tune. The noise of the lunchroom began to quiet. Kaylene nudged me.

"Music Man…Sincere." She whispered.

I shook my head. "How can you tell that?"

Her face filled with disbelief. "You doubt me? Remember who you are talking to. I can name every musical there has ever been within a few notes of hearing it." She sighed. "I should have been on *'Can You Name That Tune.'* I'd have killed it."

I smiled. Only Kaylene would reference a 1970's show. What a geek.

The brothers finished their tuning, took a deep breath and began. As with all of their performances, their voices blended with a purity of a church choir, and many 'ah's' escaped several of the surrounding girls, especially the middle school ones that were having an early lunch.

Garret started, he was the bass, "Cinnamon."

Then Josh jumped in with his baritone, "Cinnamon."

And finally Gene's tenor chimed in, "Cinnamon."

The magical blending of their voice entranced everyone especially Brooke, whose blue eyes stared wide eyed at them. They grew wider as a distant high lead voice filtered in as Christian slowly slid from behind them, "Cinnamon."

They drew out the 'N' for a few moments then stopped. The sound echoed around the lunchroom and finally faded out. Everyone was watching now.

Tears were beginning to well up in Catherine's eyes as she watched her buddy.

"Tell me how do I convince you, Blue, how can I explain to you why?"

"How….do….I…. try?" The others echoed.

"You are the sun in sunshine, Blue, your smile is so kind it makes me cry."

"Ow tell me why?"

"Will you go with me to the Valkyrie dance, let my heart jump with a yes…oh please."

Their voices stopped. The only sound was the quiet hum of the heaters in the back ground.

"How can there be any.….sin in Sincere."

Christian's lone voice broke the silence and carried on the tune with the elegance of an angel singing from a mountain top. "Surely you can see I'm…"

"Right"

"Am I not right?"

When they finished, sobbing erupted from several tables. Catherine was crying openly as she ran to Christian, who gathered her up in his arms and hugged her. Brooke had a mesmerized look on her face.

"So much for your dinner seduction plan." I mumbled to a captivated Brooke.

Applause erupted and filled the lunchroom. Even Mr. Resler and Mrs. Shoen were applauding with smiles on their faces from the back. A sigh escaped my lips.

Christian placed Catherine on the ground, she ran over to Brooke as Christian shook the brothers' hands.

"Remember, lunch on me tomorrow." He told them.

"Hope you have deep pockets," Garrett told him. "We're going to eat our fill."

Christian laughed. "I'll make sure I bring my dad's credit card."

The brothers slapped him on the back and walked back to their table as they were mobbed by their girlfriends and others when they sat down.

Christian turned back to Brooke expectantly.

I've seen Brooke express many emotions in our short four years together, but the sheer astonishment and surprise were not ones that frequented her face often.

Christian raised his eyebrows expectantly.

An awkward silence ensued.

"Brooke." I whispered.

Brooke just continued to stare at Christian dumbfounded.

"Brooke." I said again.

"Please, Ms. Brooke." Catherine pleaded. "He'd been practicing for a long time. You have to say yes."

Kaylene grabbed Catherine by the hand. "It's not whether she will or not, Catherine, it has to do with whether her brain can come out of its daze and create a coherent sound to reply. Right now, the only thing she hears is the blood rushing in her ears because her heart is racing so fast that her brain isn't able to keep up. It's called 'love'"

"Shut up!" Brooke barked finally.

"See, her brain is clearing." Kaylene laughed.

"Well?" Christian asked again.

Brooke slowly nodded, her eyes glazed in awe, "Yes."

A collective exhale of breath escaped our table.

"Jeez, took her long enough." Someone groaned.

"Thought she'd never say anything." Another said.

"I'd jumped him right now." A girl sighed.

Other comments floated our way as the table began clearing.

"Okay…everyone get to class." Mr. Resler's voice boomed above the din.

Christian knelt before Brooke. "Thank you. I'll talk to you later." Brooke nodded.

"Let's go Catherine. Mrs. Heart is going to be upset if I get you back to class late."

Catherine patted Brooke's knee as she passed by and took Christian's hand, "Naw, Mrs. Heart likes me."

They walked off together.

Brooke turned to us and the excitement in her eyes was infectious.

I was about to say something facetious when Gabe sat down next to me.

"Well, that's going to be tough to follow." Gabe sighed.

I nodded. "He just set the bar pretty high for sure. Wait, what?"

"Nothing. I'll see you after Brooke's practice." He touched my arm, which left a warm spot that began spreading to my face. I did everything I could to keep the blush that was coming from spreading to my face, though with the way the rest of the table was ogling him it didn't take much.

A heavy sigh escaped Brooke's lips. "My life is complete."

"That was beautiful." Kaylene uttered next to me. She placed her hands over her heart. "If only he were single."

Brooke's ears perked up. "He's dating someone?" Her eyes began to grow a brighter blue as they always did when she began to get angry.

Kaylene put the back of her hand in a dramatic fashion to her forehead and sighed, "If only he could see me for who I am, oh Romeo, oh Romeo where for art thou Romeo…" she let her head fall slowly to the table and sighed again.

"Uhg," the guys at the table moaned.

"O, speak again, bright angel! For thou art as glorious to this night, being o`er my head, as is a winged messenger of heaven. "

Kaylene's head jerked up as Gene walked over dramatically, knelt beside her, and took her hand, "My fair lady, I have watched you from afar with great admiration and apprehension. I would freely give my heart to you, if you would agree to take my hand offered and humbly accompany me to the dance." His big brown eyes grew even larger like in a puppy commercial.

Kaylene blushed, withdrew her hand, "Oh good sir, I am ever taken back by your kind offer. Surely there are others more worthy than an old maid such as myself."

Gene's face saddened. "I dare say, my lady, there is no one more fair or kind as thy self. The sun is not nearly as bright as your smile, nor a rose petal as soft as your skin. Your beauty rivals the night sky full of sparkling stars. I am mesmerized." He took her hand again. "Please say you will." Then kissed it.

The rest of the seniors at the table either awing or made gagging noises, all were lost on Kaylene.

"But what of your other, sir. Will she not be jealous? I will not start a scandal, good sir!"

A broad smile grew on his boyish face. "We have parted amicably nie three weeks ago…"

"Three weeks!" Kaylene shouted. "We could have been dating…" Kaylene suddenly stopped herself and looked around. She quickly recovered herself and fell right back into her role, "Such news is unexpected." She sniffed, "I . . ."

"Is this who she is talking about?" Brooke suddenly interrupted. "Is she talking about Gene or Christian?"

"I just wish the thespian geek would answer him!" A boy at the table said.

"Shut up, jerk! You 'BOYS' could learn something from those two. Ass!" Several of the girls got up and left, followed by their boyfriends, who were trying to explain themselves.

"Well," Kaylene huffed. "I dare say, we have been interrupted, why don't we discuss this further after class at the Edesia and discuss the arrangement for our meeting."

Kaylene got up, gathered her books, and daintily placed her hand on his offered arm and they strolled off.

"So, she wasn't talking about Christian."

"No, Sherlock."

The warm, lost look came back into Brooke's eyes.

"Really?" I rolled my eyes.

"Don't you ladies have class?" Mr. Resler's voice boomed. He stood at the end of the table.

"We're going now." I grabbed Brooke and hauled her off to class.

The warmness of the Edesia was a welcome relief to the cold outside. After guiding Brooke through the halls like a wayward child we arrived at Dr. Marcus's Econ class. Placing her in her seat, I sat down and lost myself in the movie that Dr. Marcus was showing about the development of beer and economics. Dr. Marcus's econ class was always an interesting time, because every lecture appeared to be about how alcohol and economics were linked interchangeably with the growth of civilization. But as I sat in the warmth of the restaurant, with drafts of cold air coming in from the ice rinks, sipping on my hot chocolate, I couldn't help but feel a little down about the events of today. After Christian's song, and Gene's melodramatic monolog, a flurry of creative and not so creative invitations to the dance took over the rest of the day. Students throughout the day were bursting into class and asking each other, or leaving messages on cars. One of the more creative stunts was performed by Luke, who got four of his buddies to paint their bodies with Susan's name on their chest and then, somehow got the mini-trampoline out of the gym and were bouncing outside Susan's class. Needless to say, Mr. Resler wasn't pleased at the disruption of daily activities. But I heard that Luke didn't get detention nor did Gretchen, who had somehow gotten Mrs. Law's class to form the letters in the courtyard to ask her date.

All in all it was a pretty sad day for those of us that didn't get asked. Not to say I didn't get asked, but all the invites were lame and none of the boys interested me. So, as warmth began to seep back into my toes and the hot chocolate soothed my belly, I watched Kaylene and Gene sitting in a booth discussing their plans as well as other couples doing the same. I only wanted to be asked by one boy and that hadn't materialized. Therefore, I sat by myself, drinking.

Suddenly the wafting smell of caramel corn caught my nose, making my heart jump into my throat. He sat down before I even saw him. His golden eyes were full of merriment. An infectious smile immediately caught onto my lips, and when he touched my hand, fire raced through my body like nobody's business.

"Guess what?" He asked.

Trying to control my hormones, I pulled my hand away. "What?"

"My dad invited your dad over for dinner tonight."

As my heart raced, I tried to sound not too excited. "What for?"

He shook his head. "Not a clue, but make sure you follow Brooke to our house." He stood.

"You leaving?"

His embarrassed blush made my heart melt. "Yes. I….I have something to attend to." Then rushed off towards the door.

My eyes bore holes into his back as he reached the door. "I'm not going." He stopped, turned and the hurt expression on his face made me want to cry. Then he mouthed, 'you have to come' and left.

Regaining the composure of my heart and filling the pit that had opened in my belly when he looked so sad, I pushed away my drink.

"I never want him to look at me that way again." My heart whispered.

Numbly I sat in silence as time ticked by, waiting for Brooke's practice to finish. The playoffs started next week and Coach Winckler was running extra practices to get them prepared. I was so deep in thought that I didn't even know when Brooke arrived until she hit me in the head with a french fry.

"Hello?"

Blinking my eyes, I stared at her. "When did you get here?"

She rubbed her shoulder. "Long enough to get fries and throw them at you."

I smiled. "Ah." A quiet pause ensued.

"Something wrong?" She asked me.

I didn't want to say anything about it, since it was stupid to think that my not going tonight would make him sad, though in my heart I hoped that it did.

"Okay, well you ready to go?" she stood and grabbed her hockey bag.

"I don't think I'll go."

She smiled. "I don't think that is going to happen."

"I can do whatever the hell I want!"

"Not tonight you can't. Besides, it's a great meal and my mom is really looking forward to seeing you." Brooke laughed. "I think she sees you as the calm daughter she never had."

I laughed back. "Well then, can't disappoint *her*." I grabbed my coat. *How easy was that?*

"I knew you would see it my way."

We walked out together in the cold and snow.

The trip was uneventful to Brooke's house. We walked inside and Cooper bolted around from the kitchen. I gathered him up in my arms, he attacked my faced in a flurry of licking motions.

"Ah JJ, my dear, come in." Mrs. Wasabi shuffled around from the kitchen and led me to the living room. Mr. Wasabi was entertaining my dad in a game of Go. From the puzzled expression on my dad's face, and the number of white stones to black, my dad was losing.

I kissed him on his forehead and sat down. "How's it going?"

He sighed. "Not well."

Mr. Wasabi laughed, "Fine for his level. It is a very hard game to master."

Dad smirked. "A diplomatic way of saying I suck."

"I'm sure you are doing your best." I said.

"I am, but, I've lost." He gently pushed the board way from him and raised his hand to shake Mr. Wasabi's hand.

"Great game, Toyo. You are a master." Dad took a drink from his glass.

"I just have the benefit of experience." He smiled and began putting the stones away.

"Ah, if this were as simple as my work. Have you ever been beaten?" Dad shook his glass.

Mr. Wasabi smiled ironically, "Only by Mr. Chance. A friend from the East."

"He must be really good."

"Your job isn't easy, Dad. You spend hours on your work." I told him.

He shrugged.

"Have you picked a college yet, JJ?" Mr. Wasabi asked me as he tied the strings on the bag of stones and placed them in the box with the board. The Go box was a beautifully carved piece of wood decorated with a gold Chinese dragon. Just looking at it, the box appeared to be made out of a single piece of wood. A dark fine grain ran the length of the box. As Mr. Wasabi picked up the box and stood, the gold dragon shimmered and appeared to move making me blink. My eyes could have been playing tricks on me since no one else seemed to have noticed.

"Um, no. Not yet."

Dad smirked. "She's leaving me Toyo. Leaving me all alone, going out of state and never coming back."

"Shut up, Dad. That isn't true. I haven't decided yet." I huffed.

He folded his arm on the table and buried his head in them. The sad, forced sobbing made him look foolish, but it elicited a smile from Mr. Wasabi.

"My baby girl's gone." My Dad sobbed, unconvincingly.

"I'd leave you too. A man shouldn't cry." Mrs. Wasabi told him in no uncertain terms as she brought in the sweet smelling orange chicken dish.

Dad lifted his head and gifted Mrs. Wasabi with a hard stare. "You are a cruel woman."

Instead of taking offence, Mrs. Wasabi smiled back at him. "It's why I've lived so long."

Mr. Wasabi nodded in agreement.

"Dinner!" She yelled.

Brooke came barreling down the stairs in her jamies and her blue hair wrapped in a towel. She plopped down in her chair and looked expectantly at Mrs. Wasabi.

"Where are your manners? We have guests!" Mrs. Wasabi admonished her.

Brooke looked around confused. "Where?" Then her blue eyes lit up. "Is Christian here?"

I shook my head. "Uhm, I think she means us."

When Brooke looked at us I pointed to myself and dad.

"Psh, they aren't guests, they're family. Where is the rice?"

Surprised, I smiled. Only Brooke would be so quick to make that statement. One of the other things I've noticed over the past four years that if she thinks of you as a friend, she'll do anything for you. But if you do something to damage that friendship, she'll be the worst enemy you will ever have.

I looked at Dad and he actually had a tear in his eye.

"Thank you, Brooke. That means a great deal to me and JJ." Then he lapped into silence as he stared at his beer glass. An awkward silence was about to begin, when Gabe came bounding into the house followed by Set.

"Someone say dinner?" Gabe said.

Set in all his cockiness strolled over, threw his coat on the chair and sat down next to Brooke. She eyed him coldly as he smiled back at her. Gabe came and sat down next to me, which made my heart race and I could feel the heat rising in my face.

"Ready to lose next Tuesday, Baby Blue." Set put a sinister smile on his face.

Brooke blew him off. "You won't be scoring on me, Set. You might be in a rare form, but your skill is no better than mine." She turned to him. "In fact, you are more limited than myself and Gabe."

Set let out a hearty laugh. The laugh was deep and full, almost like a tiger's roar. "Don't think that I'm at your level, Blue. Draco Touched doesn't make you the same as a Pure Breed. Don't overstep your importance." His brown eyes grew a deeper shade of brown, just as Brooke's grew bluer.

"Enough you two!" Mrs. Wasabi warned.

The tension in the room was growing, and I wasn't sure even Mrs. Wasabi was going to be able to contain it.

"Set," Mr. Wasabi started, "As a Pure Breed, aren't there rules for this? Enticing a young one is beneath even a black, wouldn't you say?"

"Don't patronize me Father. I don't care if he is a Pure Breed, even a Draco Touch blue is a match for them in this form." Brooke turned to Set. "I'm not afraid of you."

"Then you are foolish." Set leaned back in his chair, superiority dripping off him like water. "I have no quarrel with you, Blue. Just getting you riled is enough for me to show you how weak blues are."

"Thank you, Set." Mr. Wasabi said. He turned to us. My look and my dad's must have been the same, confusion.

Mr. Wasabi laughed. "Children." He walked off to put the Go box away while Mrs. Wasabi fumed and stared at both of them.

"Don't you have something to do, Gold!" Brooke whispered through clenched teeth as she continued to stare at Set, who ignored her.

Gabe nodded and stood. "Set?"

Set absently waved his hand at him. "Truce. I won't dirty myself with a blue."

Brooke balled her left fist and it looked like she was going to hit him.

"Brooke?" Gabe's soothing voice echoed in the room.

I suddenly felt at ease, as if the world was in perfect order. Brooke's fist loosened slightly. "You don't need to work your magic on me, cousin." She leaned back. "When I goose egg him and his team, he'll see who is more powerful."

Set snorted. "As if."

"Thank you both." He turned to me and smiled. A smile that could have melted a thousand hearts. I think mine had already turned to liquid and was running though my body. He put his hand out to me, I gently placed mine in his and he lifted me up out of the chair.

"With your permission, Mr. Ritter?" He asked Dad.

"What?" He said. Dad's face showing the same look of serenity as mine must have. "Oh, of course." He winked.

Gabe led me to the door, then opened it.

"Wait, my coat."

"You won't need it."

"What? It's like twenty degrees outside?" I complained.

"Trust me." His eyes said.

I stared into his golden eyes and I knew I'd follow him anywhere.

We stepped outside and the cold instantly attacked my body. My body began to shivering and my breath was easily seen. He placed his arm around my shoulders and began to lead me along a white gravel path that was situated behind the house. The stars filled the night sky and his sure footedness kept me from falling when I stumbled. The crispness of the night air intensified his scent that was becoming intoxicating.

Shaking my head to clear the numbness that was beginning to set in from his delicious smell, I asked about what happened earlier.

He shrugged.

"What about the names? Gold, blue, black? What's that about?"

He laughed and it sounded like chimes in the wind. "Just nicknames because of our hair color."

"What about the Pure Breed and Draco Touched?" We entered the forest. The path wound its way through the trees like a vein. The moonlight made the path sparkle and it appeared to shift in the light as if being reflected off of water.

"Nothing to concern yourself with. Just stuff they used to do when we were little."

For the first time since meeting him, I felt he was holding something back. I chose to let it go for my body, despite the warmth from his, was becoming very cold.

"Not too much further, JJ."

I nodded.

We continued along the path for what seemed like forever, deeper and deeper into the forest of evergreens. The smell of the trees mingled with the cold, crisp air and the sweet aroma of caramel began to make my eyes droop. Like a sleepover, when you stay up all night and the waxing light of the morning sun begins to pierce the bedroom through the windows, sleep finally arrives and hits you like a brick. My head fell onto his shoulder as he led me off further into the forest.

As his rhythmic breathing and the gentle walking motion lulled me further into a walking dream, a light at the end of the path came into blurry view.

He nudged my head with his shoulder, "Hey, you asleep?"

My head rolled back and forth in response, but if he had let me fall to the ground I would have been out like a light.

"Just up ahead."

The light grew in size and the outlines of a greenhouse began to take shape. The size of a small garage, silhouettes of plants and flowers flickered in the light that appeared to be moving around.

We walked up to the door and opened it. Heat blasted my body, burning my frozen skin, as we walked inside. More aromas rushed through my nose and I sneezed. Beautiful flowers of every imaginable color were crammed on the shelves, along with various plants. The sound of running water came from the far back of the greenhouse. As my eyes wandered about the place, drinking the sights of the flowers, I noticed that the lights were not just a series of bulbs strung together, but hundreds of individual lights floating and fitting about. Mesmerized I stopped and stared.

"How can these lights be floating?" I gently reached out to grab one but it flitted just outside my reach.

"Magic." Gabe whispered.

My body was warming up. "Ha, ha. Really, what are they?"

"Fireflies."

Never seeing fireflies before, I watched in amazement and then a high pitched laugh echoed around the greenhouse.

Startled I looked around, but didn't see anyone. "Did you hear that?"

"No," he said looking around. "And neither did you."

"Why did you say that, if you didn't hear anything?" I asked him.

"What? I don't know what you are talking about. I only heard your soft gentle voice and the soothing sounds of the waterfall in back." He took my hand. "And that's all I will hear."

That last didn't seem to be directed at me. He smiled, and led me forward. We came around some plants and a table was set out. A burning candle sat in the middle of the white table cloth, while two plates with steaming food sat ready for someone to sit down and eat. Suddenly, soft music began to play in the background. He guided me over to one of the gold velvet chairs, pulled it out and nodded for me to sit.

He walked around the table, pulled a bottle of sparkling grape juice out of the waterfall basin, popped the cork and poured some into the crystal flute glass in front of me.

With my eyes riveted onto his, he lifted the glass, "Ms. Ritter, I'm not a singer, or an actor. I'm a simple person, with old worldly views of how things should be done. I have talked to your father and he has given me permission to . . ."

"Yes…yes!" My legs pushed me out of the chair and into his arms. "I will marry you!"

"…ask you to accompany me to the Valkyrie Dance."

Silence. Deafening silence. My eyes grew wide with embarrassment as I continued to hug him. I stepped back, plopped down in my chair, looked around, and took a sip of my drink. Then above the din of the music, a smattering of high pitched laughter drifted in with the music.

Gabe scowled at something behind me and the laugher died away. "I'm sorry if I made you misunderstand."

My hand waved off my embarrassment as best I could, knowing that my face was still beat red and I fervently wished I was outside or anywhere than here. "Ha, I was just trying to break the tension. Just in case you were nervous." My hair covered my face as I dropped my head.

He smiled. "Thank you for looking out for me. I was nervous." His smile widened and it put me at ease. "You are a very kind person. Always willing to put someone else's feeling above your own. Thank you."

"Just trying to help."

He looked at me anxiously. "Well."

"Well? Oh," Embarrassment gushed over me again. "I . . ." Suddenly the floating lights started to move about in an agitated manner.

Gabe's face clouded.

The lights were now rushing about wildly like sparks being blown around from a forest fire out of control. They began to swarm around each other like a school of fish trying to make themselves look big. Suddenly, the ball of light shot up into the corner of the greenhouse as the crashing sound of glass reverberated down the isle of green to us. Gabe grabbed my hand and pulled me behind him. My head began to swim again from all of the scents mixing with the sound of the waterfall and despite the adrenaline rushing through my body, I heard Gabe utter something under his breath and my eyelids began to droop.

The front part of the greenhouse was drenched in darkness as the ball of light was behind and up to the right of us. Shapes began to move in the darkness as a familiar scraping sounds echoed in the darkness. Images of the creature from the alleyway began to intrude upon my mind as my tired eyes tried to focus on the movement in the shadows. High pitched chattering rambled from the light ball in the upper corner. Gabe made a few high pitched whistling noises and the ball of light began to slowly move along the wall until it was directly behind us. The reflection of the creatures green eyes moved into view like an eclipsing moon until only the greenness remained. My heart froze. I felt Gabe's body tense. His scent of caramel corn slowly began to change in intensity until my head slowly fell forward onto his back. A loud roar erupted from in front of him and blinding white light flashed that brought darkness.

Chapter Nine

Chaos before the Dance

I awoke unsure where I was. The bed wasn't my own but it slowly began to feel familiar. Light began to filter in from the window illuminating the room. My eyesight was fuzzy and objects wouldn't come into focus. I rubbed them but they still didn't clear. A headache rocked my temple, so I closed my eyes again. I breathed deep. My left arm wouldn't move. It appeared to be pinned under something and then I realized I was naked under the covers. Panic set in. *Calm down!* Slowly turning my head, my eyes focused on a silhouette next to me. *Oh my god! Tell me I did not sleep with him. Did he drug me? Is that what that white light was? No, he wouldn't have done that. He's too nice. I gave up my virginity and I wasn't even awake for it?!*

Panic was about to set in until the person turned to me and bright blue hair flopped onto my face followed by her hand falling upon my breast over the covers. Disappointment set in quickly. *Great. Groped by my best friend.* I removed her hand and jerked my arm from under her. She groaned a little and turned back the other way. My head was still throbbing. I rolled out of bed. My clothes were on a chair next to her dresser where the egg sat. While I gathered my clothes and began to dress, the swirling colors of the egg began to soothe my head. Upon finishing, I sat down in a chair and watched the egg. The warm colors that lazily pulsed to the surface entranced me. My headache began to drift away and my body felt a warm sensation begin to permeate it. While my mind drifted to last night's events, the anxiety and unease that should have created a lot of fear in me didn't manifest itself. Watching the egg, and the beautiful colors, I was able to look back at it with a calm I didn't think I possessed.

So what did happen? I remember feeling drowsy after the long walk to the greenhouse. Then Gabe leading me back to the table, with the wonderful meal, I wonder if I ate anything? I don't remember eating, since I managed to make a fool of myself. Though, I thought I played it off well. Then there were the lights. He called it magic, and the distinct sound of laughter coming from different areas around the greenhouse. And though I didn't say anything, I could have sworn I heard tiny voices around me. Then what about the lights? The way they all moved together up into the corner like that? And Gabe? Whistling and making them move behind us? How could that have happened? I didn't notice any strings attached to the lights, but I wasn't looking either. So how did they move like that?

The colors continually danced in a hypnotic rhythm that ebbed and flowed in no coherent pattern except for a stream of red that pulsed like a heartbeat. *So, what did happen? I remember seeing the green eyes and I know that it belonged to that same dog like creature that I saw in the alley New Years. But what happened? And what happened to Gabe?*

Brooke moaned, rolled over, and her blue eyes fluttered open. "Come back to bed, I'm cold."

"I don't think so."

She frowned. "You suck."

"That isn't the first time you've said that to me. Where's Gabe?"

Brooke's face clouded. She flipped up the bed covers and walked to her dresser and put on her robe.

"Why'd you strip me? Jealous of my body?"

She turned to me, opened up her robe exposing her naked body, "Seriously? This is a ten to your three."

I turned away. "Bitch."

She walked over and knelt down in front of me. "What do you remember of last night?"

The look in her eye made me realize that she wasn't joking, which stopped my sarcastic retort on my lips. "Not much." I breathed. "I remember entering the green house, sitting down for dinner, talking about the lights, then feeling dizzy. Then a crash of glass, and waking up in here."

Her blue eyes grew sad as I watched them, which opened a pit in my stomach, the likes I've never felt before. A cold sweat broke out on my forehead and I could feel the tears starting to fill up my . . .

"Hey, breakfast is ready." Gabe announced as he barged into Brooke's room.

Brooke jumped up so fast, her gown flipped open, "I'm naked in here you jerk!"

I turned to witness Gabe's embarrassment as he turned back around and exited the room in a rush, slamming the door.

Brooke huffed, wrapped her robe around her, turned her head very slowly around and looked at me while an evil grin spread across her medusa face.

"I hate you." Escaped my lips as I jumped out of the chair and charged her.

Her snake filled blue hair bounced easily to the side as she stepped back and used my momentum to push me forward onto her bed. I felt her jump onto my back, digging her knee between my shoulder blades, "Calm down."

I struggled, "You fucking bitch!"

"Awe, come on JJ. I was just having a little fun." She laughed. "I didn't really think I could make you believe he was dead." Her laughter sounded like glass being rubbed against concrete.

"I hate you!" The pillow took most of my scream, while my flailing arms and kicking feet did little in their futile attempt to get her off my back.

"I just wanted to see how much you have fallen for him. Jeez."

My face was flushing and not because of the exertion of trying to get her off my back, but because the empty feeling in my stomach had turned to an unexplained joy at seeing his face. I stopped flailing about and laid there with my face down on the pillow, wondering what had happened in the short time of knowing him that could make me feel the way I do.

A knock came at the door. "Everything okay?" Mr. Wasabi voice echoed from behind it.

"Yes, dad. Just us girls having fun." Brooke rolled off my back, but I continued to lie there.

"Okay, well hurry up and get to breakfast." He replied from the other side of the door.

"Okay." Brooke said.

While I laid there listening to Brooke getting dressed, my mind kept cycling through the same four thoughts. *What is wrong with me? Why did I feel that my world had stopped? Am I really in love with him? When did that happen?*

Brooke slapped my butt. "Let's go."

"Ow. What happened last night?"

"You got sick, but don't feel too bad. You could have done a lot worse. You could be in love with Set." Her laughter echoed down the hallway.

I crawled off the bed, stretched my shoulders to get the knot out of my back left by her knee. I didn't get sick. Something is going on, but when my face passed in front of her mirror, I didn't recognize the look that stared back at me. Normally, the face was calm, eyes calculating, relatively pretty, clear of pimples, and mostly composed. Now, the face was flushed, the eyes bright, and a silly smile that wouldn't go away. It was unfamiliar but welcomed. Winking at my reflection, I strolled off down to breakfast.

The drive home was quiet. My dad had no idea what happened last night. He and Mr. Wasabi had put back a few sake bottles and he was still asleep when I went down and sat next to Gabe for breakfast. Set wasn't there and no one seemed to be worried. Brooke was nice enough to not tease me, though she continued playing with her left hand ring finger. I ignored her.

"Can't you turn that down?" My dad moaned from the passenger side of my jeep.

"I can't do anything about the wind, Dad, it's a soft top."

"Drive slower."

"I can't." I said sweetly.

"You're in an awfully good mood." He growled.

My silly smile widened even more.

"What, something you want to tell me?"

"Not, really." I didn't think my smile could grow any further, but it did. "I'll need the credit card. I have to go shopping." Then giggled.

Out of the corner of my eye, my Dad rolled his head and looked at me. "For what?"

"Wedding dress."

If his eyes could have popped out of his head, they would have. "He asked you to marry him? That's not what he said he was going to do?!"

"Maybe?" I giggled again.

"No. I strictly forbid it." He sat up straight and he winced in pain.

I put on my most dejected and hurt face I could muster and turned it towards him.

It didn't take long for his stern face to soften, though the sake helped to break him down quicker than normal. "Honey, getting married is a big commitment," he started before I interrupted him.

"He just asked me to the dance."

"That's it?" He said disappointed.

"You hypocrite."

"What?!"

"You're disappointed he didn't ask me to marry him!"

"No, I'm glad." He settled back into his seat again, then whispered, "although, he's probably the best you'll get."

I tried to get angry, but my mood was too good. "Just give it time."

My Dad's smile matched my own.

The Saturday afternoon sun warmed the air quickly. I helped my dad up to his room, where he pointed to a cabinet with the credit card, and fell right back to sleep. Picking up the American Express Card, I walked to my room, showered, picked out something easy to take on and off, so it would be easier to try on dresses, and left the house. Normally I would have called Brooke or someone to go with me, but I wanted to pick this out for myself, so Gabe would be the first person to see me.

Sante Fe was crowded and the drive to Downtown took longer than I expected. I parked near the 16th street mall and began my trek to the store with the red dress. Lots of people were out and about enjoying the afternoon sun. I strolled along carefree and that silly smile kept making its way onto my face no matter how many times I tried to stop. The sound of conversations mingled with the sounds of the cars and busses running along the mall. Everything appeared clearer, sounds crisper and my whole body felt more alive than it ever had. My feet skipped up to the edge of the street; I waited for the cars to pass, waited for the light to turn green, then skipped across the street and stopped.

Skipping? Really? Dork. Yet I continued skipping down the mall. I stopped at the store. The bell rang loudly and the smell of cloth and perfume tickled my nose. A lady walked out from the back in a nice long green dress that shimmered in the light coming in from the window. Gorgeous, thick white straight hair hung down to her waist that framed a beautifully marble chiseled tanned face. Hazel eyes peered at me. Her walk and dress flowed like snow drifting over a dense green forest as she approached. She stopped and looked me up and down as one observed a piece of art. I lowered my head.

She placed her hand on her slender, pointed chin, "Prom?"

I shook my head. "Formal dance".

With a curt nod, she strode away.

Unsure what to do I waited. When she didn't come back right away, I busied myself around the shop looking at the expensive dresses made by some of the top designers. Dad was pretty generous with his money, since he knew I wasn't the spending type, but even these prices were beginning to make me doubt my choice. I wondered if I shouldn't just leave. As the uncertainty was settling in my belly and my feet began to walk involuntarily towards door, I heard the store lady's feet returning from the back.

"Uh, hum?"

My legs froze. I slowly turned around and in her hand was the perfect dress. The elegant red dress hung loose in her arms like a golden fleece. The softness of the color, the simplicity of the design, and the suppleness of the fabric combined to make a dress that would transform the wearer into a mythological goddess. My breath caught.

A knowing smile flashed and vanished on the store lady's face. "You like?" her deep accented voice asked.

My head was bobbing before I even realized it. She strolled over to me, gently took my hand like a mother handling her wayward child and guided me towards the changing room. She gently placed the dress on the plush cushion of the bench, then slowly, and distastefully I noticed, began to undress me. I stood there like a child until she had expertly disrobed me down to my granny underwear and woefully in adequate blue bra. Her face held the serene niceness of a person helping a valued customer, but she couldn't hide the contempt and superiority of her heightened fashion sense. Just as I was wilting under the gaze and the blandness of my body, the store bell rang.

Relief flooded both our faces.

"Are . . ." She started as I interrupted her.

"Please, I will be extremely careful with the dress." I earnestly told her. "You should help whoever is out there."

Relief flooded her face, though a concern smile appeared. "If you need anything, don't hesitate to call upon me."

I nodded. "I will."

She strolled out and I felt a huge amount of pressure leave my chest.

"Ah, Mistress Pendragon, a pleasure to have you back in my humble cave." The Store Lady's voice held much respect.

Pendragon? Ms. Pendragon?! Is she here? Panic gripped me. *I have to make this last until she leaves. How embarrassing.*

"Hello, Vanca."

"Where is Shapoc Tiberius?"

"Ah, who knows? Outside somewhere." She sounded exasperated.

Vanca's laugh was deep and full, almost like a man's. "Children will play."

"That they do. Has my dress come in?"

"Ah, yes," Vanca's footsteps recede into the distance. Then her muffled voice called from somewhere in the back. "Lady Phebos sends her compliments and wanted to know when you will be visiting her."

I was halfway through putting on the red dress, when the door busted open, and Vanca stepped in. Her voice was a controlled measure of impatience. I noticed that her white hair seemed a bit whiter.

"Done?"

"I . . ." I stammered.

"Take your time." She sweetly said and disappeared. Then her voice echoed from the store, "The changing room is occupied at the moment. Do you wish to wait?"

"No, that's fine. I'll just take it. She never makes a mistake on her dresses. Let her know it will be awhile still."

"Very good."

I heard some low talking that I couldn't understand and then the doorbell chimed.

The door opened again and Vanca entered with a smile. I immediately noticed that her body language had changed and there was a more personable air as she spoke to me.

"Let me see." She gently pulled the strapless dress up, adjusted the front, which involved a readjustment of my breasts and stared again at me critically. She then took a piece of chalk out of her dress, I'm not sure where she had it hidden, and made some marks around my butt, chest and hips.

"Please, take off."

I quickly obeyed and she left with the dress. I again found myself standing semi-naked in the dressing room, starting to feel a little uncomfortable staring at myself in the mirror. Luckily she returned quickly and I tried the dress on again. It fit perfectly, except for the extra tightness that gave me more cleavage than I normally would have. She caught me staring and she placed her head next to mine as we looked at each other in the mirror.

"He'll love it. Trust me." She said as her eyes took on a mischievous air, then for a split second I thought they flashed white with vertical black pupils, then back again. I blinked and her hazel eyes looked back at me.

"I hope so." I breathed.

She packed it up in a nice box; I paid, and walked out feeling even better than I had when entering the store. Looking up at the clock tower, the adventure had taken little more than an hour and my rumbling stomach told me I was feeling hungry. I carried the box like it were a priceless treasure and made my way to down to the Tilted Kilt. My friends give me a lot of grief about this place, notably because of their notoriously scantily clad waitresses, which has been pointed out to me are worse than Hooters, but I go for the food. Brooke does it because she knows she's more beautiful than anyone there.

The hostess showed me to a vacant seat out on the patio that was in full sunlight and on the rail, so I could look out onto the 16th Street Mall. I gently placed the box next to me on the chair to my left, picked up the menu and waited to order. It wasn't long before a voluptuous waitress with a huge tattoo on her back amid several others scattered along her arms approached.

"Hi, my name is Ester, what can I get you to drink?" She asked.

"Coke"

"Pepsi okay?"

"Yep"

"Do you know what you want to order?"

"I'll take a Big Arse burger, medium, Swiss, mushrooms, and fries."

"Garlic fries?" She inquired.

"No thanks."

"Very good."

She took my menu and left. I watched people walk by. Tons of people were out and about, a bunch of them were couples. A smile come to my face knowing I'd be one of them soon. Not much later my lunch came, with a refill on my Pepsi and I ate my fill. I only got through three quarters of my hamburger, but ate all of my fries. I asked for a box that was brought presently along with my check. I didn't pay right away as I wanted to sit and enjoy the sun and the good feelings that penetrated my body.

Then something strange happened. While finishing my drink and getting ready to pay my bill, a man walked up to me on the other side of the rail.

"Hello, miss." He said.

"Hello." I said politely.

"May I join you?"

I wasn't sure what to say, when Ester walked up and greeted him warmly. She even gave him a hug over the rail.

"Hello, Cedric." Ester squeaked. "Your regular meal?"

"Please, Ester," then he looked at me. "May I?"

I waved to the chair to my right.

He hopped easily over the rail and sat down. His blond hair was well kept and short. He had on a nice flowered Hawaiian shirt with khaki shorts and running shoes. He had an air about him that was arrogant, but tempered with a wisdom that seemed beyond his years. Despite his easy demeanor, he had several worry lines between his brows, though overall he seemed kind enough.

"Are you a modeling agent?" I asked.

His laugh was full and deep, though it appeared it didn't come naturally to him. "No."

"Photographer?"

This time he just smiled. "An inquisitive mind, I see why the gold is attracted to you. But are you intelligent?"

My eyes narrowed. "You can leave if you are going to be rude." I growled.

His eyes lightened. "Feisty. That explains the blue." He placed his hands together on the table, leaned forward and stared at me. "But why the black?"

"Black?"

He leaned back in his chair as Ester brought him a dark beer and a basket of fries.

"That it?" Ester asked him.

"Yes. Thank you my dear." He stuffed a few fries in his mouth and took a drink of his beer. He winced slightly as he swallowed. "Not nearly as good as Random's." He sighed.

"Nor is the food." A woman's voice said.

Turning, Ms. Pendragon stood on the other side of the rail. She was holding onto the hand of a very handsome man. His black hair was pulled back into a ponytail and his almond shaped green eyes glistened with merriment as they watched Cedric and the surrounding area. The odd thing that caught my attention was that even though they were holding hands, the man was behind Ms. Pendragon like they weren't exactly equals.

Cedric's body tightened a little as if he was expecting something bad to happen to him. He tried to control his voice, but it was easy to hear the fear and awe wrapped up in his words. "Just having lunch."

"Where is Aguavey?" Ms. Pendragon inquired.

The man nudged her shoulder, which made her scowl slightly, and motioned his head in the direction down the street. A man was standing on the corner watching us, intently. He was dressed in casual clothes and had dark sunglasses on.

The man with Ms. Pendragon shook with excitement. "May I go and play?"

Perturbed she spoke. "Just a moment, Tie."

Tie calmed his body, but it sagged a little disappointed.

"You are breaking the Law, Cedric." Ms. Pendragon coolly said.

He laughed. "*You* lecturing *me* on the Law, Piccolo?"

Piccolo? That's Ms. Pendragon's first name?" I thought.

A nasty snarl, one many students would have given their lives to avoid, appeared on Ms. Pendragon's face. "You presume to lecture *me* on the Law?"

"Don't forget who the keeper of the Law is, Piccolo. It's the only thing keeping order," Cedric snarled.

She laughed. "And that's why we are where we are. You and the others insistence that order is something to be controlled. Order is stagnant. Order is decay. Order is death."

The argument sounded old, like a regurgitated worm, as she spoke, but her grip on Tie's hand firmed and it was turning white. The merriment never left his eyes.

"Then the alternative would be chaos? That may be good for the gray, but the rest of us need some resemblance of balance." Cedric said. "You thought the same at one time. Remember?"

Ms. Pendragon let go of Tie's hand. "Go play."

Tie sprinted off down the street faster than I've ever seen anyone run before. The other man looked surprised, then bolted off down a side street.

"Why are you here, Cedric? This is my territory under the Law. You are not here with permission." She stepped up to the rail and the hair on the back of my neck rose.

"The Law states that the Law Keepers can travel to opposing territory if a need arises."

"I know the Law, I helped write it." Ms. Pendragon said.

"With as many clauses as Selckar put in the original Law."

"Lord…" Ms. Pendragon hissed.

Cedric's eyes flared slightly with fear, "Lord Selckar." He amended.

I hadn't noticed that I'd pushed myself back into my seat until a person behind me asked me to move. I apologized and slid my chair forward just a bit.

"Well?" she asked.

"Anything out of the ordinary been happening?" Cedric asked.

Her eyes narrowed. She stared at me, which I wilted under, then looked back at Cedric. "Yes."

Cedric nodded. "Someone has broken the agreement. I was sent to reassure you that it wasn't Them."

"Do you mean the Law Keepers or the Observers?"

"Both."

"Do They know who it is?"

Cedric shook his head. "No. They believed you might have some information, you might be willing to share."

"They thought it was me." She folded her arms.

Cedric shook his head. "Actually, They knew it wasn't you. That's why I'm here and not anyone else."

She barked out a laugh. "Everyone else is afraid, you mean."

Now Cedric barked a laugh. "Blame them? You destroyed our home."

"I should k…" She started but stopped as she caught sight of me. Ms. Pendragon took a deep breath. "I'll return our home to us."

Cedric nodded. "So you have said. You've gotten a little side tracked with your crusade." He rose. "Maybe you should refocus on that."

"I have not lost sight of my goal." She hissed. "If you would quit interfering, maybe I could get to it sooner."

Cedric shrugged. "It should be your first priority." He hopped over the rail and threw a hundred dollar bill on the table. He looked at me. "That should cover your lunch and mine. Nice to have met you, I'm sure we will meet again. I hope you choose wisely." He turned to Ms. Pendragon.

"They said not to say anything, but I will." Cedric drew in a long breath. "They are going to come for you."

"Let them." She chuckled.

"This would be much easier if you would change your mind. We used to be friends,"

Ms. Pendragon scoffed at this point.

"And I'd like to think we will be again. Our goal is not that different, but the methods are very far apart. Chaos is not an option."

"Neither is complete order." She sighed. "I still don't understand why they think I want complete anarchy. That has never been my goal. But I will put an end to the senseless selfishness that cost us our home. I will make them pay."

Cedric smiled. "And that is why They oppose you. The universe cannot function without them."

"And it isn't functioning well with them." She said. "Tell them, no. If they think they can do anything about it, let them continue to try. But let them know, when our armies meet, I will not hold back this time."

Watching her, I could have sworn that the gray streaks in her hair actually grew in the intensity of their gray color.

Cedric watched her as his eyes narrowed. "I truly hope that it will not come to be. For if that happens, no one will win."

He turned around and walked in the same direction that Tie had gone.

Ms. Pendragon watched him go as her face hardened. Then she whispered, "Tie."

Tie immediately ran back the way he had come, side stepping Cedric. He stopped by her, he panted mildly.

"And?" She asked.

He frowned. "They haven't improved. Sad."

Ester came back to the table. I handed her the money, she smiled brightly at the ridiculously huge tip and left. I rose from the table.

"Ms. Pendragon?"

"Forget what you heard today. Just gibberish from an ex-friend. Nothing more." She turned to me and put on her best smile. "Are you ready for the dance?"

The smile that spread across my face made it hurt. "Very much."

"Tsk. You like him that much, huh."

I blushed badly.

"Only a gold could do that." Tie said merrily.

"No doubt." Ms. Pendragon lapsed into a moment of reflection. "Oh, well. Can't be helped." She placed her hand on my shoulder. "Make the right decision when the time comes, JJ. You'll only get to make it once."

I blushed so hard that it spread throughout my body. *Does she think I'm going to have sex with him? How embarrassing.*

"See you at the dance." They walked off together as they did when they arrived; Ms. Pendragon in front leading Tie by his hand.

Chapter Ten

Playful Antics

My chariot raced home with my red treasure tucked safely in back. The jeep bumped into the driveway and skidded to a halt. I leaped and landed upon the driveway in my superhero pose only to see the great beast Cooper come racing around the house. I quickly laid the trap of burger on the ground, which distracted the beast, and continued on towards the dungeon house. His raunchy burp caused me to pause, knowing it foreshadowed the awful gas he'd have tonight. Undaunted, my mind made my body stop at the great door, which blocked my path towards the sanctuary of my room. My breath slowed. Peeking through the living room window; the T.V. was off. With fingers crossed and fervently praying dad was working in his study up-stairs or hopefully, (I prayed real hard on this one), that he was still sleeping off his Sake drunk from last night,

I gently pulled back the screen door. Placing my key into the door lock; the key turned agonizingly slow, and with the stealth of a ninja, quietly pushed open the door. The screen door close slowly behind me until it latched and I didn't bother closing the front door, since my objective was to reach the sanctity of my bedroom before arousing the denizens of the dungeon. The living room was empty. Having passed through the first obstacle, my feet carefully made their way across the threshold and out into the living room. *Good, now just to get upstairs.* Like a thief in the night, my stealthy journey across the living room to the stairs proceeded without so much as a squeak of the floor. My escape to my room to bury my treasure was almost assured and I was halfway to the stairs when a tank hit the door rattling the glass in the screen door.

"Honey, will you let Cooper in, please." My father's voice floated down from the second floor.

Closing my eyes and cursing under my breath, I let out a sigh of frustration. "Okay."

Cooper was jumping up and down with excitement as I opened the door. He rushed in and sprinted for the kitchen. His water bowl sounded like a bell being rung for church as he drank. When I turned back around, Dad was standing at the bottom of the stairs looking at me with his usual 'my daughter is mental if she thinks she can out smart me' look accompanied by his silly grin.

He stepped off the bottom stair and casually strutted towards me with his best 'I know what you are up to' walk and stopped in front of me.

"Next time," he started, "If you want to hide something from the old man, maybe you shouldn't skid to a halt under his window."

My whole demeanor deflated and I cursed myself for forgetting his study window overlooked the driveway.

"You got me, again." I said sheepishly and hung my head in defeat. "Can't out smart you, Dad."

"Well, I am the best." He flopped into his favorite chair swiveling around to face me. "So."

"So…what?" I said.

He pointed to the box that I had tried to casually conceal behind me with little success because as he brought his attention to it, it slipped out of my hand and fell to the ground with a loud 'thunk'.

Cooper came racing around the corner with his mouth dripping with water and raced towards the box.

"No!" I screamed turning and protecting the box with my life.

Dad grabbed Cooper around the chest and pulled him in saving my treasure from ruin.

"That…what." My Dad nodded towards the box. "How much did you spend? God, I hope you are not like your mother in that regard. She didn't shop to shop but when something caught her eye…boy…" He trailed off without finishing his sentence. He often did that when talking about Mom.

"Well, don't worry. You can afford it for your little girl." I smiled at him.

His face softened. "I'd buy you the moon if it would make you happy." He told me.

And I knew he would. "Well, it didn't cost you that much, but you better put some extra time in on your work."

He winked. "I'll do that. So, let's see it."

I hesitated.

"Honestly!? You aren't going to show me?" He sounded actually hurt.

I stood there torn between wanting to show him and not wanting to show him. This was actually causing me a lot of stress and the biting of my lower lip confirmed it.

But he bailed me out.

"Fine." He got up. "If you want this Gabe character to see it first, I'll just have to wait in line." He grumbled some other thing under his breath about being mistreated, and that life wasn't fair, and something about wanting to play golf, as he passed me by.

"Dad." I called.

He stopped at the bottom of the stairs. "Yes." He said dejectedly with his most pathetic, comical, pout.

"I love you." And smiled at him

His face immediately brightened. "I love you more than anything, Sweetie. Don't ever forget that."

"I won't." Cause I love him more than anything too.

"Honey?"

"Yes?"

"Do we need to have the…" He put up his quotation finger, "play safe talk."

"Dad!" I blushed so hard. "No. I took the sex education course at school."

Relief flooded his face. "Good. The video I found wasn't very good. I. . ."

"Go." I shooed him up the stairs. "You are so embarrassing at times. Way to ruin our moment."

"I want to be a responsible parent, JJ. I don't want any rug rats running around." He continued. "Though a granddaughter would be nice." He yelled from upstairs.

"You are insufferable." I yelled at him and plopped down into his chair. Frazzled, my fingers fumbled opening the box and the gleaming red dress brought back the joy I had been feeling all day.

"A little girl would be nice."

"That's what I'm saying." Dad yelled down.

"Go away!" and laughed as I closed the box.

"You going to eat that?" Brooke said.

I shook my head. It was Monday and the lunch period was a complete and utter disappointment.

My treasure had been hidden safely in my closet that day, taking steps to make sure Dad wouldn't go snooping, not that I thought he would, but he can be snoopy at times, then went to bed. Sunday went by without any of my Dad's usual teasing, which I was grateful for and found myself in bed early in hopes of getting to Monday faster. My mind fell into one of those beautiful dreams; large fields of rice blew gently in the wind, along with cherry blossoms floating freely upon the wind. Contented, I rose early before my alarm, dressed, put on a bit more make-up than usual, and suffered through my friends making fun of me, because they of course notice my nicer clothes and extra make up, just to find out that Gabe wasn't at school today. What a disaster.

"He's sick, whatcha going to do." Brooke said gobbling down my dessert.

"Yeah. It's still three weeks to the dance." Kennah offered. "You'll get lucky before then."

"Shut up." I growled.

They laughed. My mood grew darker.

"Hiya." Kaylene said bopping up to the table. They greeted her, I continued to brood.

"What's up with JJ?" Kaylene looked around the lunch room. She always watched the activities going on. She loved watching people.

"Lover is sick." Brooke teased. "She's heartbroken." She sighed and fell into Kennah, who laughed and pushed her away.

I ignored them.

"Oh, how cute." Kaylene cooed.

She loves a good love story.

My mood changed when, just as another round of comments were about to commence, Christian started to walk our way. It was clear that Brooke hadn't seen him and I sat calmly as she continued to levy incendiary comments at me.

"And..." she began when he touched her shoulder. Her face lit up like a beacon in the night and I pounced.

"Is that red, I see." I laughed.

Brooke's cheek turned even deeper red.

"H-h-hi." She stammered.

"Something wrong with your voice?" my voice sounding concerned. "You didn't have any trouble just a few seconds ago." I turned to the others. "Did something just happen?"

Kennah creased her brow. "Did it just get hot in here?" She asked. "Seems to be a lot of heat coming from a certain direction… passionate heat."

An overloud giggle escaped my lips.

Christian turned his head slightly toward us and his eyes appeared brighter and had a red hue like a picture taken with a flash. Confused by the sight, I wondered if any of the other girls had seen it. Suddenly a funny smell reached my nose like really bad BO. I looked around to see who could be so stinky.

"Let's go." Brooke said in her best dismissive voice. They left and went to sit at another table.

"I don't think that's far enough, it's still hot in here." Kennah yelled.

As we laughed, Mr. Resler walked over to our table.

"Any reason to be yelling, Ms. Knowles?" He asked.

"No. Sorry." She said embarrassed.

He nodded and walked away where he sat down next to Brooke and Christian much to Brooke's annoyance. While I watched them, my mind raced to remember all the insults I would say to her to make up for her forked tongue comments, when his eyes flashed red again. Stunned, I turned to the others to see if they had witnessed it. They hadn't and the smell had dissipated too.

"Did you see that?" I asked them.

"What? Brooke seething." Kaylene said.

"No. Christian's eyes."

"I've been watching his eyes since freshman year. They are beautiful." Kennah sighed.

"Auh." I turned back to them, Mr. Resler had gone and they were both absorbed with each other. *Must have been my imagination. Light is streaming in from the open windows in the walls. They must have hit his eyes right and made the illusion. But, there isn't any light over at their table.* I shrugged. *Must have been a reflection.*

The bell rang and the lunch room cleared. Brooke wandered over to us, clearly light of foot and feeling good.

"You sicken me." I said to her. "What did Mr. Resler want? If you could pull yourself away from Christian long enough to listen."

"Something about the game on Wednesday." She cooed. Clearly she was still in her warm thoughts and not thinking of answering my question.

As an afterthought. "Did you notice anything interesting about his eyes while you were talking?"

She stopped and looked very seriously at me. "You know....I did."

Oh my god. She did see them turn red!

"My reflection." She smiled, turned and walked to her class.

"You suck." My voice carried over the din of the lunchroom.

She flipped me off in response.

On Mondays, I sub in the administration offices during Fifth period. Mrs. Douglas was a nice elderly woman that pretty much ran the office. Everyone knew that if you wanted something done in a timely fashion, you went to Mrs. Douglas for it.

I entered the office, Mr. Resler's door was cracked and he appeared to be in a meeting with someone.

"Hi Mrs. Douglas." I greeted her walking up to her desk.

Her Kenny Chesney calendar hung behind her as she turned to me. "Ah JJ. How are you?"

"Okay." I sat in the chair at the end of her desk.

"Ah, young love." She placed her hand on her heart.

My face turned hot. "I'm not in love."

"Of course not." She winked at me.

"Does everyone know about this? He just asked me to the dance." I complained.

Her eyes sparkled. "We are a small family, JJ. We take interest when one of our students suddenly begins dressing and acting differently. Least in your case it is a happy occasion." She turned around and put away a file.

I knew she was making reference to Loralee Phippin. She was a senior last year and had gotten into some really bad stuff off campus. If Mr. Resler and the staff hadn't taken matters into their own hands, despite her parent's denial that nothing was wrong, Loralee would most likely have killed herself. And in gratitude for saving her life, her parents brought a nasty lawsuit against the school. Mr. Resler and the board never flinched in fighting it. It is still in litigation.

Mrs. Douglas handed me a file. "Go sit outside Mr. Resler's office and give him this file when his meeting is done, will you dear."

I frowned. "Do I have to sit outside his office? It will look like I'm in trouble."

"Are you?"

"No."

"Then don't worry about it." She waved me forward.

I rose and wandered the fifteen feet to his office and sat down. With my body turned inconspicuously away from the hallway, trying not worry about who might come down the hall and see me, my ears picked up the conversation going on in Mr. Resler's office.

"Mrs. Intolerantiae, I assure you that Mr. Gibson is following the curriculum set by the Regents."

"Then there is something wrong with the curriculum, Mr. Resler." She said. "I believe that Mr. Gibson is wrong in forcing my child to dress that way."

"Mrs. Intolerantiae, I can tell you that no one is forcing anyone to do anything. The point behind the Cultural social studies class, which is an elective, is to teach tolerance among the different cultures by exposing our students to their culture."

"I'm not upset about the exposure, but having my child dress like a Muslim is just wrong." She complained. "I don't want him dressing like them."

"Wearing traditional garb is a way of showing them the prejudices associated with first impression because of the way they dress. It isn't any different than the stigma associated with rappers, rock stars and politicians." He told her. "The point of the class is exposure. You received the release form that was sent home?"

"Yes, but..." Mrs. Intolerantiae started.

"Then you know that your child could have opted out." He said.

Mrs. Intolerantiae's voice rose a little. "Then he would have been humiliated by not participating. That is unacceptable!"

"Choices are made every day with consequence. This is one of them. I'm not going to rewrite a curriculum for one child's discomfort, no matter the popularity or unpopularity of the class." Mr. Resler explained. "If you disagree with our curriculum, then *you* have three choices. Opt your child out of the class, don't have your child participate, or leave the school."

The silence was deafening. I was on the edge of my seat leaning in.

"Mr. Resler, I've talked to my lawyer . . ."

Mr. Resler interrupted her. "I'm sorry, Mrs. Intolerantiae our meeting is done."

Even outside I could tell that Mrs. Intolerantiae was at a loss for words. Footsteps approached the door and then it opened.

"Janice, will you contact Mr. Hatzenhueler our lawyer and take Mrs. Intolerantiae's lawyer's information and pass it along." He turned to me.

"Ah, JJ. Will you go and get Jacob Intolerantiae from Mr. Gibson's class, make sure he understand how to get his assignments from the school website and bring him back to the office. Janice, please call Mr. Winckler to the office too."

"Mr. Resler," Mrs. Intolerantiae began as she exited his office.

He cut her off. "I'm sorry Mrs. Intolerantiae, since you brought up your lawyer, our lawyer has instructed us to discontinue our talks until both of our legal counsel representatives have talked."

Her demeanor softened. "I wasn't trying to threaten you, Mr. Resler." She assured him.

Which was a lie of course. It was clear she was trying use the lawyer card to intimidate him and get her way. Even I could see that.

"I'm not suggesting you were, Mrs. Intolerantiae. You made your choice to bring him up and I'm showing you the consequence of your choice." He turned to me. "Aren't you supposed to be going and getting someone?"

"Yes, Mr. Resler." I handed him the file before scurrying out of the office as he dismissively waved her towards Mrs. Douglas and shut his door.

The hallways were empty while I walked towards the Middle School portion of the building which occupied the middle three floors. The stairs were vacant, which was to be expected during classes. I opened the fifth floor door and proceeded to Mr. Gibson's classroom. Stopping at Mr. Gibson's classroom, I observed through the door's window that the kids were dressed in traditional Muslim garb. I opened the door to music playing quietly in the background while class sat on the floor listening.

Mr. Gibson waved to me and walked over quietly, which was a feat because of his size. He was a gigantic man, 6' 7", broad shoulders, dark moppy hair and a large grin. The kids call him The Bear outside of class.

"Hey, JJ. What's up?" His deep voice reverberated through the class. Several of the students opened their eyes, but one look from The Bear and they closed their eyes quickly.

"Jacob Intolerantiae is asked to come to the office. His mom is here." I explained to him.

He frowned. "Does this have to do with the Muslim garb?"

"I believe so, but I wasn't told."

He shook his head. "He wanted to dress up but his mom wouldn't let him." He looked over the class. "Jacob." His loud whisper was almost the volume of a normal voice.

A young boy reluctantly got up. He had a turban around his head but had on his regular clothes unlike his classmates.

"I gave him that so he could participate." He reached out his hand.

Jacob took off the turban revealing his cropped brown hair underneath.

Mr. Gibson got down on one knee. "Hey, buddy. JJ here is going to take you to your mom. She's waiting for you…"

"I don't want to go." He complained.

"You have to. Remember our discussion on responsibilities?"

Jacob nodded.

"Okay. Do what your mom asks." He said.

Jacob nodded but resentment appeared in his eyes.

"Come on." I pushed the door and he stomped out. I waved to Mr. Gibson and he waved back. "Tell Mr. Resler I'd like a meeting."

"Okay. We need to get your stuff from your locker." I told Jacob.

He stopped, stunned. "I'm being suspended?"

My smile did little to relieve his apprehension. "No. You just have to get your stuff. You know how to get on-line to get your lesson, don't you?"

"I'm not stupid." He grumbled.

That tone made me stop. "Hey. You don't need to be rude."

Defiance rose in his eyes.

"Let me tell Mr. Resler how you acted." I walked forward.

He reached out. "No, please don't. I'm sorry."

"Okay. I forgive you. Just don't worry. Mr. Resler will always look out for us." I told him.

He didn't smile but his demeanor relaxed. We picked up his coat and stuff from his locker and made the trip back to the office, where is mother, Mrs. Intolerantiae fumed. As we walked into the office, Mr. Resler's door opened and he greeted us.

"Everything okay?" He asked.

I nodded. "Yes. He knows how to get his assignments on-line, he has all his stuff, and Mr. Gibson asked for a meeting with you."

"Already e-mailed him." He turned to Mrs. Intolerantiae. "Thank you. I hope our lawyers will be able to work something out. Jacob is an important member of our school."

"Mom! You called a lawyer because of some stupid clothes?" Jacob appeared beside himself.

"Don't you raise your voice to me, Jacob!" Mrs. Intolerantiae grabbed his arm.

"Jacob. Remember our Tenants. Respect." Mr. Resler told him.

"But…"

"No buts. We are having a disagreement. That doesn't mean you get to be rude." He said.

Jacob bowed his head. "Yes, Mr. Resler."

Mr. Resler smiled. "Thank you Jacob for being a gentleman. I look forward to a swift resolution."

Mrs. Intolerantiae nodded curtly and stormed out of the office with Jacob in tow. I felt bad for the little guy.

"Will he get to come back?"

He winked. "He'll be back tomorrow I suspect. You have to pick your battles, JJ, and sometimes all the battles are the right ones." He actually cracked a smile then quickly regained his usual stoic demeanor. "Don't you have something to do?"

"Yes, she needs to go out to the west gate and deliver these passes for the game Wednesday night." Mrs. Douglas held out the passes. "And the south gate."

"Both of the Bunkers?" My whiny tone didn't do anything but get a mocking smile and nod from her.

Grabbing the passes I head off outside. The day was warm. My walk along the road toward the south gate wasn't really all that bad. When I approached, Kim and Mark were working on homework inside the South Bunker.

"Hi guys." I handed them the passes through the window. "These are the passes for Wednesday night's hockey playoff game against Valor."

"Oh, man, I can't wait." Mark pumped his fists. "We are going to kill them."

A smile appeared on my face.

"I don't know, they got that new kid that just transferred in." Kim said looking up from one of her physics problems.

"Who?" I asked.

She looked up, "uhm, I think his name is Cret? Tret?"

"Set?"

"Yep, that's it. I'm not very good with names." She said.

"Unless its epsilon or omega or tangent." Mark rolled his eyes. He mouthed 'boring' to me.

"Whatever." Kim said going back to her book.

I smiled. "Have fun you two."

"I'd rather have a stick in my eye!" Mark yelled to me as I continued down the Trail of Tear toward the West Bunker.

It wasn't long before the P.E. class came running around the trail at the corner of Broadway and Dry Creek. The fourth graders were huffin and puffin with Mr. Carter yelling at them from behind.

I cut across the grass to stay out of their way and waved to Mr. Carter. *I wonder if Brooke's feelings about Set playing have changed.* I shrugged and continued on. The West Bunker came into view and the two girl students occupying it, I didn't recognize. Since the gates are part of the junior class community services it wasn't surprising I didn't know them. Even though Apollo Academy was small, you don't always get to know the transfers that come in. I introduced myself.

The two girls smiled back. "Hi, I'm Julia and this is German Julia."

German Julia waved.

"Are you an exchange student?" Figuring that could only be the reason for such a name.

The blonde girl nodded.

"Nice to meet you. Here are the tickets for the hockey game on Wednesday, do you guys know where you need to store them?" I asked.

"Yep." Julia pointed to the floor safe.

"Good. Nice to meet you two, bye." My feet led me away from the bunker and back towards the school.

"And you." They said together.

The floor safe never has money in it, but they do keep cameras on them in case they get vandalized. My phone beeped reminding me that the bell was going to ring soon.

I rushed into the office, grabbed my back pack, said goodbye and headed off to my next class. The rest of the day passed by without much excitement and I couldn't keep my thoughts off of Gabe.

Even though he wasn't around, my mind continually thought about him and not much else. So, when the last day's bell rang, the hallways crowded quickly with exiting students talking about the big matchup for the Wednesday hockey playoff with Valor. I think the most excited were the elementary students and the seventh graders. The eighth graders tried to appear more cool but even they couldn't keep the excitement from filling their faces. Since this was a big game, the administration had reluctantly agreed to have a late start day on Thursday for postgame celebrations. But everyone knew the faculty were just as excited or even more than the students.

I stopped at my locker, pulled out my books for classes that had homework, and shoved the others back in. A quick checked of my hair in my little mirror told me it looked great and then freaked when red eyes appeared over my shoulder. I spun around. Nothing. Nobody stood behind me as my eyes scrutinized the passing student. *What could have done that? Christian isn't around and besides, his locker is on the other side of the star. I remembered the night at Gabe's with the red eyes, but could I be hallucinating about them? I…*

"AHHHHHHH!" My screamed would have made any horror movie goer proud. Everyone in the hallway stopped and teachers came rushing out of their rooms.

"Holy shit, little jumpy are we." Brooke laughed.

My heart pounded so fast and loud that I thought I was going to drop to the floor and begin hyperventilating.

"Everything okay?" Mrs. Wallace asked.

I waved to her indicating it was, even though my breath was still having trouble entering my lungs.

"She's okay, Mrs. Wallace. Just a little love struck." Brooke smiled and Mrs. Wallace smiled back.

The hallway returned to normal but even the students from above and below came to look about the scream. And there were plenty to fill them in on who did it.

I leaned up against the locker. "God, I hate you when you do that." My breath moved in and out of my lungs real slow.

Brooke snickered. "I've never made you jump like that. What's wrong with you?"

"Nothing," slamming my locker shut. "Shouldn't you be at practice?"

"Yep. On my way there now. Just wanted to stop and see if you were up for going out afterward. Going to head to Cold Stone for some ice cream."

"No." I didn't really feel like going out after I got home. "I have too much homework to do. Plus Dad has some really important conference call to do, so I said I'd make him dinner."

"That's even a better reason to go out. You don't want to disturb him." She winked.

I smiled. "I don't think so."

"Okay." Her tone changed just a little. "But a certain someone… just might be disappointed….if a certain someone…didn't show."

My heart started pounding again. "Okay!" The word blurted out of my face even before my brain fully registered what was being said.

She clapped her hands together in victory. "You are so easy… and I'm not talking about manipulating you either. Though, that's pretty easy too." She skipped off down the hall. "I'll text you."

Why do I let her do that to me? I hung my head. A solemn walk punctuated with moments of skipping took me to my jeep; backpack tossed into back, climbed up, sat for a moment before looking at my review mirror and there it was: That happy smile. I winked at my newfound self and headed home.

Chapter Eleven

Oh…there be Dragons here

Copper jumped up on me when I came through the door.
"Hey, boy. How's my little puppy dog." Scratching his ears, we walked over and put my backpack on the couch and sat next to it. I pushed Cooper to the floor and rubbed his belly.

"Honey, do you know where my tie clip is?" Dad yelled.

"Try the dish in the bathroom. Right side." I yelled back.

"I looked there!"

"Your other right."

"Ha…Ha…oh!"

I smiled knowing he had found it. Cooper jumped up and raced to the stairs as Dad walked down them.

He was neatly dressed in a maroon shirt, silver tie, and his favorite Avalanche hockey tie clip. But what really made the outfit were the gray track shorts he had on and his Monty Python bunny slippers. I clapped.

"You are a fashion Faux pas." Standing, I walked into the kitchen to start dinner.

"I know. That's why all the ladies love me." He kissed me on the head as he went to the fridge.

"I was wondering if I could go out with Brooke for some ice cream after her practice."

He placed a fruit drink next to me. "As long as you have all your homework done. You know I don't mind." He gulped his down. "But I thought we were going to have dinner together?"

I pulled the shrimp and veggies out of the fridge, poured some oil in the pan and began to stir fry them. "Would you get the noodles, please."

He placed them on the counter next to me.

"We are. They are going to have a long practice with some extra film time. So it will be a few hours or so. Brooke's going to text me." A little more sauce was needed in the stir fry pan.

"A few hours, huh?" He looked at his watch. "I could join you."

The bottle slipped from my hand onto the stove, spilling sauce everywhere. Copper rushed to my feet and began licking up the sauce that had dripped to the floor.

"Unless, that would be a bad idea, for some reason." He handed me a dish towel to clean up with.

Occupying myself with cleaning up, so I wouldn't have to answer right away, my mind raced. "No…that would be great." My voice sounded a little more confident than I thought it would. "Why don't you call Sydney, and have her come too."

Luckily Dad appeared surprised by the invitation and he didn't know what to say. Sydney was a lovely lady that Dad had met at a Christmas party. They had gone out a few times, but Dad was still not ready to seriously date someone. And to tell the truth, I wasn't sure I was ready either.

I took the opportunity to complete the clean up and put the finishing touches on the stir fry.

"Plates?" pointing to the cabinet.

He still seemed puzzled as he quietly handed them to me. I piled on some noodles, smothered them with the stir fry, handed the plates back to him and pointed at the table. It isn't often that I make my Dad speechless, but I do relish it. He walked over to the table like a zombie, as I grabbed two sparkling juices out of the fridge and placed them on the table.

"Well?" I said after taking a bite of the stir fry. *This is good. I am such a good cook and I'll cook every day for Gabe!*

"Uhm," He said.

My face appear as uninterested as I could make it, since I didn't really want him to come with us to get ice cream and ruin my alone time with Gabe. But watching him struggle with whatever emotional path I accidently sent him down, made my heart ache. I didn't think my offer would cause him this much distress. It was clear that mom's memories were still a deep wound.

"Don't you like her?" I asked between mouthfuls. "I thought you liked her?"

"I do. Do you?" He said concerned.

I shrugged. "I guess so. She seems nice enough. Beautiful, smart. She is a doctor after all. Not quite sure what's she's doing with you, though." I chided him.

This appeared to wake him up. "Ha. You so funny."

"Thanks, I get it from you." I gave Cooper a shrimp.

"I guess I could call her." He didn't seem too enthusiastic about it.

"At least this way you wouldn't be out of place." I stood, washed my plate and placed it in the dishwasher. "I've got homework. Don't struggle with it for too long, you might not be ready for your conference call. I don't want to live on the street." Kissing him on his head, I grabbed my backpack and headed upstairs.

My homework could have been done much sooner if watching my stupid phone hadn't taken most of my time. I groaned for the millionth time, but my phone stayed annoyingly quiet anyway. Even Rumpelstiltskin would have complained about how agonizingly slow Time was behaving. But being afraid of missing the text, which of course was stupid since my phone's sound volume was all the way up, my pen barely made scratches on the paper. I couldn't help but continually flipped my phone over every time my imagination though it saw the flashing red light of the text alert. A sigh escaped my lips. But then again, I didn't want to be sitting downstairs either, because that would have just made it worse. So, I finished my homework and picked out a new outfit to wear to kill time. Then as I took off my fifth outfit change, the light lit up and my waiting text showed. I reached for the phone on my desk, missed it and pushed it onto the floor with my elbow, where it landed and exploded. Panicking, I quickly assembled it, waited for it to come alive, retrieved it and died: 'I'm tired…Not going….C-ya tomorrow….'

My body fell onto my bed, my heart bleeding, my head swooning, a cold sweat breaking on my brow, when my phone lit up again. 'Jk…outside…hurry up. ☺'

I rushed to my window and threw it open. "I hate you!" I screamed at her car.

Brooke waved from the driveway. I quickly changed, flew downstairs, where my Dad sat on the couch.

"Have fun." He said.

"Not coming?"

"No. I've got something to think about. Do you need money?" He said.

I shook my head.

"Have fun." He smiled.

"You too." And ran outside.

Brooke's smile didn't alleviate my mood any. I piled into the back seat with Kaylene, Serina, who was another cheer, Kennah, and Alexa. Brooke was in the passenger side and Mr. Wasabi was driving.

"Hi, JJ." Mr. Wasabi greeted me cheerfully.

"Hi, Mr. Wasabi. You have a very mean child." My eyes burned holes in the back of Brooke's head.

"It's what Blue does. Just ignore her." He assured me.

"You'd think she'd learn that by now." Kennah agreed. "That was a very good scream though. Just like today, I heard.

"Shut up." I growled.

"Oh, someone is in a bad mood." Brooke chirped from the front.

I ignored her.

The girls talked away while I silently sat wondering why Gabe wasn't in the car with us.

After we arrived at Cold Stone and piled out, I pulled Brooke aside.

"And?" I whispered.

"And what?" Brooke said confused.

"You know what."

"Oh. Yeah, he's still sick." She apologized.

I was beside myself. "You said he'd be here." We came to the door. She opened it.

"What can I tell you?" She shrugged.

Pissed, I stomped in and caught my breath as Gabe, Set, John, and Steve sat at one of the tables. He looked up at me and smiled. My heart melted, the world turned bright again, and I forgot why I was pissed at Brooke.

"You can thank me later." She whispered.

Like a little girl walking towards something new and wonderful, Brooke guide me to the table where they sat. She set me in a chair next to Gabe, his caramel corn smell immediately washed over me sending me into heaven.

"Hi JJ." His musical voice spoke to me like a god from heaven. I didn't answer.

"JJ?" He said again.

"Yes." I breathed.

"How are you?" He asked.

Pain shot up my arm. "Ow!"

"Show some restraint." Brooke rolled her eyes.

The pain snapped me out of whatever trance I was in. "I'm good. Thank you. You?"

He smiled. "I'm better." He turned to ask Steve something, but didn't hear what he asked.

"How was practice?" Alexa asked John.

John was one of the defensemen and the only one that Brooke had any respect for.

"Tough. I don't know what's worse, Coach Winckler yelling at us or Brooke." He said jokingly, but the truth of his statement could be heard.

Brooke smiled. "You know which is worse." She winked.

John smiled.

"It won't do you any good." Set commented confidently.

Kennah and Serina were giving him their full attention, despite Kennah and Serina both having boyfriends.

"Don't think I'm going to lie down and let you score a ton of points." Brooke informed him. "You are the only thing they have."

Set leaned back and placed his arms around Kennah and Serina. "That's all they need."

"We'll see." Brooke got up and went to the counter. Kaylene followed as did John and Steve. Set turned to Kennah and Serina, leaving me with Gabe.

"Is Mr. Wasabi coming in?" I asked.

"I believe he is meeting Mrs. Wasabi for some late dinner. Shall we?"

"Oh. Okay." We rose and went to the counter.

"Shall we get something together?" He said looking up at the menu.

My heart leaped into my throat. "I…"

"Gabe. That's not a good idea." Brooke called from down the line.

"Oh…" He started but I interrupted him.

"No…that's okay. I can't…"

"No." Brooke said emphatically.

Gabe nodded. "She's right. I forgot. We'll just get two smalls. What do you want?"

"Whatever." I stared Brooke down who ignored me.

Steve ordered, paid and sat back down. My laser beam eyes burned holes in the back of Brooke's head and was melting her brain as she ordered.

"It would have been interesting to see." Set mused from the table.

"No, it wouldn't have." Brooke told him.

"What are you talking about?" Kennah asked.

My attention turned away from the menu board as the store bell rung. Two young men, probably in their early twenties walked in. My eyes narrowed. An unpleasant smell wafted over me, which made me scrunched up my nose in disgust. The two men surveyed the scene. They were in dark cloths and steel tipped toe guards sparkled in the shop light. One of the men nudged the other as his gaze fell upon Set.

Set was about to kiss Kennah while her eyes rolled back in her head, lips puckered forward, and limp in his arm, when one of the men's hand flashed forward. It was a blur of a motion just as Set's hand was coming up. Set caught the knife blade mere inches from his left cheek. Annoyed, Set turned his lips way from Kennah, who appeared to have fallen asleep in her chair, and set black eyes upon his would be attacker.

"Gabe?" I said confused.

"What?" Gabe answered.

I pointed at the two men and then at Set.

Gabe's eyes widened in concern. "Brooke!"

Brooke turned from the counter. "Somnus!"

Suddenly, the worst fatigue overcame me. I staggered to a table next to me and fumbled with the seat. Strong hands helped me into the chair as I tried to keep my head up. My vision began to blur. Kennah, Steve and Serina were asleep at our table. I swiveled my head and Kaylene, John and Alexa were asleep at Brooke's feet. Brooke cautiously knelt down in front of them like a shield. The store clerk couldn't be seen and I surmised she must have fallen asleep behind the counter.

One of the men moved forward. His eyes turn red like a stop light and leaped towards Set.

"Going to kill you Draco. Kill all your kind." With one smooth motion he pulled a long jagged knife from behind him.

Set easily sidestepped him and in one gesture with his arm, set the man flying across the store.

"Seriously." Set turned to the other man clearly upset. "I was about to get some."

Gabe moved in front of me like a shield and placed his hand on my shoulder. I leaned into him.

"Set." Brooke moved back.

I couldn't see the two men now because Gabe continued to be in my way. His caramel sent was beginning to make me even drowsier.

My eyelids were beginning to droop as my head rolled forward and back as I tried to stay awake.

"I'm going to hurt you, man." The other man yelled.

My head rolled to the side and I saw the other man pull a gun.

"You have no idea what trouble you have gotten yourself into, punk!" Set smiled. "I'm glad I'm going to get to send you to the hospital or whatever hell hole you crawled out of. Your choice if you and your friend want to go alive or dead back to your master."

"Set." Brooke cautioned.

Why isn't she asleep? Why is Set acting this way. Just let them rob the place and let them go.

Set looked at me like he had read my mind. His disgust etched his face like the carving of a stone.

My eye sight began to blur. Set moved forward. Gun shots rang out. A scream. Set's shoulder flinched back. Then his other one. Like makeup being scrapped away to reveal the blemish underneath, black skin appeared where the bullets hit him. A scream lodged in my throat. Brooke turned and looked at me; her eyes widened. A motion caught my attention, Set laughed but it sounded like it was coming through water. His eyes turned black and he moved with inhuman speed disappearing from my view because Gabe continued to block the scene. Another scream rang out, and another, each deep and frightened. Then silence. I pushed myself away from Gabe. He turned and as his eyes focused on mine, stars erupted in my vision and everything went black.

I was cold when I woke. Air streamed in from the open window of Brooke's car. My mind was foggy with the events of…I didn't know what time it was. The phone in my hand read eleven thirty two p.m. I closed my eyes again trying to remember when we had arrived at the ice cream shop. Fuzziness continued to cloud my mind, while the foggy images of what had happened tried to assert themselves through the haze. The emptiness of the car crept upon me. I opened my eyes; Brooke sat in the front passenger seat, Gabe was driving and Set sat next to me.

My mind snapped.

"Oh my god!" I yelled.

The image of Set being shot crashed down upon my consciousness like a hammer smashing down upon a nail head. I grabbed Set, who appeared annoyed at such an aggressive move and shoved me back.

"Control your girlfriend." Set scowled.

"We have to get you to the hospital!" Panic gripped me. I'd never seen anyone shot or had them die. "We gotta put pressure on those wounds!" I frantically searched around the car but nothing presented itself as a useful bandage.

"JJ." Brooke calmly said from the front. "It's okay."

I stared at her like she was crazy. "No it's not! He's been shot!" My jacket easily slid off.

"Don't do that." Brooke insisted.

Set smiled. "I don't mind."

I ripped the sleeve off my shirt, leaped at Set, ripped his shirt open and stopped. The black spot that I had observed earlier was nearly closed over with normal skin color. I fell backwards.

"Don't stop." Set winked. "I told Gabe I'd get you before he did." His laugh was filled with spiteful superiority.

"Enough, Set." Brooke looked at me. "JJ. What do you remember from the ice cream shop?"

My mind tried to wrap itself around her question but it couldn't grapple with the reality of what I'd just saw with Set.

"What are you?" The whisper was lost to the open window.

Set buttoned his shirt. "Nothing you've seen before or will again." He laughed.

"Set!" Brooke yelled at him.

His eyes turned black again as they had in the ice cream shop. "I'm getting tired of you thinking you can boss me around, Blue. Secundarius are inferior. Don't push your luck."

My eyes were wide. "What are you!?"

"I'll boss you around all I want if you choose to ignore the Law!" Brooke warned him. "Or should we take it before the Mage?"

Even with the state of his eyes being completely black, fear rush into them at the mention of the Mage.

Silence filled the car.

"I want out of the car." I whispered.

"We are almost to your house." Gabe said.

"Where is everyone else?" I put my coat back on. The anxiety inside me was beginning to grow at an inexplicable rate and threatened to overtake me. The car felt small. The air stuffy. My breath was coming in small gasps.

"My Dad took them home. They're safe." Brooke assured me.

My mind was having trouble focusing. "Let me out."

"Not yet…"

"Now!" fumbling with the car door.

"Grab her Set." Brooke ordered him.

He raised his hands. "This isn't my concern."

My hands were like a child's dealing with unfamiliar objects while my brain raced at a hundred mile per hour without any coherent though. I was in an instinctive flight mode and just wanted to escape the car.

"Gabe, pull over." Brooke grabbed my coat just as the door flew open. The white line of the road raced by my head. I'd have tumbled out if Brooke hadn't had my coat. The car screeched to a halt and she let go. I rolled through the door out onto the pavement, scrapping my hands. I jumped up. The neighborhood was unfamiliar to me in the dark and in my current state of panic, I wasn't sure I'd have recognized it anyway.

Gabe and Brooke both got out and tried to flank me on each side.

"Stay away from me!" I warned them.

Brooke looked quickly around at the lightless houses. "Shh. You want to wake up the neighborhood? You stupid, bitch."

This brought me up short. "I'm a bitch!? You are the fucking bitch!" my voice screeched. "He's supposed to be dead! I saw him get shot three times." I stormed over to her and put up three fingers in her face. "Three times, Brooke! What the hell is he? Are you the same?" and turned to Gabe. "Is he!?"

That thought broke my heart in two. The mere thought of losing Gabe crushed my will and quickly dropped my anxiety to the bottom of a well. The ground rushed towards me as I swooned and felt every desire leave my body.

The familiar smell of caramel corn filled my nostrils as his strong arms enwrapped me gently catching me before hitting the ground.

"Oh my god! Can you be any more melodramatic? It's not like Set is an alien or some kind of vampire or something." Brooke sighed. "He's just different."

"If he's not already dead, Brooke." I began. "Then how can he be alive? I saw him get shot! Nobody just walks away from that. And how is it that his skin is different under his…..skin?! He's an alien. You are an alien and you are…" I started to sob.

"Seriously? You think we are going to eat your brain now." Brooke said disgusted. "I've known you for four years. You think if I had wanted to eat your brain I could have done it by now. Not that it would have helped me any."

"Shut up, bitch. I'm 10th in our class. You aren't even in the top twenty. So shut it." And sobbed again.

"That is just sad, Blue." Set commented from the side. "To let them think you are not superior is a disgrace even to your kind."

My eyes popped open. "See…see…you are aliens." My world was spinning out of control and I couldn't get a grip.

"JJ. You are being ridiculous. We are not aliens." She looked at me annoyed.

A light popped on.

My hand reached up to Gabe's warm face. "You wouldn't lie to me, right Gabe? You like me. You will tell me the truth."

"Golds don't lie." He assured me.

"But they will stretch the truth." Set interjected.

I ignored Set. "Tell…me. Are you an alien?" I sniffled. "Are you going to eat my brain or make hybrid babies with me?"

His warm smile spread across his face like the sun rising in the morning. "No, JJ. I'm not going to eat your brains or have a hybrid baby with you even if I wanted to." He paused. "We are….dragons."

"Half." Set corrected him. "I'm a full."

Chapter Twelve

Dragons are People too

"You don't want to have babies with me?" My life ended at that moment.

Gabe's eyes popped open at the unexpected response; clearly that wasn't what he thought I would ask. Set laughed and Brooke looked incredulous.

"That's it? You don't want to have babies with me? That's all you have to say after the revelation he just told you?" Brooke was beside herself. "I can't believe this. We finally tell you…and the only question you can ask is if he is going to take your virginity?" Brooke started walking around agitated.

"That isn't what I meant." My face burned with embarrassment. "And I didn't say anything about my virginity, which seems to have been brought up a lot more than I'm comfortable with these last few days, thank you."

I pushed myself from Gabe's arms, wiped my face and rose. *Okay. Let's try and get a hold of yourself here. I don't know what kind of alien Dragons are, but they haven't eaten my brain yet.*

To buy me some time to think, I walked over to the car.

"I'll take your virginity and make some babies with ya, if the Gold doesn't want to." Set smugly said.

I slapped him, hard. The excruciating pain traveling through my hand and up my arm stifled my yelp on my lips. I wouldn't give him the satisfaction of seeing the pain in my eyes, so the thought of moving over to the car presented itself and I took it. The car was cold as my limp hand laid upon the trunk. *I think I broke my hand!* Breathing in deep gulps of the night air, I fumbled with the door handle, and after some struggle, opened it and slid into the car.

They remained outside talking amongst themselves, well, Set and Gabe did little of the talking and Brooke did the majority. I couldn't hear what was being said. They were talking in low tones, and my hand hurt so bad that I didn't really hear anything outside of the pain that seemed to throb throughout my whole body. The clock on the dash said eleven thirty.

Brooke got on her phone. Talked very shortly, and hung up. A few more words were exchanged and then they all climbed back into the car. The clock on the dash read eleven thirty four before Brooke turned to me.

"We are going back to our house." She informed me.

"I'd rather go home." I told her.

"I don't think that is a very smart idea." She said.

My anger flared. "I don't care what you think. I want to go home!"

"Listen. You have to realize the danger you are in now." She insisted. "Now that you know, there will be others looking for you."

My eyes widened. "There are more aliens!"

Brooke's head hit the seatback in resignation. "Yes. More aliens. Bad aliens. That will try…"

"And eat my brain!" I gasped.

"You are impossible." She turned around.

I felt an uncomfortable stare focused on me. Slowly turning, Set stared at me with his eyes as black as a new moon. "I… personally…like my human brains…pickled." His gleaming white smile filled his face as he leaned towards me.

Before I fainted, screaming with as much volume as my vocal chords could muster and sure that I'd never see the sun again, Brooke spoke.

"Nice going Set. Now she will never believe us."

"Come now, dear." A kind voice called to me across the blackness of fatigue. "Your Dad would be very disappointed that you are so soft." The kind voice said. "He has prided himself on how tough his little girl is. Don't disappoint him."

The voice sounded very familiar. It was old, soft, and as rare as a Green Jade. My eyes fluttered open to see Mrs. Wasabi over me with a wash cloth, cleaning my face. My heart relaxed and I wondered if I hadn't been dreaming the whole thing. I began to sit up, when my vision fell upon the aliens that were going to eat my brain.

"Don't let them kill me, Mrs. Wasabi. I won't tell anyone. I promise." I clung to her arm with my head buried in her side.

"What is this? You have your father's imagination for sure." She gently, well, not as gently as you would think for a small Japanese woman, pulled me away from her and looked at me. "You need to listen. Nothing is going to happen to you. Do you understand? Would you like some tea?"

She got up without me answering, meaning that I did want some tea. I've been around the Wasabi household to know that much. Everything else was suspect now.

I pulled my feet up next to me, hung my head, and looked my feet. "My Dad isn't going to let you get away with this. He knows I'm with you."

"He also knows that you are spending the night and we'll be taking you to school."

My eyes stared at Brooke with surprise.

She smiled. "He appeared to be happy that we called, since it sounded like he had some company of his own."

Sydney!

"I..." but Mrs. Wasabi returned with my tea.

Mr. Wasabi entered and took up a seat next to Gabe. Even though I tried to not notice, he had been watching me the entire time and his eyes appeared to be generally upset at my distress.

In Mr. Wasabi's hands, he held the multi colored egg. Its colors were swirling with the harmonious hypnotic patterns that had enthralled me when I had first discovered it after break.

My eyes widened and terror like nothing I'd ever felt before flooded my body. My hands trembled but the cup remained calm and I couldn't rise. Incomprehension pierced my mind as to why I couldn't stand. Then I notice Mrs. Wasabi's arm around my shoulders and her hand on my wrist that kept the cup steady.

"Please don't put that in me." I whimpered.

"Pay up, Blue." Set laughed.

"God! I didn't even think *she* could be that dumb." Brooke took a twenty out of her jean pocket and handed it to him.

My eyes pleaded with Gabe for him to save me. To be not like the others. That my love for him was real and that he felt the same thing. He sat motionless.

"JJ." Mr. Wasabi started. "First, nothing is going to happen to you. They are not aliens or anything that is extraterrestrial," He bobbed his head in uncertainty. "Mostly."

"Mostly?" I blurted.

"Yes. To say that they are originally from earth would be a slight stretch." Mr. Wasabi explained. "But they have been on earth long enough to call it home."

I stared at Brooke. "How old are you?"

"Eighteen." Brooke said.

"Eighteen thousand!"

"God, no." Brooke said incredulous. "I'm not like Set."

My gaze went to Set. "How old are you?"

"Thirty thousand or so. I've lost track a few times." He answered.

Thirty Thousand? How is that possible? "How?"

"As I tried to tell…" Mr. Wasabi cut Brooke off, who acquiesced without further word.

"Okay. I'm going to tell you a story. It's going to be hard to believe, but I'd like you to try and keep an open mind. It should all become clear." Mr. Wasabi assured me.

"Does my Dad know about any of this?" My concern for my dad quickly filtered out my own fears.

"No. And I'd like to keep his friendship, just as Brooke and the others want to keep yours. It's important to have good friends, really good friends." He appeared sincere in his sentiment.

"I don't care." Set said off handily.

I stared hard at Set. "So you are not going to hurt me." I asked. "Or make me forget, eat my brain, breed with me, or any other things the movies say aliens do."

"Because the movies never lie." Gabe smiled and I eased a little.

"The breeding part still stands for me." Set smirked.

"Set." Mrs. Wasabi cautioned.

Set bowed his head in deep respect.

Mrs. Wasabi nodded. "Understand dear, we cannot make you forget what we are about to tell you. This knowledge will be with you for the rest of your life. It is very valuable to certain people."

I nodded. "Brooke mentioned something about that."

"Good." Mr. Wasabi said relieved. "Now, before I tell you the story. You have two choices. One…you can walk away right now without the story. We will disappear and you will never find us and you can tell whatever story you want to."

My heart jumped.

"Two…you can listen, believe it or not, and understand that we are placing our lives in your hands as you will be placing your life in our hands."

I paused. "I don't understand. How could your lives be in my hands? I don't even understand what is going on."

"The reference Brooke made about the people that could try and kill you is very real. Those two things at the ice cream shop were with those that would like to hurt us. They will torture you for the information, for they don't want Brooke and Gabe's kind or Set's kind to help in the war. And above all…They want this." He looked down at the egg.

"What war? What does a lava lamp have to do with it?" I asked.

Mr. Wasabi shook his head. "You have to choose, first."

Okay…my curiosity is certainly peaked. And I really want to know what is going on and if possible not to lose the man of my dreams, who smells so incredibly good. But I don't want to get Dad in danger or myself really. I studied the others. *Brooke and Gabe clearly wanted me to choose option two. Set was a tougher read, and from the short time we have been together, I don't really think he cared one way or the other. I just don't know about the whole friendship thing. Brooke has been lying to me for four years. So have the Wasabi's. Do I trust them?*

"Will I be able to ask questions afterwards and then still choose?" I asked.

"Come on, JJ. Would I willingly put you in danger? I've been your best friend for four years. That does not come easy for my kind." Brooke said.

"You have lied to me for four years as well." I countered.

She looked a little dejected like it actually bothered her. "I didn't want to, JJ. Really. I love you. I really meant that you and your dad are family to us. I wouldn't hurt you." She got that mischievousness in her eye. "Besides, I've been preparing you for this day." She sat back.

That actually made me smile. "If I agree. You will answer all my questions, no matter how weird or dumb."

"We've been doing that." Set snarled.

Mr. Wasabi nodded a scowl at Set, who turned up his nose.

"And, this won't involve my Dad. I want him to be safe."

Mr. Wasabi's face became very serious. "I will do my very best, JJ. I treasure your Father's friendship very much and I would put my life on the line for him. But I can't completely guarantee that he will be safe. The only way for that to happen is for you to walk away."

Surprised by the answer, I could tell he spoke from his heart. But, when Mr. Wasabi said he would put his life on the line for Dad, I had already made my decision.

"I'm not sure it's right for me to make this decision for my Dad, but with you looking after him, I believe he is safer than he is on his own." I took a deep breath. "Okay. Let's hear it."

Brooke rushed to me and gathered me up in her arms. "I knew you would do it. From the moment you could smell Gabe, I knew you would join us." She pulled away and looked to be on the verge of tears, which *never* happens to Brooke.

"BFF's. Which reminds me, why does he smell so good."

"He's dying." Set announced.

"What?!" My heart stopped again.

"He's just kidding." Brooke assured me. "Well, technically he is dying, but it won't be for a while still. But that is why his smell is so overpowering. Normally, we smell just like any other human. But since he is older, his smell is stronger."

My heart returned to its normal beating rhythm.

"Why do you do that Set?" I said.

He shrugged. "When you have been alive for as long as I have, you take pleasures in the little things." His cruel smile told the truth as he walked upstairs.

"He is so mean." My eyes burned holes in his head.

Brooke agreed. "True Breeds are." She turned to me. "Ready?"

Excitement grew in me. "Yes."

"Oh. I have to bite your neck now." Brooke said seriously.

"What?" Laughing nervously.

"Yeah. I have to bite your neck to turn you into one of us." She said again.

"But you aren't vampires?" I looked nervously over at Mr. Wasabi. "Are you?"

He shook his head. "No, Brooke is having fun at your expense. Normally that is a Green trait but the Blues have an odd sense of humor too at times."

I turned back to her and gave her my best evil eye. She laughed at me, then almost as swift as Set had moved, she was upon me and bit my neck.

"Now you are one of us!" She howled into the night.

Chapter Thirteen

To Further the Tale of the Gods War Chronicle

"You are a real bitch at times. That hurt!" I rubbed my neck and wiped her over produced saliva from my neck on Brooke's shirt.

"Hey."

"It's yours." I continued wiping saliva off me and onto her.

"Brooke." Mrs. Wasabi said.

Brooke jumped up. "Yes, Mother." She went off to the kitchen leaving me with Mr. Wasabi and Gabe, who smiled continuously at me.

I blushed.

"Thank you, JJ. Not many would take up this cause. It is rare and greatly appreciated." Mr. Wasabi bowed.

"You are very welcome. I just hope I can help." I said.

"I have no doubt." Mr. Wasabi leaned back in his chair holding the egg.

"May we start with that?" Pointing at the egg.

He smiled. "Certainly. This is a dragon's egg. More correctly, a Gold Dragon's egg."

I looked at Gabe.

"No. It isn't his. His kind cannot produce eggs. Only Set and his kind can."

"Brooke mentioned about his 'Kind' before. What makes them so different? Aren't they both dragons?" Not really grasping the whole 'dragon' part yet.

"No. They are very different. Set is a full dragon, who has changed his form to appear as a human. Gabe and Brooke are Dimidius or half dragons." Mr. Wasabi explained. "Do you understand the difference?"

I shook my head. "Not really? You mean half, like a dog that is half one breed and another?"

An ironic smile set up residence on Gabe's face and Mr. Wasabi's smile took up his whole face.

"Not the most elegant of statements but theoretically correct." Mr. Wasabi agreed.

"I'm not a dog!" Brooke yelled from the kitchen.'

"But you are a bitch!" I yelled back.

Mrs. Wasabi's disapproving look made me drop my head. "I'm sorry."

She smiled. "That look isn't for you, dear."

That made me feel better. "So?" I prompted.

"Ah, yes." Mr. Wasabi was clearly determining whether Mrs. Wasabi's look was for him or Brooke. "Let me continue. Brooke and Gabe are the offspring between a dragon in human form and a person. Someone like your father or you."

"How does that happen?" My mind conjured images of a dragon having sex with a damsel in distress. I shuddered. "Is that what they meant when they said they were Dragon Touched?"

Mr. Wasabi appeared surprised. "Yes. When did you hear that?"

"A while back. Brooke and Set were arguing about the hockey."

Mr. Wasabi eyed Gabe, who shrugged.

"So, how does a dragon have sex with a human?"

"Just like anyone. Once a dragon takes on its human form…"

"Which Set is and Gabe isn't."

"…correct, they take on the characteristics of a human…"

"Meaning that Gabe can't have children." *Which means I can have all the sex with him I want and not get pregnant. Oh, my, god! How is this not a good thing! So what if he is like a hundred years old. He is sooooooo gorgeous!*

"Get your mind out of the gutter, you slut!" Brooke yelled again.

Mr. Wasabi eyed the kitchen door. "With some exceptions."

Don't tell me he CAN get me pregnant!

"Such as, not getting hurt when being shot." I offered first.

Mr. Wasabi nodded slowly. "Yes. Though, you should have been asleep during that accidental transgression."

"But I wasn't."

"And that is why you are here."

"Because I didn't fall asleep?"

"Because you have a resistance to Dragon Charm." Gabe said.

His golden eyes peered at me. *Not your charms.*

"I still don't understand." Shaking my head. "Dragon Charm?"

Mr. Wasabi nodded. "Yes. All dragons have a natural aura around them that people react to. Black dragons create fear, Gold dragons exude a sense of peacefulness…"

"And Blue dragons are bitches?" Offering this statement loud enough for Brooke to hear.

There was a momentary silence until Brooke roared from the kitchen. "I'm going to punch you in the face! I know where you live!"

The tirade would have continued but Mrs. Wasabi coughed lightly and the noise stopped.

I smiled. *It is so easy to push her buttons.* Gabe winked at me in appreciation of my talent.

Mr. Wasabi laughed. "I've never seen anyone with that kind of power over a Blue. You are good."

"I try."

Even Mrs. Wasabi had a slight hint of a smile.

"Okay. So, each dragon has a charm that affects people. How many different kinds of dragons are there?" Trying to grasp this whole charm thing.

"Seven and one. Gold, silver, black, blue, red, green and white. Each has a different attribute that accompanies their personalities. I don't need to go into each, but since you know three…gold are inquisitive and pragmatic. Black dragons are mischievous and manipulative and Blues' are…"

"Let me guess…..bitches." I laughed again.

The silence lasted just a while longer before the outburst of rage. "I am sooooo going to punch you in the face!"

"Belligerent is a better term." Mr. Wasabi said.

"Dad!" Brooke whined.

I nodded my head to him. "Okay. She's a little aggressive. Do the Dimidius have the same powers?"

"No. They are faster, smarter, healthier and a bit more durable than normal people, but they are just as vulnerable as anyone else. Only true dragons retain most of their power. They just aren't as powerful as if they were in their dragon form."

"I see. So that is why Set didn't get hurt. His dragon hide wouldn't allow normal bullets to go through." I said.

Mr. Wasabi agreed. "Yes."

I shuddered. "Did he kill those robbers?"

Mr. Wasabi shook his head. "They weren't robbers. They were servants of the Two. But no. He just incapacitated them. And don't worry about your friends or the store owner. They won't remember a thing."

"How is that? Magic?!"

He laughed. "Not quite. Just a potion."

I was a little deflated with that. I have to admit, I was hoping for the magic angle, but I guess that is still relegated to books. "So are you and Mrs. Wasabi Dimidius?"

"No. We are like you and your father, but our families have been involved with the dragons for centuries, raising and caring for them until they can go on their own. That is why Brooke is with us and now this egg."

The color's swirled excitedly as if it knew what was being said.

"When will that hatch?" I asked very interested.

"At the end of May." He became very serious. "That is why Set and Gabe are here. To help protect it until it hatches."

"And that will be a half dragon?"

Mr. Wasabi laughed. "Oh, no. This will be a full dragon. Those like Brooke and Gabe, are born to real parents, but are then taken away by the Gray Mage." His voice became low and respectful when he uttered that name.

"But the Gray Mage helps you? Where does he come from?"

"She." Mr. Wasabi shook his head. "No one knows. There are rumors, and no one really can say what she looks like either. Her power is unmistakable when you meet her, though."

"But she looks out for the True Breed too?" I asked.

"Yes. Much to their annoyance. But getting back. Both of them will leave when the egg has hatched."

"Then they will leave?" My heart dropped. *How can I live without him? I have to have him in my life. Oh god, what am I going to do?!*

"I'll be around for a while." Gabe assured me.

My heart eased.

"So, there are seventy one dragons. That's a lot?" I said. "How do you keep track of all of them?"

"Not seventy one, JJ. Seven *and* one." His voice dropped a little and was very serious.

I was confused. "Isn't that seventy one. Seven and one."

"No. There are seven true dragon kinds and one other." Set walked down the stairs. His demeanor had changed. A true hatred filled his eyes, not like the contempt he had for Gabe and Brooke, but a deep seeded hatred that appeared to emanate from his soul.

"What is this other dragon then? What kind are they?" I wasn't ready for the outburst from Set. It was loud and nasty.

"Not they… one. It isn't even a true dragon." He stomped forward until he stood before me with his finger pointed at my face. "It is an abomination! A monstrosity of wickedness conjured from the deepest parts of the universe. It lives to consume. It lives to destroy the very existence of all life. True dragons shun it because of its sinister nature. IT…Is…Evil!"

I was so absorbed in Set's story that it wasn't until Brooke nudged me with a drink in her hand that I heard her mocking laughter. Set scowled deeply at her.

"You laugh, Dimidius, but it would devour you as well. It doesn't respect our kind, it won't give your half breed brethren a second's thought."

"Oh, Set. The arrogance of the True Breeds are only overshadowed by their notion that they are the most powerful creatures in the universe, which I believe has been disproven more than once." Brooke's tone clearly indicated that she believed Set's kind were far inferior to her. "The Gray is no threat to us. Only the True Breed fear it because it can kill, and I'll use your words, your *kind* without a thought."

Set stepped up to her until the only space between them was the breadth of a hair. "You think you have power, Half Breed?" Set clenched his teeth. "Care to try?"

Somehow Brooke was able to get her finger on his chest. "I'm not afraid of True Breeds, Set." Then she stepped back and put on her most innocent and charming smile that had won her the hearts of many boys over the years. "The Gray Mage protects me."

Again, the fear that leaped into Set's eyes at the mention of the Gray Mage overshadowed any anger or hatred that had been there before.

"She causes this much fear in Set?"

"She is the Dragon Master." Brooke said. "She rules…"

"Cares." Mrs. Wasabi interjected.

Brooke nodded at the correction. "She cares for all the dragons and those defenseless against the tyranny of oppressors."

"She protects us and cares for us." Gabe said. "We aren't that many, maybe a dozen in a hundred years' time. Most True Breeds don't bother with humans, but there are a few who enjoy their company. But when we are born, most human parents can't understand or deal with the difficulties of raising us. Only people like the Wasabi's, who are specially trained, can. It is very difficult."

"But why do you fear her, Set? If she is a friend to the dragons, shouldn't you be thankful?"

Brooke laughed. "True Breeds aren't thankful for anything. They are selfish and mean. They fear her because she is more powerful than them. Their egos can't allow them to understand the good work she does. And only *SHE* can control the Gray Dragon."

Set hissed. "You are a fool." And left by way of the front door making sure to slam it hard.

Brooke had her superior smile on, a familiar look when she knows she has gotten the better of someone; Gabe had a sad smile, and Mr. and Mrs. Wasabi appeared unaffected. Clearly, there were other things going on, much of it I didn't understand between the Dimidius and the True Breeds, but the ace card was clearly the Gray Mage.

"So, how did the dragons get here? Did the Gray Mage bring them?"

Mr. Wasabi nodded. "Their planet was being invaded by a rival god and his army. The Gray Mage defeated them, but their planet was wrecked. She brought the survivors here."

"God? God is real?"

"Yes. All gods are real, JJ. They are just very powerful beings." Brooke smirked. "There is more going on in the universe than just the formation of planets and galaxies. War between Gods are happening all over. I can't explain it, for I don't know all of it. But the Gray Mage is the calm in the chaos. She leads our war against the Observers." Brooke's blue eyes burned with admiration.

"Who are the Observers? Are they the ones that are so dangerous?"

I looked to the others for answers.

Mr. Wasabi nodded his head. "They want to kill the Gray Mage. They believe she is a threat to the entire universe." Hatred dripped with every word spoken about the Observers from him. "The Two… believe the Gray Mage intends to destroy the existence of all the gods, when in truth the Gray Mage only wants to restore balance back to the universe."

"The Two?" I asked.

"An evil, ruthless pair that were supposed friends of the Gray Mage, until they betrayed her on the battle field and destroyed her home." He explained. "Now they wage a war to rid the universe of her presence and enslave the dragons and dragon kind so they may sow their evil across the universe."

The entire universe? How can a conflict engulf the entire universe? "How is this possible? They work with the other gods?"

"It's unclear. Their combined power is very formidable. They join with rouge gods to hunt Set and Gabe's kind. Now they are trying to destroy the eggs of any dragon on this planet."

"Then the things that attacked us in the green house?" My gaze fell upon Gabe. "The alleyway on New Year's Eve and now the ice cream shop?"

"Were minions of The Two." Gabe nodded. "They are coming for this egg. They will do everything they can to destroy it. As for the alley," he looked at me with a deep concern I've only seen from my dad. "We could have lost you. You shouldn't have been able to move once you walked into the alley, and certainly not have seen the Doppelganger. If Cerasina hadn't been already tracking those two Deev we couldn't have gotten to you. You were very foolish."

Gabe's disapproving look was crushing me. I didn't want to disappoint him or have him think badly of me. "I was just trying to find you." I mumbled.

"And you almost died." Mr. Wasabi said.

"Was that the claw marks I saw on the side of the wall? I remember seeing something up there when I ran from the alley."

Brooke nodded. "Yes. She is young, but a great tracker. I like her a lot more than some of the other dragons." Brooke gave a sidelong glance to the front door.

Suddenly, everything seemed to crash down on me. The figure I saw that night on the road was a part of it too. The whirlwind must have been Cerasina tracking them and I just happened to be near Brooke's home. For the first time, I started to doubt myself for agreeing to this cause. Originally, I agreed to do it just to be with Gabe, but now as the enormity of the circumstance filtered through my feelings, I felt I was getting into something way over my head.

"And the trips to Japan?"

"Meeting with other caretakers like us." Mr. Wasabi said.

I lowered my eyes. *What am I doing?*

Seeing my distress, Gabe got up and knelt in front of me.

"I won't let anything happen to you. I'd give my life for you as well."

Staring into those golden eyes made my heart beat harder in my chest. "I'll do whatever I can."

He smiled.

Chapter Fourteen

New Suspicions

It wasn't long after my history lesson that I laid in bed across from Brooke staring at the ceiling.

Mr. Wasabi had concluded his story with a warm hug. Brooke had pushed me upstairs with the intention of going to bed since the big hockey game was tomorrow. While she grabbed my hand and pulled me upstairs, my eyes never left Gabe's. I knew right then that I couldn't ever be without him.

Brooke brushed her long blue hair in the mirror. My head rolled over to look at her. Even without the story, she had always been so beautiful and perfect. Now to think that she had actual dragon blood in her made her even more beautiful and perfect. I wondered if all the really attractive men and women were Dimidius. *What about all the really fantastic actors, politicians, singers, and athletes? Were they half dragons too?*

"What's it like?" I mused. "Being this way?"

Even from the side, Brooke's smile filled her whole face. "It's fantastic. I'm not going to lie to you, JJ. I don't pity humans, nor do I have a disdain for them as the True Breeds do. But being this different is really awesome. I never get sick, I'm not afraid to go out at night or anywhere by myself. The dark isn't a scary place. I am really lucky." She turned to face me. "I've heard that some Dimidius have a really hard time accepting their true nature. They feel so different that they can't accept who they are."

A sarcastic grin came to my face. "I can't understand that. You are perfect. You have everything that anyone could possibly want. Looks, intelligence, health. What is the draw back to that?"

A sardonic smile came to her face. "Never having a family. Watching the person you love die. Right now there may not be any drawback, I can't really say. I'm just as old as you. But those that are like Gabe have watched many of their friends die."

She got up and came and sat down next to me. Her demeanor was a solemn as I have ever seen.

"Are the stories true? The tales of dragons." I asked.

A small smile appeared. "For the most part. There is a bad history between True Breeds and humans. Even some with us. But most have been blown way out of proportion. Hollywood isn't even close. But there is some truth." Her face turned solemn again. "Remember when I told you that I was sorry for you about Gabe?"

"Yes. I didn't understand why you would say such a thing."

"It's because, he meant what he said tonight. He will protect you with his life." She leaned forward. "Do you understand what that means?"

I thought I did, but with the earnest look in her eye, I wasn't sure anymore. I shook my head.

"It means, he will never leave you, JJ. Gold's are the most passionate of the dragons too. True Breed Gold Dragons take only one mate for life. They have been known to die when their mate dies unexpectedly. This trait has carried over into the Dimidius. Some of the greatest love poetry and sonnets are written about Gold Dimidius who have inspired those writers." She placed her hand on the side of my face. "And what about me? I've reached the age where my body will now age much more slowly, but you will continue to age normally." She now took my face in both her hands. "I will have to watch my best friend, someone I love very dearly, grow old and eventually die."

A deep blue tear ran down the side of her face. I reached up and wiped it away.

"Not for a very long time, Brooke." My smile told her that it will be okay.

She smiled. "I hope so." She went and turned off the light and crawled in bed with me next to the wall. She draped her arm over me and held me tight. It was very comfortable and I felt very secure until, in typical Brooke fashion, she ruined the moment.

"Wanna make out, before Gabe ruins you?" She whispered.

I chuckled. "Not even if I was a Dimidius too." And elbowed her in the gut. As she sucked in air to laugh I found myself wishing that I was one too.

The next morning came too early. During the night, Brooke had pushed me out of her bed and onto the floor. I went and climbed into her cold bed and fitfully fell asleep. My dreams moved in and out of the realm of the fantastic. They cycled between the cloudy encounter with the strange beast in the alley to Christian's eyes turning completely red and devouring me whole.

"Wake up, sleepy head!" Brooke punched me in the arm.

"Ow!" I woke immediately and rubbed my arm. Brooke was in her towel, her blue hair hanging wet around her shoulders. "You pushed me out of the bed, you know." My feet swung over the bed and yawned.

"Should have given me some love." She said off handedly rubbing her hair dry.

"Ha, ha. You don't even like girls." I grabbed the towel she had left for me on her mirror chair.

"Who says?"

"Me. I'm the only girl who is your friend." And laughed.

"Psh. You wish. I left the water running for you." She flung off her towel and dressed. "Hurry up before the hot water runs out. Breakfast is almost ready too." She rushed out of the room.

I made my way down the hallway to the shower. Steam filled the bathroom. It was hard to see in the mist, and while I began to undress, the water stopped and a gentle cough made me spin around.

"I think I'll be going." Gabe emerged from the shower with a towel around his waist and his muscles rippling with droplets of water.

My face flushed immediately and wrapped the towel around me, but I couldn't pull my eyes away from his body. Goosebumps sprang to life all over me.

"Ah…ah." I stammered.

He smiled as he gently passed me, despite my mind racing erotically about him taking me right here on the countertop. Gabe opened the bathroom door and Brooke's laughter rose from down stairs. He nodded in understanding while he closed the door behind him.

Standing there, my heart raced, by body tingled like it never had before, and my mind was racing in so many different directions that it paralyzed my body. Gulping in the warm wet air, beads of water ran down my body and all I could do was imagine they were his fingertips.

"Hurry it up!" Brooke's voice thundered from the other side of the door. Breaking me out of my trance, I climbed into the shower, my body still tingling, and didn't care that the cold water froze me. Once done, I dressed quickly, wanting to get some breakfast in. Brooke still had her mischievous smile on until she took a good look at the clothes I was wearing.

"Hey. Those are my clothes. Wear your own." She complained.

A wave of my hand dismissed her statement. "Mine are dirty. So I borrowed yours." And sat down.

Mrs. Wasabi placed some eggs, bacon, and couple of pieces of toast in front of me. Normally, this would have been too much breakfast, but Mrs. Wasabi's cooking was too good to pass up. Brooke and I were the only ones at the table.

"Juice?" Mrs. Wasabi asked.

"Please." The bacon melted in my mouth. "Where is everyone?"

"Why, didn't you get enough of Gabe?" She snickered. "Did he fill the right spots?"

I looked confused at her. "What? I haven't seen him today. That's why I asked."

She eyed me. "You didn't see him when you went to take your shower?"

Again, the confused looked. "No." I tried my best to keep the color from coming to my face and it must have succeeded because Brooke stopped teasing me, but then again it could have been the gentle cough from the kitchen too.

"Are you ready for tonight?" Mrs. Wasabi returned with my juice.

Brooke's face lit up. "Hell ya!"

"Brooke."

"Sorry, Mother." She leaned forward. "Hell ya." She whispered.

I smiled. "What about Set. Won't he have the advantage?"

She looked hurt. "Do you doubt my skill? You think I'd let a True Breed get the better of me?"

"No. Of course not. Just asking." My head swiveled around.

"You better not." Brooke corrected me. "He's gone. So stop looking and focus on me."

My attention returned to her. "Of course, Master."

She giggled. "I like that. Master Brooke."

"You are insufferable."

Mrs. Wasabi brought more juice, I drank it down in record time and headed out the door as Mr. Wasabi called to us to take us to school.

We turned onto the road that lead to the first check point off of Broadway. It was clear that someone, most likely the Counsel of Twelve of each class, had been hard at work. The South Bunker, was decorated with the school colors of maroon and blue. Great big letters adorned the top of the bunker spelling out Valkyrie Pride. Ribbons, tape, and various other items in the school colors were also hung in various positions around the school grounds. Some of the elementary pictures were hung as well. Each picture represented one of the hockey players and their number. Everyone knew that the third grade class was heavy on girls and Brooke's picture outnumbered anyone else on the team. It also helped she had been spending time in their class all semester. An observation that Brooke's noticed.

"I am a superstar." She informed us from the front seat.

While we pulled up to the bunker, Jen and Steve were manning the post.

"Hi guys!" Brooke called. "Did you see all my pictures?!"

"How could we miss them? Third graders have been filing out all morning to put up their pictures of their favorite hockey player." Steve grumbled.

"Don't encourage her." I complained.

Jen laughed. "Then just wait. *It* gets worse."

Brooke beamed. "Oooh, do tell?!"

She shook her head. "Just wait."

"It's pathetic." Steve moaned. "There are other people on the team you know."

"Yeah, but none of them are as beautiful as me." Brooke flipped her blue hair back.

"This place will not be the same without you two." Jen started to cry.

"Yes it will. You'll take good care of it for us." Surprised at the outburst of tears.

Jen was one of the junior mentors for the lower grades, she shadowed with me last year and we became good friends. I will miss her too.

She nodded, sniffling back tears. "Hello Mr. Wasabi."

"Hello, dear. May we move on?"

Steve waved us through. "Good luck tonight!"

"Luck is already with us." Brooke assured him.

We followed the road around to the front of the school. Cars were backed up as the underclassmen were being dropped off.

"Drop us here, Dad." Brooke told him as she started to open the door.

"JJ. Your Dad will drop the jeep off tonight. If you want to go home before the game, I can come and get you."

"No. I'll text my Dad and tell him to bring a change of clothes." I got out of the car with a strange feeling rumbling in my stomach as I thought about it.

"Come on, JJ." Brooke leaned in. "Love you, Dad."

"You too, Blue."

We rushed off toward the school.

You would have thought the circus was in town with all the outfits. One of the things I loved most about our school was its pride. Colored faces and shirts were proudly displayed on students and lots of costumes of Valkyries were around too. Some of the guys dress ups might have been a little overboard, but everyone knew that if it wasn't done with taste, Mr. Resler would be sending them home. You'd also miss the game and that was paramount to death.

We greeted other seniors with a wave and I looked especially for Kennah, Alexa and Serina. I didn't see them.

"Are you sure the others were okay?" I whispered to Brooke as we made our way through the hallways to our lockers.

"My dad is a potions master. Taught by a Green Dragon himself. He could put the whole school asleep and no one would be the wiser. Quit worrying. They are probably in class already." Brooke rushed up the stairs.

"Why are we in such a hurry?" Trying to keep up with her, but she kept bounding up two steps at a time. The climb to the sixth floor was taking its toll on me. "Slow down, I'm not a dragon."

"I bet you wish you were now." She called over her shoulder, disappearing around the corner of the next set of stairs.

I stopped to catch my breath. *I don't know why I'm running. I've got ten minutes to Dr. Daugherty's class. What is her deal?* Taking in a deep breath, while passing students greeted me, I climbed the rest of the way. When I exited the stairwell, the reason became apparent. Christian stood at our locker talking to her. Brooke had her back to the locker with one foot on it and she played with her hair like a little girl. She giggled and laughed and the whole thing made me want to vomit.

Christian waved to me as I approached slightly out of breath. A smell began to infiltrate my nose that didn't quite fit. The hallways always contained odors that weren't readily recognizable with this many students and their differing tastes in fragrances. But this odor had a foulness to it that even was odd for the hallways. I stopped some distance from them, wondering if Brooke's clothes were the source of it. Nonchalantly, I look around while smelling my armpits and shirt. Nothing seemed out of the ordinary, but looking back at Brooke and Christian, he was watching me intently, while Brooke blathered on about something.

Cautiously I approached them and the odor increased and began to grow fouler. I've never smelt a decaying corpse, but the literature Dr. Daugherty's has had us read describes it pretty well and this is what it must smell like.

"Something wrong?" Christian asked.

My head turned to the side. "Something smells foul. Do you smell it?"

Christian's eyes narrowed at my statement.

"I only smell love." Brooke said dreamily.

"Oh, god." My fingers fumbled with the locker combo.

Throwing my stuff into the locker, I grabbed the other books I'd need for the first part of the day. "Do you want me to leave this open?"

"What?" Brooke continued to stare at Christian.

When I turned around, Christian's eyes bore into me. Not like an upset look but a calculating look as if my worth had become more important. The smell grew.

Christian laughed. "Oh, that must be me." His face flushed with embarrassment though it looked contrived. He pulled two small bottle of cologne out of his back pack. "The guy at the store said that the *Rugged Man Musk*, would turn the women wild. I was trying to impress Brooke." He sprayed the other cologne and the smell instantly disappeared.

"Oh, now that is nice." Brooke agreed. "What is it?"

"Devil's delight." Christian's face flushed even deeper in color.

My eyes narrowed. His flushed skin looked strange. I couldn't understand what I was seeing, but it looked like his skin was covering a deeper colored skin, almost like a mask. Just as Set's had. *Was he a dragon too? Can't be. Brooke and Gabe would know.* The red coloring disappeared just as fast as it had come. *Strange though.*

"I'd say you got taken. Hope it didn't cost too much?" The after smell still lingered like diet coke in your mouth.

He dropped his head. "Fifty bucks."

"Ouch." Brooke patted his shoulder. "It's alright. Thanks for trying, but you don't need to impress me." She fluttered her eyelashes.

"God." I slammed the locker door shut. "I'll see you in class. Hurry up, you know how Dr. Daugherty treats tardiness."

"Don't worry, he loves me." Brooke winked at me.

I glanced back before rounding the corner; Christian was staring at me. A shiver ran up my spine.

Dr. Daugherty was standing at the window with the rest of the class.

"Dr. Daugherty, Brooke might be running a little late."

"Because of this?" He pointed out the window.

Kennah was standing with the others, so I quickly put my books down on my desk and went over to her. "How are you?"

Kennah smiled. "Little sleepy. Can you believe this?"

"Do you remember anything from last night?"

She looked at me. "Just you getting sick and Mr. Wasabi taking us home. Are you okay?"

Surprised, I fumbled with my answer. "Ah, yeah."

"As if her ego wasn't big enough." Cameron sighed.

"What?" I stared out the window.

From Dr. Daugherty's class room, you can see the primary school's playground. Down in the middle of the playground, a bunch of blue haired students were aligned together to spell out Brooke's name and 'we love you'.

"Are you kidding me?" I sighed.

"What's everyone looking at?" Brooke's voice sounded a bit different.

Dr. Daugherty sighed. "A spectacle of ridiculousness propaganda. But in retrospect not for you."

"What?" She pushed her way to the window and she squeaked with enjoyment. "Oh, that is so sweet!"

"I think it's adorable. They need good role models." Carrina said in her thick Italian accent.

"Yeah, but, Brooke?" Cameron questioned.

"I'm adorable, Carrina said so. And Italians know adorable. Can…" Brooke didn't even get the rest of sentence out before Dr. Daugherty commented.

"Try to be back before the end of class bell."

"Thank you, Dr. Daugherty." Brooke went to give him a hug, but he shooed her away before she could.

We waited for her to run around the building and make her grand entrance. I noticed a person standing by a car in the parking lot that overlooked the playground. On cue, Brooke came running around the building, as fast as I've ever seen her run, past the man without a glance, and entered the playground. You would have thought Taylor Swift had entered a concert hall.

The blue haired students erupted into a silent scream and several seconds later the yells of excitement crashed upon the open windows with the force of a thunderstorm. They all swarmed around her. She reveled in it.

"If we don't win tonight, I think her popularity is going to die." Cameron said.

Dr. Daugherty returned to his desk. "I think you underestimate her influence. We could lose badly and they will still adore her."

Cameron scoffed. "Why?"

The class began to return to their seats. I lingered a while at the window watching the man Brooke passed. He turned his gaze up at me, nodded to me, and walked around the building and disappeared. My neck hair rose up, which made me shudder.

Who is that? Do I know him? Oh my god. Could that be one of the people after the egg? I better tell Gabe when I see him.

"Ms. Ritter, will you return to your seat, please." Dr. Daugherty said politely.

"Sorry." I returned to my seat and sat down.

Dr. Daugherty continued answering Cameron's question. "Simple, Cameron. She represents something special to them."

"But what? She isn't anything special. She's athletic, but she's an average student, not even in the top twenty of our class."

"Sounds like someone is jealous." Kennah chirped from the back of the room.

Cameron shot her a nasty look but kept silent.

Dr. Daugherty smiled. "You are missing the point. And thank you for not falling for Ms. Knowles trolling. One, she is a successful woman in a man's sport. Two, have you watched her out on the playground with them? She knows every one of their names, she knows their histories, and she takes the time to listen to them."

"We all do that. It's one of the Tenets of the school." Cameron grumbled.

"Yes, that is very true. But have you done it with any other class besides the one you were assigned to your junior year?" He asked.

Nobody answered.

"Those third graders are not part of her group, but she can tell you their names, the fourth graders, second graders, first graders, and the kindergartners." He took in a deep breath. "I'm not saying she is perfect."

That drew several laughs from the class.

"We all know she's impulsive, outspoken, tactless at times, and a pain in the administrations ass when she thinks she's right."

That reference would pertain to the commotion Brooke caused our freshman year. So, here is the story I didn't go over earlier about how she came a part of the boy's hockey team. Since we have a girls' hockey team, Brooke was supposed to play for them our freshman year. But she knew her skills were far too good for the girls' team and when she was told she couldn't try out for the boys' team, all hell broke loose. She petitioned the board, wrote Mr. Donahue, the Governor, and was about to set up a meeting with Senator Udall, when the board relented. When she got the chance and was clearly the better goalie, she took a lot of grief from the upper classmen and the girls' hockey team. But to her credit, she took it in stride, said very little about the teasing, and was always supportive of the girls' team.

"She inspires them to take a stance, but to do it the right way without slinging mud at the opposition. A lesson our congress could use." He finished.

No one spoke. Dr. Daugherty was right. There is certainly a way to have a disagreement and find common ground.

I raised my hand.

"Yes, Ms. Ritter."

"You know she is going to get into a fight tonight, especially with her cousin, Set."

A wide smile came to his lips. "I never said she didn't make mistakes. I trust she will make the right decision when the time comes." He winked. "And everyone knows, sometimes bullies need to be popped in the nose. Go Valkyries!"

The class cheered.

Chapter Fifteen

The Hockey Game

Brooke returned to class just as the bell was about to ring. She beamed with pride and excitement. Nobody teased her when she came in and she looked a little disappointed about that. Dr. Daugherty passed out the homework assignment for the next day, knowing full well that it wouldn't be turned in until the following Monday.

We headed off toward second period. Excitement permeated the halls as students chatted about tonight's game.

"Hey, I'll see ya at lunch." I told Brooke.

She nodded. "Save me a seat."

We hugged and parted ways at the fifth floor stairwell. My next two classes were pretty entertaining, with each teacher showing their pride in very different ways. Finally, when the fourth period bell rang and everyone headed to first lunch at around twelve thirty, the buzz was beginning to get even more pronounced. Even though the game wasn't until seven o'clock, you couldn't get away from the enthusiasm. Going through the lunch line was like going through a buffet for royalty. The culinary students had fixed up something special for the day, and clearly Mr. Donahue must have told them to go all out. Since our school was named after a Greek god and our mascot from a Norse myth, lunch was a combination of foods from Greece and Sweden. Needless to say, the calorie count was thrown to the wind for the day, and everyone feasted upon authentic dishes. My personal favorite was the lamb stew with fresh bread and some kind of fruit tart that was to die for.

Kennah, Kaylene, Alexa and Howard, a junior thespian, came over and sat down.

"Hi, ladies and gentleman," wiping stew from my chin.

"Hey, JJ." Howard greeted me.

"I love this school!" Kennah bit into her tart and moaned with pleasure.

"I will certainly miss the food." Alexa agreed.

"How you feeling?" I asked her.

"Tired. Are you okay? You got pretty sick last night. Should you be eating all that?" she asked concerned.

I nodded. "Yeah, must have been some kind of twenty four hour bug. I felt really good this morning." My thought was to keep up the charade since the two of them appeared to believe the same thing.

"How's Serina? I haven't seen her today." I asked them.

"She must have gotten the same thing, but didn't fare as well. She's at home sick." Kennah said between mouthfuls and moans.

This concerned me, but I guessed that some people might react differently even to natural herbs just like medicines. "Will she be at the game?"

"I think so." Alexa answered taking a bite of the fruit tart and moaning with pleasure.

"Did you see the Third Graders?" Howard asked. "It was a circus over there."

"Yeah, we watched it from Dr. Daugherty's class."

"No, what happened." Kaylene asked.

"I was greeted like a queen." Brooke announced as she walked up.

I explained to Kaylene what happened.

She smiled. "Only you, Brooke."

Brooke sat down. "They adore me, what can you do."

She reached over to snatch my tart, and was met with a slapped hand. "Go get your own."

"You need to learn how to share." She said in a huff. Her eye caught sight of Christian. "Don't wait for me."

She got up and walked over to him. He greeted her with a hug, but his eye caught a hold of mine and we locked stares. Again, an uncomfortable feeling washed over me, but I wasn't able to give it any real meaning.

"Have you guys noticed anything different about Christian?" I asked.

"Beside the fact that he is gorgeous?" Alexa acknowledged.

"Yeah, beside that." And laughed.

"No. Usually, he is very quiet and doesn't say much. I'm kind of surprised he's interested in Brooke. She is much too boisterous for him." Howard said.

"I don't know." Kaylene countered. "I've seen Christian get a little out of control at some of the parties. But on a whole, I'd have to agree that Brooke is a little outside his normal zone."

"What? Are you saying Brooke isn't normal?" I mockingly said.

"I'd say she is really different." Kaylene said seriously. "She just does things that seem so….unnatural."

My heart increased in rhythm. "What do you mean?"

"Well…" But before she could continue, Gabe came and sat down next to us.

The girls at the table smiled at him, even Howard had a pleasant smile.

"Hi." He said.

"Hello." The table answered in unison.

"Nice to see you with your clothes on." Gabe said.

My face turned four colors of red as 'oohs' came from the table.

"Nothing happened" I blurted out. "Just a prank that Brooke played on us this morning."

"Your look doesn't suggest you were opposed to it." Kennah teased.

My body was on fire from embarrassment. I was speechless.

"My cousin can be very mischievous at times. A most embarrassing moment for myself as well." Gabe explained.

"Speaking of your cousin, Valor believes that Set will win them the playoff game tonight." Kennah said. "My boyfriend said the school is having a huge assembly today."

"So what?" Howard huffed. "Brooke is the best goal keeper in the state. We'll win it easily. Has she said where she is going to college?"

Gabe answered. "She got accepted into a college in Japan."

"Japan?!" The table said.

He nodded. "Yep. It's where my Uncle and Aunt attended."

"What kind of university is it?" Kaylene asked.

"Business." Gabe said.

"Do they play hockey in Japan?" Howard asked.

"I think her playing days are over after this." Gabe announced. He started to continue when Ms. Pendragon stepped into the lunch room and waved to him.

"Hey, I have to go." He got up.

"I need to talk to you about something." I told him.

He looked over at Ms. Pendragon and back at me. "I'll see you tonight." He waved.

I watched him go. My heart filled with joy.

"Well?" Kennah said.

I turned to her. "Well, what?"

"Is he?" She moved her hand together and then apart. Clearly trying to get me to answer how well hung he was.

"Girls don't kiss and tell." I said smugly.

"She doesn't know." Kaylene smirked. "Her left eye twitches when she is lying.

My hand shot up to my left eye. "You guys are as bad Brooke."

They laughed and we ended our lunch talking about the game.

The rest of the day was pretty normal if you don't include the strange ways that each teacher expressed their own pride in the school. The one that stood out the most and got the most talk of the day was Dr. Zang's Latin class having to go and recite the Spartan oath of Brotherhood from the amphitheater.

When classes were over, people scattered to do what they needed to do before the game, and I waited out front for Dad. Brooke had to go to a meeting for the team, so I wouldn't see her again until after the game. I didn't see Gabe after lunch, and since he had transferred out of Dr. Daugherty's class to be in my Ms. Pendragon's class, this had put me in a bad mood. Cars honked incessantly as they left from the student parking lot. Windows were painted with graffiti proudly showing school pride. Dad showed up in the jeep with his bike attacked to the rack in back.

"Hey, sweetie." He hopped out of the jeep and kissed me on the forehead.

"Hi Dad." Tossing my backpack into the passenger side.

He put his hand on my forehead. "How you feeling? Toyo called me and said you were sick. Something you ate?"

"Uhm, must have been." Not sure what else to say. "Dad…" I started, when Mr. Wasabi's warning came to mind. I hate keeping secrets from my Dad. It's something that we both agreed upon when Mom passed away. But I didn't want to put him in danger either. My stomach felt as if it had a huge hole in it.

"What JJ?" He asked concern filling his face. "You feel sick again?"

"No. I just wanted to say sorry for not coming home last night." I blurted out. "I feel kind of stupid about getting sick."

He smiled. "It's okay honey. It happens." He took the bike off the rack. "I'm going to go and get Sydney, have some dinner and then come to the game. You want to come?"

"You like her don't you." I asked.

A silly grin came to his face. "I do. But you have to too. If you don't, then I'll break it off with her." He cupped my face. "No one or anything is as important as you, JJ."

I knew that he meant that and my inner conflict rose to the surface again. "I like her. She is really nice. I hope I find someone like that. What you and Mom had and what you have with Sydney."

His face grew solemn. "Understand, JJ. No one can replace your Mom. She was the most perfect woman I have ever known. Just like you." He smiled. "But I like Sydney too. I think you will find someone. Besides, don't you have someone?" He nodded in the direction behind me.

I turned and Gabe was walking toward another car.

"Not a shabby pick." He winked.

"Yeah. I just hope he feels the same way about me." I mused.

Gabe waved at me before getting into the car.

"I bet he does." Dad kissed me on the head. "Okay. I'm off. See ya tonight? You sure you don't want to come and eat with us?"

I shook my head. "No. I have homework to do. Plus, you know how good the food is here."

He nodded. "True. Oh, here." He reached inside his bike shorts and handed me a fifty dollar bill. "Just in case you want to celebrate tonight."

"Is this your way of paying me off not to come home?"

His face grew innocent. "I am not suggesting any such a thing." He got on his bike and as he rode off, he called back. "I'm not responsible for any nightmares you might have from the noise." He waved.

Gross. "TMI, Dad!" I shook my head. It made me wondered if any other parents talked about sex as openly as my dad did. They probably should and maybe there wouldn't be as many pregnancies. I have to say it was refreshing.

"Love you!"

He waved back.

I climbed into the jeep and drove off toward the ice rink. There was plenty of parking since the game wasn't for another three hours and I wasn't worried about what to do during that time. My homework will take up most of it and I'd get to eat and people watch. Then my friends would show, we'd get ready for the game and then some time with Gabe during the game. A glorious evening for sure.

The CHSAA T.V people had been setting up all day. There had been talk that ESPN would be here but Mr. Resler quickly put the kibosh on that rumor. Parking near the South Bunker, I grabbed my back pack, and headed into the restaurant. Connor was behind the counter and I waved to him.

"Usual?" He called to me.

"Yes, please." I found a corner that overlooked the parking lot, settled in, pulled my homework out and started.

It wasn't long before Connor brought me my Blackberry tea and chili fries.

"Are you going to get something else?" He asked.

"I'll probably get some chicken tenders later, but I'll let you know. Thanks."

He waved. "No problem. Remember, they have the Cherry Creek, Mullen game earlier."

"Oh, crap! I totally forgot about that!"

Normal policy was that students couldn't take up the tables when events are planned. Since students are notoriously renowned for getting the cheapest stuff on the menu. The school does like to have the revenue from the restaurant. The restaurant helps offset school cost, so the school can remain free to the public.

"Okay, just tell me when I need to leave." I stuffed some chili fries into my mouth.

Connor shook his head. "Don't worry about it. I'm not going to kick you out. Just try and keep your friends down to a minimum."

"Don't worry. Most won't be here until the start of the game. I'll stay incognito." I put my book up to hide myself.

Connor laughed. "Okay. Just wave if you need anything."

He left to help some customers that had come in. I wondered who else might be working tonight. With the other game, he would need some help. Soon, some freshman came running in and went behind the counter. Connor barked some orders at them, and they began their duties in earnest. Soon though, my homework lost interest as crowds began to funnel in through the restaurant doors. I watched them. The school bus from Cherry Creek pulled up and the familiar red and blue of the Bruins piled off the bus. Cars drove by honking to the players, who returned the yells from their fellow students, whose cars were as painted as the students faces. Like a river that gets its flow from the first drops of rain, so did the river of people that started to flow from the parking lot. Mullen arrived in several vans, their gold and blue shone in the early evening sun. I frowned at the throng of people.

I wonder how many of them know about the dragons or the half dragons. Were all these people as blissfully ignorant as I was about the dangers out there in the world? Or even the universe. There is life out there! I was literally told there was life outside our solar system and now I've seen it. Well descendants anyway. How would the world react to something like that? Are all the rumors of UFO's and creature stories that people read in the newspapers and tabloids anywhere close to being true? My mind reels with the possibilities of what this means. Civilizations older or even younger are out there. How cool is that!

"Hello! Earth to JJ." A voice broke my contemplation of my place in the universe.

"What?"

Alexa, Kaylene, and Avery stood at the front of the table. Both Avery and Alexa were dressed up in their school colors, with faces painted, but Kaylene had taken it to a whole new level. Her hair was blond and in long braids that spilled out the sides of her Valkyrie helm. Two huge ivory horns stuck up on either side that tapered into nasty points. Her chainmail, leather under garment, leather boots, leather belt and sword looked like it could have easily been manufactured in the thirteenth century. It was amazing.

"You look fantastic!" Complementing her.

"Thank you. I have a friend down at the museum that lent me the stuff. It's a little tight in some areas and pinches in others…" She ran her hands over her breasts. "If you know what I mean."

"I'm thinking Geoffrey is going to be pissed if he sees you." Avery said.

Geoffrey wore the school mascot costume. Also a thespian, he took his duty very seriously.

"That's okay." Kaylene said. "He's in love with me. It will make him think I like him too."

"What about Gene? Isn't he your new love?"

Kaylene waved away the remark. "Love em and leave em."

"He knows you are a lesbian." Alexa commented.

"Bi would be the correct term, but the guys keep hoping. I actually liked Gene enough when he asked me to the dance, before sending him on his way. Besides, he said he wasn't ready for all this!" Kaylene drew a circle around her face before turning to me. "You are not going like that?"

"Oh, no. I've got my stuff in the jeep. Just waiting." I explained.

"For what? The game starts in forty five minutes? What have you been doing?" They all looked at me.

My eyebrows scrunched together. "I just got here." The half empty glass of tea and the empty tray of chili fries corroborated their story. "I guess I lost track of time."

Wow, I must have been in some deep thoughts. I slid out from the booth and stuffed my back pack with my books. "I'll be right back."

"Hurry up!" Alexa urged.

I rushed through the restaurant and as I was about to exit, my gaze fell upon a man sitting by the left side of the entrance. His face was turned from me, but something seemed familiar as I walked past him. Quickly dismissing him, I hurried to the jeep, put my pack away, grabbed my bag and went to change. The girls came into the locker room and in short order my face was half blue and maroon, my hair tied up with ribbons and my Valkyrie t-shirt and pants put on in record time. I stuffed my bag into Alexa's gym locker and headed out with the girls. We paid our five dollars to get in and even with the game some thirty minutes away, the arena was almost filled. The student section was already filled, which made we wonder if we were going to find a spot. My fears were put to rest as Kaylene moved deftly down the aisle towards the middle of the student section where five empty seats were reserved. The triplets and Jeremey waved Kaylene over.

"Thanks guys!" She told them.

"No hurt feelings?" I whispered.

"No. Just the dance…Nothing more." She winked.

"No troubles, certain privileges when you are requested to sing the National Anthem." Gene smiled.

"Doesn't mean you should get special treatment." Tyrone yelled from behind us.

"As if the football team doesn't get special treatment." Kaylene told him.

"Yeah. Who got to be first in line for the state lobster dinner?" Teasing him.

Tyrone smiled big. "Yeah, but you guys aren't even on a team." He playfully whined. "Not the same."

"Team or fan. It's all the same." Alexa assured him.

"Sweet costume, Kaylene." A girl yelled from above.

Kaylene turned and her helmet almost stuck a few people including me. "Thanks, Emily!" She waved.

"Hey, watch it. I don't want to lose an eye." Several students said in unison.

"Sorry." Kaylene apologized.

As the arena continued to fill, I found myself watching for Dad and Sydney to arrive. Mr. and Mrs. Wasabi were already in their seats, over on the other side, in between some of the other hockey parents and there were two empty seats next to them. I waved frantically to them but to no avail. I hoped Gabe would find his way down to our seats, even though there wasn't enough room for him. But I'd make room. My face flushed.

"Thinking about your man?" Kaylene teased.

"No." But my lie didn't work. "What makes you say that?"

"That stupid, 'I'm in love' grin you have on your face."

My eyes narrowed. "You can be as mean as Brooke. You know that?"

She nodded. "She told me to do it."

Before I could come back with a sizzling retort our hockey team came out onto the ice and the arena erupted in a chorus of excited yells and boos.

Directly across from us, but on the second level, were the students of Valor High School. Various boos and hollers were traded across the arena and then they reversed themselves when Valor skated out.

"That's our cue." Josh said.

"Good luck!" Kaylene slapped each of them on the back as they passed by.

"Ow, you beast." Gene said.

"You like it." Kaylene winked at him.

The teams skated around. I looked for Set and found him quickly. He was just a little taller than most of the other Valor hockey team, but it was clear his skill was leaps above the others. Instead of taking shots at the goal or flipping the puck around to his other players, Set busied himself with tricks of the sticks for a few girls that were clearly in college and sitting by the corner ice. He leaned his cheek into the glass as one of the girl's kissed it. This sent her into a crazy frenzy of joy, just as if a rock star had kissed her. I laughed.

That's when Brooke skated out of our end of the ice towards Set. An action not lost on the other hockey players. They stopped what they were doing to watch. From this distance I couldn't tell if Set knew she was coming but just before she got there he calmly turned around towards her. Brooke lifted her helmet, which was painted as a Valkyrie helm, and pointed her stick at him and clearly said something. Set said something back to her and even from this distance it clearly pissed Brooke off, for her stick trembled angrily in her hand. Some more words were said and that's when Coach Winckler sent one of his players over to get her. More words were exchanged before Set gave her the middle finger, which caused three more of our players to skate over to restrain her. Clearly the referees didn't see it but our student section burst into shouts directed at Set, who ignored us and went back to chatting with the girls.

"Oh, man this is going to be good!" Tyrone cried from behind.

"Isn't that Brooke's cousin?" A junior asked me.

"Yep. Distant cousins. Very distant." I said.

"Does he know how good she is? She holds the record for the most shutouts in CHSAA history." Another said.

I sucked in a slow breath. "Yeah, he knows. That's why I don't think this will be a low scoring game."

Everyone turned to look at me as if I had just said the most idiotic thing on the planet.

"You're joking." Alexa disbelief written on her face.

Another chimed in. "She shut them out twice during the regular season."

And another student said. "Aren't you her best friend?"

"Which means I'm also more aware of her cousin's talent. He's been around for a very long time." My voice had dropped very low.

"You mean, he's been playing juniors or pee wee wherever he is from?" Someone behind asked.

I nodded. "You could say. He's just very talented."

"Where is he from?" Someone else asked.

"Japan."

"Is he a ninja?" Tyrone said sarcastically.

"Not quite." I was trying to find a way to explain, but the angry looks from the students were starting to accumulate into more than just a few. Looking to my left, the elementary section had clearly caught wind of what I was trying to explain and were staring at me as if I had leprosy. I chose to sit down rather than continue explaining.

Kaylene nodded in approval. "Yeah. I'd shut up before you get burned for heresy."

Soon the announcer came on.

"Welcome ladies and gentleman to tonight's semi-final playoff hockey game between the Eagles of Valor…"

Boos and cheers went up. More boos I might add.

"and your Apollo Academy Valkyries!"

The place erupted.

After the din died down, which took several minutes, the announcer named the individuals from each team. The announcer started with Valor and scattered cheers went up until they got to Set and then the entire student section of Valor rose and cheered. Set skated out and like a returning King from conquest far away, and drank the adoration whole heartedly.

While the Valkyrie team got more cheers for their individual players than did the Valor players, when it came time for Brooke to be announced, the Third graders were already screaming their heads off with the rest of the crowd. Brooke made a special point to acknowledge the Third graders and they grew even louder.

Once all the introductions were finished and the CHSSA code of conduct of sportsman ship read, the announcer introduced the triplets. They walked out to a polite applause and a few scattered 'I love you' that were yelled from the student sections of both schools.

Garrett started with a soft alto 'oh' that grew in volume until Josh added his bass voice an octave lower. Gene joined with a perfect third harmony that resonated and brought the other two voices into sync. Their voices grew in volume until, even without the mic, it would have sent shivers down your spine. Once this one word reached a fevered pitch they continued on with the Anthem. Their voices intertwined like vibrant colors on a painter's canvas. Each brother's voice a perfect stroke of harmony and color that cascaded up and down the registry while blending volume and pitch in perfect unison creating vibrant pictures of the battle in your mind. Even as individuals joined in, the harmonies of the brothers captured each off tune voice and brought them together like a baker combining spices to create the perfect blend.

When they reached the conclusion of the song and the last note trailed off their lips, the audience in the arena remained silent until their harmony faded away to the whir of the HVAC.

Not until they bowed did the arena erupt into thunderous applause. There wasn't a dry eye around me including the tears I wiped from my eye. Suddenly, I wondered if they were also Dimidius. I'd have to ask Gabe or Brooke next time, since I couldn't image any persons having that effect on people.

"I want to have their babies." A girl cried out in euphoric passion.

"God they are good." Kaylene smeared her mascara around her eye.

"You are leaking." I told her.

"Well, your face isn't any better." She said.

I nodded knowing that the blue and maroon were smudged. "I'm not trying to impress anyone."

She nodded towards a row in front of me. "You sure?"

Down in front was Gabe sitting with Kennah, Serina, and several of their friends.

"I guess she *is* feeling better. Good thing your face is covered." Alexa smiled.

"What?!"

"I thought you guys were dating?" Kaylene asked.

It took me a moment to respond since the sound of my heart beating was washing out all other sounds. "No." Was all I got out.

"Oh, then you won't mind that Serina is trying to hold his hand." She smirked.

My eyes widened with anger as Serina's snake fingers tried to intertwine with Gabe's.

"Don't touch him, you, bitch! You have a boyfriend!" The scream was out of my mouth before my consciousness could stop it.

Everyone turned towards me with an amused expression. I sank back in my seat trying to disappear. Gabe turned around and waved; he got the ignoring treatment.

"That outburst doesn't say you aren't hot for him." Alexa and Kaylene laughed together.

"Ha, ha." Knowing I'd be in for a long evening if he stayed down there. The drop of the puck didn't come soon enough as the teasing from the people around me about my outburst was piling up. But when the puck dropped, the teasing stopped immediately, which I was thankful for. Each team skated around the ice without much action until Set came in. He came out on the third line, which seemed odd to me considering his skill, but it was clear that the Valor coach had put some thought into it. Since each lines skill diminished with each consecutive line, Set's skills put him on a plane of existence far above the others. He moved and passed with the precision of a pro, which made it hard for even his teammates to keep up. If I hadn't known his true origins I would have been as impressed with his skill as the crowd was. Oohs and ahs accompanied each move as he passed to himself off the walls or through the legs of the Valkyrie lines. I watched Brooke with interest. She only seemed concerned when Set was on the ice. It was clear that he was just out there having fun and when the first period came to an end with the score tied at zero.

The announcer brought the crowd to their feet with his enthusiasm as the Zamboni came out onto the ice to refurbish it.

"Oh, man. That was good." Alexa exhaled before falling back in her seat.

I nodded. Most of the game was lost on me since I was watching Gabe and Serina. She continued to try and get close to him, but he deftly kept his distance from her. He got up with the crowd, said something to her, which made her shoulders slump in disappointment and I internally yelled with excitement. My composure of uninterested was tested while he moved out into the screaming crowds of fans moving towards the exits to get something from the concession stand.

"I'm going to go get something. You want anything?" Kaylene asked me.

"Are the triplets coming back?" I enquired, keeping a side long glance at Gabe moving towards me.

"I don't think so. They are probably up in the box with Mr. Donahue." She told me.

"Oh. No, I'm good."

"Okay. Alexa?"

Alexa got up. "Yep. Need my red vines. They keep me energized."

I moved out of their way as they pushed past me. Fans were moving around when I caught sight of my Dad waving at me from across the arena. I smiled and enthusiastically waved back at him and Sydney.

He sat back down next to Sydney and began talking to her while gesturing toward the ice. She laughed and appeared interested and my heart felt really good for him.

"Seat taken?" A voice inquired.

I stared into Gabe's golden eyes and with the firm intension of tell him yes, my mouth betrayed me and uttered, "No," instead.

"Hey Gabe." Tyrone and some others greeted him.

Gabe said hello and talked to some of the other students, which irked me a little, but he quickly returned his attention back to me.

"How are you?" He asked.

"Not as good as you, it would appear." Waving absently towards Serina.

He raised his eyebrow in confusion. "What?"

"Did you have fun down there?" I'm not sure why I was being such a bitch but it seemed to just jump out of me.

"Oh, you mean down there." He pointed at Serina, who was looking back very unhappy.

My triumphant smirk, made her turn away pouting.

"Yes. Serina is very funny. She was just being friendly. It wasn't anything. Why?" He asked.

"I don't know? I . . ." My sentence trailed off.

I'm not sure what I was thinking. Nothing had been talked about us being together. As far as I knew, Gold's put their lives on the line for anyone. Doesn't mean I'm special or anything. This made me sad.

"JJ…" He started but I stopped him.

"Don't say anything. I know." I had to concentrate to stop the tears welling up in my eyes. Kaylene and Alexa returned.

"Hey Gabe." Kaylene hi fived him. "I'll sit on the other side. I just texted Gene and they aren't coming back. So stay."

"Red Vine?" Alexa offered one to me.

Like a striking cobra, I snatched it out of her hand and took a bite, so I wouldn't have to say anything.

"You're welcome." She muttered.

"Sorry, thanks." I said in between munches.

The start of the second period unfolded very differently. Our team scored a quick goal, which brought a tremendous roar from the home crowd. This appeared to excite Set, for he started taking more control of the puck. In a brilliant move around a defenseman, Set broke free and skated at Brooke. Brooke skated out to cut the angle down. Set shot the puck at the goal clearing the tiniest of opening between Brooke's pads and tink'd it off the side bar and out on the ice. Set passed Brooke and blew a kiss at her and chased after the puck. The crowd went ballistic.

Gabe sighed beside me.

"What?"

He shook his head.

Five more times through the period Set tink'd it off the crossbar at impossible angles or through her pads only to smile or blow a kiss at her each time. And each time he did this, Brooke's body language grew more agitated. Then it dawned on me.

"He's playing with her." I said.

Gabe nodded. "He's patronizing her. This game would be over if he were playing for real, but he wants to humiliate her. She knows he's purposely hitting the crossbar and there isn't anything she can do to stop it."

"Why is he doing that?" Starting to get angry at my friend's treatment.

"Because she had the audacity, in Set's eyes, to believe she is as good as a True Breed and he's showing her how wrong she is." Gabe answered.

The second period came to an end. Brooke rushed out of the goal and skated toward the Valor bench but Set had already gone inside. Mr. and Mrs. Wasabi spoke to each other as my Dad and Sydney got up and walked toward the concession stand.

"I'm going to have a heart attack." Kaylene had taken off her helmet midway through the period because it kept falling as she jumped around at the missed goal opportunities.

Alexa had been so nervous that she had unknowingly finished off her Red Vines in record time and now sat feeling a little sick.

"Are you going to be okay?" Rubbing her back.

"Yes." She breathed deeply looking a little pale.

Tyrone laughed. "I'll get you some water."

She waved a weak thank you as she put her head on Kaylene's shoulder.

"Don't be sick on me." Kaylene warned her. "I'll never get that red dye out of the leather."

"I'm not going to be sick." She grabbed her stomach. "Not yet anyway."

Gabe watched the Zamboni on the ice.

"You think he's going to humiliate her more?" I asked.

"I guarantee he will. This isn't the first egg that Set and I have helped protect together. I've learned over the years that he is as snobbish as they come." He mused.

"I know he has been around for a long time, but is he typical of the True Breeds? Are they all like him?"

Gabe smiled and my heart melted. "No. But he is one of the older dragons. He came of age when they used to hunt those like Brooke and I down and kill us."

My heart leaped. "They hunted you?"

He nodded. "Yes. Rumors say that the ancient dragons used to create us just to hunt us for sport. But I haven't been able to confirm that, besides, the Gray Mage would never have let that happen. I believe more that they just saw us as inferiors of their kind. Dragons are very conceited."

"So I've noticed." I couldn't imagine what kind of life that must have been. "What do you think he will do to her? Don't you think she has a chance to stop him?"

Gabe shrugged. "Whatever he is going to do will look like an exceptional feets of talent and will be incomprehensible to your eye. As for Brooke, she's young, but far more talented than most her age. Must be her Blue blood." As he stared at the ice a mischievous glint came into his eyes. "Though, I'd give her an outside chance if it's a straight up contest of her going one on one with him."

"Like a break away?" I asked.

"Yes."

Soon the teams took to the ice and the arena filled. An underlying buzz of excitement brewed in the arena as everyone watched each team battle back and forth. Throughout the twenty minutes of play time, Set hit the side and cross bars five more times, each one a little closer to going in than the last. It was an incredible display of accuracy that neither team could match. When anyone other than Set shot the puck on goal, Brooke made the save as easy as if she were playing with children.

When the time reached three minutes of play and the score was still one to zero in favor of the Valkyries, Set's line came out on the ice. Coach Winckler countered with his first line, but even they couldn't match Set's skill. The puck flew down into Valor's side and was chased in by a Valkyrie forward, who shot it around the boards. Time ticked down to two minutes and twenty-four seconds. A Valor defenseman scrambled for the puck, won it and shot it out towards the middle. The Valor forward came in to pick it up, but in a blur of speed, Set snatch the puck and weaved in and out of the Valkyrie forwards. He crossed the blue line and easily eluded the Valkyrie defensemen too. Set barreled in on Brooke and closed the gap with amazing speed. It was clear none of the skaters were going to catch him and it was the one on one opportunity that Gabe had said would take place. The crowd was silent as Brooke moved out from her goal to stop him. And just like Gabe had predicted, the ultimate insult occurred so fast that no one could believe it had happened until the goal light flashed on.

The Valor crowd erupted like a sleeping volcano.

From behind me someone in disbelief whispered. "Did that just happen? To Brooke?"

I blinked my eyes to see if they were even open.

"How could anyone stop the puck and control it that fast?" Alexa breathed.

Gabe just shook his head. When the replay came up on the overhead display, even in slow motion it looked fast.

The closest defensemen was just crossing the blue line as Set moved across it. He skated in from the blue line, shifting the puck back and forth on his stick. Set pivoted to his right, flipped the puck up on his stick so it laid flat on the blade. He then stopped on a dime beside Brooke as she tried to hit his stick with her catcher's glove, which looked incredibly slow in comparison to the movement of Set's stick. Then he lifted the puck past Brooke's face, so she could get a good look at it, turned his stick side ways and the puck slid onto the back of Brooke's mask. It rolled down the back of her mask and then her back and into the goal like a boulder rolling down the side of a mountain. Immediately after, Brooke dropped her stick and round housed Set in the chest that sent him careening into the back wall and her to the ice. Set dropped his stick and rushed forward but the linesman had come in with the referee and stopped them. Brooke received a misconduct penalty for four minutes.

I think they would have tossed her, but Coach Winckler talked to the referee and probably explained she was just upset and slipped on the ice. I'm not sure the referee bought the whole story, but it only cost the team a power play, which lasted the last two minutes of regulation play and two minutes into the overtime. Brooke stopped all the shots on goal except the ones Set continued to tink off the posts.

"He's waiting for the shootout, isn't he?" At some point, I grabbed Gabe's arm and was holding onto it for dear life.

He didn't seem to mind. "Yes."

My stomach turned with uncertainty and the crowd around me was equally anxious.

Once the first overtime period came to an end, five skaters came out from each side. The announcer came on and explained that each team will have five shots on goal and the team with the most at the end will win. If the score remained tied, then the next shoot out will be a golden goal.

"He's going to miss isn't he?" I sat nervously watching Brooke.

Gabe nodded. "He will. He wants it to go to the golden goal round. That's where he'll want to humiliate her again."

Valor won the toss and made our team go first. This allowed Valor to have the last shot if the score was tied. Set was last in line and was for sure to take the last shot on goal. Each goalie defended their goals without letting in a goal. Then, as Set skated forward, he did the same thing as before, but whether Brooke got something on it or Set intentionally missed, the puck flipped up, landed flat on the crossbar. Brooke moved back pushing the puck over the net.

Either way, the crowd moaned or cheered respectively, but each side was on the edge of their respective seats. With the first shoot out over, they lined up again. The arena was silent as Valor now had to go first.

Brooke stopped four goals and the Valor goalie stopped four. As Set skated to the middle of the ice and waited for the referee to give him the go ahead, Brooke retreated into the goal like a bear moving into a cave.

"Can she do that?" Someone asked.

"No." Gabe said. "She has to be out of the goal before he crosses the blue line."

Set started towards the blue line. Brooke didn't move.

"What happens if she stays in there?" Another asked.

"They get the point." Gabe explained.

Brooke sat there and just as Set was about to cross the blue line, she emerged with a ferocious roar of pure guttural rage that echoed loudly through the arena and put goose bumps all over my body. She skated well out in front of the crease with Set moving towards her with incredible speed. He faked to the right, but Brooke countered and moved to her right, baiting him to shoot at the exposed net. Cries of anguish erupted from our section. Set moved to his left, flipped the puck up, Brooke jabbed through his legs at his stick. Set closed his legs, spun and her stick flew out of her hand. Set continued his rotation, Brooke used the extra energy to spin around the opposite way. The puck left Set's stick, Brooke brought her blocker pad down catching the puck on the seam and pinning it against the ice with her face down.

The crowd was dead silent. Neither Brooke nor Set moved. A moment passed. When the goal light didn't come on, the Valkyrie crowd shouted in euphoric hysteria and started to jump around. I ended up in Gabe's arms, just where I wanted to be, and enjoyed the celebration.

Brooke got up from the ice. Set faced her. They exchanged words without punches being thrown and then he skated off. Brooke picked up the puck, looked at it, and held it up like the severed head of a fallen foe. The Valkyrie fans shouted and the chants of Brooke's name began to reverberate around the arena.

Needless to say our guy scored the winning goal. Then the team won the state championship the next week. I had asked Brooke what Set had said to her, but her only response was a wry smile.

Chapter Sixteen

Orientation

May was upon us. The euphoria of the State Hockey championship lay behind us, the back to school dance as well. I didn't end up going to the dance with Gabe, and Brooke didn't get to go with Christian. Both Brooke and Gabe were called back to Japan during that weekend, but each promised their dates to go to prom in the spring. When I asked Brooke about her trip, she just said it was dragon business and nothing more was said. Therefore, my beautiful red dress hung in the closet for a few more months until it could be brought out and displayed like the ancient artifacts of old. With Prom in two weeks, Graduation in four and Orientation at the end of this week, needless to say, my overactive imagination and teenage desires were in overload. My body was fighting my mind. Doing homework in the sleep lounge was a feat not accomplished by many. Between drooping eyes, and forced concentration, I sat in the sleep lounge finishing up a rather difficult assignment for Dr. Zang's Latin class, while listening to several loud snores coming from across the room. Dean was snoring the loudest, while Heather was close behind. I didn't envy their respective spouses when they got married because no one would be getting any sleep.

"Sequi ones cor sequi ones fatis." I mumbled

"Thinking of anyone in particular?" Dr. Zang plopped next to me on the big pillow couch. She rocked up and down. "This is a comfy couch."

"Not really." I lied knowing that Gabe rarely left my imagination. We hadn't seen each other much lately and when I asked Brooke about it, she just mentioned they were watching the egg.

Dr. Zang looked over at Dean. "Hate to be married to that one."

I nodded. "Yeah. Never get any sleep."

"For sure." She looked at my work and nodded approvingly. "Nicely done. Need any help?"

"No. I think I'm getting it." Finishing up the sentence.

"Not the conjunctive, use the feminine plural form. Then you will see the difference."

I nodded.

"Mr. Resler wants to see you." Dr. Zang said after a few moments of appreciative prodding and probing of the pillow chair. She sighed as she reluctantly got up. "I'm going to have to come back here and try this out."

"You've never slept on the Teddy Bear?" That's what the students called the pillow couch.

"Only rumors." She smiled.

"Dr. Daugherty is in here all the time." Giving her a smile. "More than the students."

She smiled back. "What do you expect from a Literature major. They are lazy."

"I'm going to tell him you said that." I teasingly said.

She waved. "Go ahead. I tell him that all the time at the staff meetings."

My laugh was short but full and continue to finish my homework. After I was done, I gathered my scattered books, shoved them into my backpack and left the snoring duo behind. My thought wondered through the day's event, and couldn't understand what Mr. Resler would want with me before my class, especially since I'd be coming to the office for class later that day.

"Hi, Mrs. Douglas."

"Hi, JJ. Go on in." She told me.

"Do you know what he wants? Am I in trouble?" I couldn't think of why he would want to see me.

"Have to wait and see." Her smile did nothing to alleviate my tightening stomach. The door was partially open, but I knocked anyway.

"Come on in JJ." He announced in his strong voice.

He was behind his desk writing on a parchment of paper. He motioned for me to sit in front of his desk as he continued writing. Patiently waiting for him to finish, my gaze kept going to the fish clock on the wall, knowing that class was going to begin in ten minutes.

"Don't worry. Dr. Daugherty knows you will be late." He told me.

"Am I in trouble?" I asked.

He shook his head. "No. Should you be?"

"No!" My voice sounding shocked at such a statement.

He smiled.

It was a rare sight to see Mr. Resler smile, since he was a solemn man and took his job very seriously. So if you were presented with a rare treat of seeing him smile, you knew things would be okay. I liked him very much. Most students found him unfriendly and a bit of a dream killer. But I always thought he just gave his honest opinion when I've talked to him. He certainly didn't sugar coat things.

He finished up his work, laid his pen to the side, placed his hands on the desk and crossed his fingers as the class bell rang. He directed his attention to me. I sat up straight, which was expected when addressing any teacher or administrator and waited for him to begin. I wasn't keen on missing Dr. Daugherty's class, but it must be important if he told Dr. Daugherty that I would be late.

"Ms. Harbinger..." "Nancy?"

He nodded. "Ms. Harbinger is sick and will be unable to attend the orientation on Friday night at seven. You know the Orientation is only for new students and their parents."

I nodded.

"She was going to announce the factuality to our new parents and take any question they might have before. Would this be something you would like to do in her place?"

I sat back a little surprised. Normally this honor was only for the Counsel of Twelve Junior Class to do. Nancy was the class president.

"Shouldn't Kammy or Lindsey do this? They are the V.P. and Treasurer of the Junior Counsel."

He agreed. "Yes. But neither has been through our program since Kindergarten, such as you." Mr. Resler held up his hand to forestall my question. "The Senior Counsel of Twelve will be doing other things during Orientation. You don't have to, but you have been an excellent student here at Apollo Academy and I thought you might like the privilege."

"I am really honored. I would very much like to do it." I beamed. Dad would be all sorts of proud too.

"Good. I'll see you at six. You may go to class now." He stood and shook my hand.

"Thank you Mr. Resler." I grabbed my bag, waved to him and left.

"Congratulations." Mrs. Douglas congratulated me.

"Thank you. I hope I don't mess it up."

She shook her head. "You'll be fine. If you can read then you won't fail."

"I can read." Laughing I went off to Dr. Daugherty's class.

When I got to class, Dr. Daugherty was writing something on the board, therefore, I quietly let myself in and took my seat.

"Welcome back, Ms. Ritter." Dr. Daugherty said as he continued to write on the board.

"Thank you. It's nice to be back." I said.

Brooke hissed at me. "What happened?"

"I got picked to give the opening speech at the Orientation." I told her.

She gave me two thumbs up.

"God, I hope you do a better job than Robert last year. I thought Mr. Resler was going to get up and toss him off the stage.

We laughed.

"He might be a good leader, but he isn't very good at public speaking." Tina agreed.

"Neither was Abraham Lincoln when he first got into politics." Dr. Daugherty turned around. "Don't underestimate him. He's got a good sense for politics."

Robert was really good. Everyone said he was a natural at soliciting ideas from other students and getting them to agree on one.

"Okay. Turn to page one hundred and sixty nine of your Chaucer book and we'll jump right in."

The entire day, plus every chance I got, I practiced the speech given to me by Mr. Donahue's personal assistant, Tatiana. She was a really nice person that appeared very at ease around people. I'd never met her before when Mr. Donahue came to the school but she was a beautiful shadow that was always by his side. A small woman of five feet four inches or so, dark brown hair, big brown eyes, and a smile that went from ear to ear. Tatiana didn't seem to have a last name because no one ever used her last name when they addressed her. Not even Mr. Resler, who called everyone by their surname. Tatiana told me to be ready on Friday by five thirty when the limousine would pick me up.

I sat on the back porch reading the speech to Cooper, who laid asleep on the lounge chair next to me.

"You want soy sauce on your noodles?" Dad yelled from the kitchen.

"You know I do." I yelled back.

Soon he appeared with two plates full of egg noodles, steak and chives. He set a plate down on the table next to me. Cooper jumped up as he shooed him off the lounge chair.

"Get out of here, you mutt. You have your own food." Dad fought Cooper off with his elbow.

"Cooper." My voice commanded sternly.

He trotted over to my side, sat, laid down and put his head on his paws.

"Wish he'd listen to me that well." Dag grumbled stuffing noodles in his mouth.

"You wish any woman would listen to you that well." I snickered, sneaking a noodle down to Cooper.

"Ha, ha." He gulped more noodles down. "You ready?" He said after chewing and swallowing.

"I hope so. It's a really long speech."

"You'll do fine. Just remember if you get nervous, they say to think of the audience all naked like." He smiled.

"Yeah, that's going to help me." I ate more noodles.

"It might. You got something nice to wear?" He said.

My head nod made a noodle whip up and slap me in the nose. I wiped off the sauce. "Yeah."

"Good. I can't wait to watch." He finished up the last of his noodles and steak.

"You are not coming!" I told him.

"You bet your ass I'm coming. I'm so proud of you. This is a great honor and I'm not going to miss it." He got up.

"Just don't heckle me from the audience." I handed him my plate.

"I hadn't thought about that. Thanks for the idea."

"Oh, god."

All day Friday my mind consciously walked through every kind of scenario that would make me look foolish up on stage. All the while my nervousness followed me like a bad shadow to my classes creating an environment of sever unfocusness. It would have been nice to see Gabe, he would have put my nervousness at ease with just a look, but unfortunately, I hadn't seen him during passing hour or anytime during the day. When I got home, I rushed to take my shower, fix my hair and put on a nice spring blue dress that was light and airy. The limousine arrived right on time. Dad walked me to the limousine, he kissed my head, said how proud he was and helped me in. The limousine arrived in plenty of time; the limousine driver helped me out, complimented me on my dress, and I walked to the auditorium.

When I arrived, Mr. Resler greeted me.

"Hello Ms. Ritter."

"Hi Mr. Resler. Is there anything you want me to be doing?"

Senior Counsel was busy placing chairs on the stage for the Regents and doing whatever Tatiana seemed to be telling them.

"Just go on up and stand at the podium so the sound engineers can get a good reading for the audience. Then tell them how fast you want the teleprompter to scroll. Tatiana will take care of you." He turned and left.

Doing as told, I walked up to the stage, Tatiana greeted me and we got started.

Fifteen minutes before the start of the Orientation, I found myself wandering out front of the auditorium. The officers of the Counsel of Twelve were busily passing handouts to those parents that were arriving early. Punctuality was one of the top Tenants that governed our school. Classes, meetings, plays, sporting events, everything started when it said it would. The Counsel of Regents believed that promptness was a quality that should be taught at an early age. Tardiness was a crime that was punished swiftly and without mercy at Apollo Academy. Many students have been expelled because of their inability to follow this simple rule. And tonight will be no exception. I moseyed over to the holding room and greeted Ted.

"Hey Ted. Ready for the angry parents that come in late."

Ted was a wiry young man with red hair and a big nose. His blue eyes looked apprehensive as he sighed. "I was hoping that I'd get one of the easier jobs, but at least I have Mr. Winkler and Mr. Marion with me."

Mr. Marion was the wrestling coach

"You are in good hands then." I said.

He smiled.

Checking the clock, it read seven till seven. "I have to go. Good luck."

"You too."

Moving down the side hallway to get backstage, Tatiana greeted me.

"Ready?" She led me to the podium without me answering.

On stage behind the curtains sat the Counsel of Regents: Dr. Zang, Dr. Daugherty, Mrs. Shoen, Mrs. Hannity, the Civics teacher, and Mr. Harlon, the music teacher. Next to them sat Mr. Donahue and Mr. Hatzenbueler, Mr. Donahue's lawyer for the school. His reputation for being an aggressive lawyer was well known around the school due to the cases that he had argued, some even in front of the State Supreme Court. Rumor also said that his wife, Mrs. Hatzenbueler had argued cases in front of the Supreme Court of the United States. Both of his little girls go here as well.

Each sat quietly talking among themselves, joking softly as the noise of the audience cancelled out anything they said from being heard. The green teleprompter came on.

"We are about ready to start." Tatiana said behind me. "You good?"

I nodded nervously.

"Don't mess up, JJ. I've got twenty saying you will." Dr. Daugherty chuckled.

"Psh, don't listen to him, JJ. I've got you covered." Dr. Zang said.

"Thank you, Dr. Zang." I stuck my tongue out at Dr. Daugherty.

The doors closed amid several angry protest before the lights went down. The audience quieted and the curtain opened. Spot lights sprang into life, startling me as I began to read from the teleprompter. I won't go into detail about my speech. It basically covered the founding of the school, its philosophy, and its dedication to the development of future leaders. My part lasted about thirty minutes or so, at which time the audience clapped very politely, combined with a very loud clapping from my dad up towards the doors. Dr. Daugherty slipped Dr. Zang a twenty with a shake of his head.

"I'd like to introduce to you, our principal, Mr. Resler." I stepped away from the podium clapping and Mr. Resler came on stage.

"Thank you, Ms. Ritter." He nodded to me then raised his hand to quiet the crowd.

I walked off stage and sat down next to Tatiana. She slapped me on the knee. "Good job."

"Thank you. I was sweating badly up there."

She waved off my remark. "Couldn't tell."

I thanked her again and listened to Mr. Resler as he introduced the board, Mr. Donahue, and Mr. Hatzenbueler.

"As was so eloquently stated by Ms. Ritter, a product of our education since Kindergarten through her senior year, here at Apollo Academy, we strive to teach a sense of understanding of the world around us, while molding future leaders that aren't afraid to change things. This Orientation is for parents to come and ask question about our program and to see if Apollo Academy is a place for their child to grow and learn. One of the first lessons that is taught is promptness. Our belief is that employers along with other industries want employees to have good time management skills. As you take a moment to look around you, you will see that there are a few empty seats."

Mr. Resler paused giving the audience the time to look around them. I counted thirty seats out of the one hundred and fifty seats were empty.

Mr. Resler continued. "At our academy, tardiness is treated very seriously. Each of those empty seats represents a lack of courtesy for our school and for each of you and is punishable by expulsion from the academy."

A gentleman raised his hand. "For being tardy? Isn't that a bit excessive."

Mr. Resler shook his head. "An employer isn't going to want an employee to be late. Each tardy is subject to review by our Regents."

"This isn't a job." A woman commented.

"I disagree. You can never be too young to learn ethics." Mr. Resler explained. "The sooner bad behavior is consequenced, the sooner positive behavior will be reward and reinforced. That is our goal."

He waited and continued. "As each of you have had contact with one of our counselors, you understand that your child can be dismissed from the academy for any action deemed inappropriate along with the action of the child's parent."

Another hand went up. "I'm still unclear about that. Can you clarify 'inappropriate'?"

"Of course. The rule that gets students dismissed the most is being rude to faculty or to other students. Bullies are dealt with swiftly and so are disruptive students. The academy isn't here to discipline your children. That is your job." Mr. Resler paused and waited for the customary reaction of nods of approval and vigorous shakes of the head in disagreement. "Let me reiterate that. 'We are not here to discipline your children. Their action can be consquensed. i.e. dress code violation, behavior, Tenant code violations, and anything a faculty member deems inappropriate. Did I answer your question?"

"No. The faculty can come up with anything? What if they don't like the kid? Can they just make stuff up and they will get dismissed?" The father said.

Mr. Resler nodded. "That could happen. But all dismissals are reviewed by our Regents along with a neutral party and that list can be found in your student/guardian handout."

"But that doesn't mean your neutral party won't go along with whatever decision the Counsel makes." Someone said.

"Then you clearly have not done enough research on the Academy. Those individuals are leaders of industry and pillars of the community, they wouldn't risk their reputation just to satisfy a petty complaint." Mr. Resler shook his head. "Besides, this is how we run the Academy. We look upon our Regents as the Supreme Court and their ruling is final. We don't require a fee for attending the Academy. If any family finds these rules to be unacceptable, you may leave at any time. Just as we can dismiss your child at any time."

There was a ripple of disquiet among the parents of the new students. The parents that have children at the Academy were busily talking to their neighbors to ease their fears. Even Dad was chatting with someone in the back.

"What if we think the ruling is unfair or prejudice? We can sue you to reinstate our child." A mom smugly commented.

Mr. Resler was about to respond when Mr. Hatzenbueler politely interrupted him. He stepped to the front of the stage.

"Madam. If you feel your only recourse is by suing, then you are encouraged to seek whatever justice you need for your child. Unlike the public school system that shies away from frivolous lawsuits because it might damage their reputation or whatever their cowardly administrators believe. I have no such qualms." His voice held a subtle menacing quality that seemed to cowl the woman. No one else said anything about suing.

Mr. Resler waited politely for the buzz to die down and for Mr. Hatzenbueler to return to his seat. Mr. Donahue patted his shoulder, leaning in and sharing a joke.

"I hope our position is clear. We expect our students to abide by the rules, within an atmosphere of individualism and cooperation. We expect our students upon leaving here to achieve whatever goals they have. Lawyers, doctors, artists, social workers, community activists or whatever. No one is a failure in our eyes unless they fail themselves by not following their joys."

Again, Mr. Resler paused here to let his words sink in. When he resumed, the Orientation continued for about another hour before he concluded.

"I want to thank each of you for coming and choosing Apollo Academy. We have refreshments in the cafeteria and the Senior Counsel, and our Reagents will be on hand to answer any questions. Please feel free to ask whatever you think is necessary. I look forward to seeing all of you at the start of summer term."

The applause went up and he bowed graciously. The curtain closed and everyone began to stretch and leave.

"Nice job as usual Mr. Resler." Dr. Daugherty said. "Now, I can't wait to get to the eats. Rumor has it the Culinary Class planned something special. Coming?"

Dr. Zang nodded. "You know it." They left.

"Mr. Resler. Is it okay if I leave?" I asked.

He nodded. "Thank you, Ms. Ritter. Good job tonight. See you on Monday."

"Yes, sir."

I peeked my head out of the curtain as the people were filing out of the auditorium. My Dad waved to me and I waved back. Stepping down off the stage, I fell in behind some people and caught up with Dad.

He grabbed me and kissed my head. "I love you. Great job up there." His smile warmed my heart.

"Thanks. Nerve racking if you ask me. Even reading the prompter was weird." The prompter seemed to move much faster than when I was practicing.

"You going to the cafeteria for the free eats?" He asked.

"I think I'll head on home. This wore me out."

"Okay, I left the jeep out there. I'll find a way home after some of that great food. That is one thing I'll miss around here. The food." He rubbed his belly.

"Psh…I'm sure you will find a way to come back."

He grabbed his chin. "Maybe you need a little sister?"

When my jaw dropped he laughed. "Sucker." Patting my shoulder he left.

"You'll be sorry when I drop from a heart attack sometime when you joke like that!" I yelled.

"Who said I was joking."

Speechless, I walked off toward the parking lot and my jeep. The light of the full moon mingled with the florescence parking light poles. Fishing my keys out of my purse, my nose caught whiff of a strong stench. It took me a moment but I recognized it as the same stink of cologne that Christian had earlier in the year. I looked to see if he was around when I spotted a man over by the light pole. His features were lost to the shadows of his hat, but my pulse began to increase noticeably as he looked at me. He pushed himself away from the pole and began to walk slowly toward me. My breathing increased as I fumbled with my keys to open the jeep door. In my mind's eye he was running towards me, but in reality it was a very slow deliberate walk. That didn't keep me from panicking in trying to open my door.

"C'mon, JJ. Open the damn door please." I whispered to myself. I turned to look at him and he was much closer when I felt a hand on my shoulder. My body froze in terror convinced I was about to be raped.

When the warm scent of caramel corn washed over me, my knees were about to give out.

"Stand still, JJ." Gabe's voice spoke.

"Your time is up, Old Man." The hiss of the man's voice echoed softly in the air. Green eyes suddenly materialized from the shadows around the man's feet as deep yellow colored eyes lit up the man's face.

"Get in your jeep, JJ." He whispered to me.

"Gabe?"

"Do it." Gabe stepped forward.

Unbelievably, my door opened and I scrambled inside.

"You don't want to do this. There isn't any need for anyone to get hurt." Gabe warned.

The man's laugh was a mix between a smoker's cough and a growl. "With the girl out of the way. We can move freely again. Then we'll come for you and the egg."

"She isn't important. Leave her out of this. You can't get to the egg, best you just leave."

The man shook his head. "We already have our in." He laughed then. "Dimidius are so stupid. You have all this presumed power and you still fall prey to the basic instincts of a human. Pathetic."

"It's what makes us better than the Dragons." Gabe retorted. "We remain human. Who are you? Did the Observers send you?"

The man sneered. "It makes you weak." Then he spit at Gabe's feet. "They are weak as well. You will learn about us soon enough. When we start turning the dragons into slaves, our Master's revenge will be complete." His next word was barely a whisper. "Attack."

The green eyes at the man's feet materialized into the strange dog creatures that had attacked me in the alley last year. Two of them moved with unbelievable speed as the tentacle on their backs whipped forward trying to strike Gabe.

Gabe's reflexes were also incredibly fast. He avoided the tentacles and moved away as they slapped the hood of the jeep and the screeching of claws on metal rang like a bell in the night. I screamed.

Gabe moved away from the jeep, while keeping an eye on the man, who appeared to be calculating when it would be best to move toward me. I fumbled my phone out of my purse and hurriedly called Brooke. When she picked up, the words coming out of my mouth rambled on so fast that I didn't even know what I was saying.

"JJ!" Brooke screamed into the phone.

"We are going to die!" I yelled on the verge of sobbing.

"Where are you?" Brooke said.

"School." My eyes darted around the area as Gabe moved in and out of the dog things. The Man watched me closely as I rambled on the phone.

"JJ. Calm down! Do you still have your bat?" She asked.

"What? Bat? Why would there be a bat in my jeep!? He's going to die, Brooke! Don't let him die!"

"He isn't going to die, unless you let him. Calm down and think!" She chastised me.

That sobered me up. *I'm not going to let him die! I love him!* "I'm going to help him!" I started out the jeep door when Brooke's voice yelled again.

"No! Then you will get him killed! Just get your baseball bat and stick it out the jeep window enough for him to grab." She instructed me.

I nodded, even though she couldn't see me. In the back, behind the seat, my dad had put an aluminum baseball bat in case I was ever attacked. My hand fumbled around for the bat, while I kept my eyes on Gabe. Finally, grabbing it, I rolled the window halfway down, and stuck the grip end out.

"Gabe!" I yelled.

The man saw the bat and raced towards me. Gabe was further down engaged with one of the dog things. He saw the man, leaped over the one of the dog things, but its tentacle grab his leg and slammed him to the ground.

Where the hell is everyone! I thought to myself as the man rushed my jeep. I began jabbing at him with the bat end and got a good shot into his face that staggered him backwards.

"Hang on JJ. We are almost there." Brooke assured me.

I dropped the phone onto the other seat. "You are too far away. Hurry!" as I used both my hands to keep the man at bay. His face appeared normal in the light of the lamp posts. But his yellow eyes had a sick hatred that came from deep within him. The stench of rotting eggs began to overpower me and my strength was quickly giving out. Suddenly, the bat ripped out of my hands and banged against the jeep door. Stunned, the man flew sideways as Gabe's fist came smashing in and the sound of breaking cartilage intermingled with the beating of my heart.

Gabe flipped the bat around and as if I couldn't fall any deeper in love with him, he began to wield it like a sword defending his princess against the forces of evil. (Hey, this my story, I get to embellish)

With broad sweeps and precision blows the dog things went down in heaps of dead weight. The man advanced, but it was clear that he wasn't any match for Gabe. Two, three hits and the man fell to the ground unconscious or dead. I couldn't tell which. Brooke's instruction from the phone went unheeded as my knight moved from the man to the dog things making sure they were dead or unconscious. In an uncharacteristic emotional traumatic response, I leaped out of the jeep and ran, throwing my arms around him. His heart wasn't even beating heavy as his strong arms engulfed me.

"You okay?" he asked.

"I'll always be okay with you around." I breathed. The emotional rollercoaster was beginning to wane and I felt weak. Gabe gathered me up, opened the door, and placed me back inside the jeep.

"I don't think you need that, Son. I'm pretty sure she likes you." My Dad's voice said.

When I looked behind Gabe, the man and the dog things were gone.

Chapter Seventeen

The Week before Prom

"You are absolutely right, Mr. Ritter." Gabe apologized lowering the bat.

"Why do you have my daughter's bat?" Dad looked at me when he asked the question.

"Uhm."

Gabe shook his head.

"He was showing me his sword moves that Mr. Wasabi taught him." I lied. It killed me to do it.

Dad's interest perked right up. He turned to Gabe, "Really? Show me." He leaned up against the jeep and that's when Brook's voice screamed through the phone on the seat.

I quickly picked it up. "Oh, Brooke. Sorry I dropped the phone."

Dad watched Gabe run through some motions with the bat.

"Shut up." I whispered. "My dad's here."

"Are they gone?" Brooke said.

"Yes. They disappeared. How did they just disappear, Brooke?" My voice trembled.

"I don't know. We are turning into the West Bunker." She hung up.

The headlights of the car came screeching around the corner startling my Dad and I. Mr. Wasabi, Brooke and Set got out of the car. Set immediately began walking around the area where I first saw the man. Mr. Wasabi cautiously scanned the area as Brooke came over to me.

"Hi Mr. Ritter." Brooke waved.

"Hey Brooke. Thought you would have been here tonight. State MVP and all. I for sure thought Mr. Resler would want to show you off." My dad hugged her and then shook Mr. Wasabi's hand.

"Naw. Even that couldn't get me invited to Orientation. You know how they only want the Counsel of Twelve there." She smiled. "It's okay. I'd rather have my weekend to myself. We were just on our way to pick Gabe up. It's cool they asked JJ to present though. Quite an honor."

Dad beamed at the compliment. "Yep. That's my little girl." He turned to Mr. Wasabi. "What brings you here?"

"I had to come and get Gabe." He lied rather convincingly.

"Oh. That is really neat how you taught those sword moves to him. Very impressive. He acts like he has done it all his life." My dad complimented him.

Mr. Wasabi smiled. "He is a natural."

"Here you go, JJ." Gabe handed the bat back to me.

"Thanks." I put the bat away. "Well, I should be going home now. How was the meal?"

Dad shook his head. "I haven't been yet. I forgot to tell you that I won't be coming home tonight."

"Oh." Brooke said, which made my dad blush.

He leaned in towards Brooke and covered his mouth next to her ear but spoke loud enough for me to hear. "Going to make a little sister for her."

Brooke laughed as I shook my head.

"You are impossible." My Dad is crazy.

"So, I just wanted to let her know it is just going to be her and the dog tonight." He smiled.

Concern filled my face, a fact that wasn't lost on my Dad.

"You okay? I don't have to."

"I can stay with her." Brooke jumped in.

My heart felt relieved. "That's okay?"

Dad smiled. "Of course." I think he was more relieved than I. He said his goodbyes to Mr. Wasabi and Gabe and walked away.

"Good luck with your endeavor." Brooke laughed.

Dad waved and disappeared into the dark.

As soon as he was out of sight, Brooke turned to me with concern. "You okay?"

I fell back against the jeep and put my hand to my face. "I don't like lying to my dad, Brooke. But I don't want him and Sydney in danger either. Is this going to continue?"

Mr. Wasabi walked over to me. "I'm afraid so, until the egg hatches. What do you remember?"

I squeezed my eyes shut and remembered. "Nothing much. I smelt the rotten eggs again and then I saw the man by the pole where Set is. After Gabe showed up he called him an old man and said I was in their way. Once I was out of the way, they could continue unnoticed. What does that mean?"

My staggered breathing showed how deeply frightened I was. The thought of what I'd gotten myself into was eating at me, but the man and those dog things brought it into a sharp focus and I questioned my decision.

Mr. Wasabi looked very concerned. "Unusual for the Observers to use doppelgangers, but not unheard of."

"He said he wasn't from them. He is working for a new Master. They are after the dragon eggs to turn them into slaves." Gabe said.

Set nodded coming over and joining us. "The man, as JJ says, used a type of magic that the Observers don't." "That doesn't mean they aren't allies. The Observers are known for their deceit" Brooke whispered.

"The Observers use the same magic as the Mage. This is very different." Set explained.

"Don't you insult the Gray Mage by comparing her to those freak Observers." Brooke hissed.

Mr. Wasabi held up his hand. "Either way. We'll need to be more vigilant these last few days. Then, he turned to me. "I'm going to ask you to stay as close to Brooke and Gabe as possible. Once the egg hatches this should all go away."

One look at Gabe and I knew I'd have no problem with this plan. "Okay."

Mr. Wasabi nodded. "I'll have Set and Gabe alternate watching your house during the week."

I wasn't happy with Set being around, but any extra time with Gabe before the dance was going to be great.

"Are we still going to the dance?" I asked.

Gabe nodded.

"Hell ya. Have you seen my date? Dreamy." Brooke sighed.

Mr. Wasabi nodded. "Set will be able to watch it for one night. I'm glad you weren't hurt, JJ. Again, I'm glad you are with us but sad you will be in danger this week."

I shook my head. "My choice. I am curious about the smell thing. Why can I smell them? Which is really disgusting."

"I don't know. You have an over sensitive nose. The way you can smell the Dimidius is an example. If you do smell anything, please let us know. Have you smelt it before?"

"Just with Christian and some guy that was in the restaurant a while ago." I said. "But I have caught whiffs now and then."

Brooke came to Christian's defense. "He told us why he smelled that way."

"Very good. Just let us know if you smell it again." He said.

I nodded. "Okay."

With that our little conference was over. Brooke climbed into the jeep, Gabe went with Set and Mr. Wasabi, and the terrifying night came to an end.

The weekend proved uneventful, which I was grateful for. Brooke stayed Friday and Saturday and when she went home I was happy. You can only take so much of Brooke at any one time and I was really waiting for Gabe to take his turn. Unfortunately, that didn't happen until Wednesday. Monday and Tuesday at school were actually really fun. Events were planned the whole week with Greek day on Monday, the 80's on Tuesday, the 20's on Wednesday, the Victorians on Thursday, culminating with the Romans on Friday.

Wednesday came very early. Set had watched both Monday and Tuesday outside the house. He kept to himself out front and didn't bother even looking up at my window from what I could tell. This really suited me just fine. He might be a full dragon in human form but his personality rubbed me the wrong way.

I climbed into my Victorian dress with its hoop skirt, corsets, chemises and instantly felt forty pounds heavier for my troubles. Walking carefully downstairs, and accompanied by several missteps that almost sent me rolling on to my back, where I would have become a turtle flailing around, my path finished at the kitchen. I grabbed the keys off the counter, found my backpack and went to the jeep. The jeep, once a source of comfort and freedom, now was a small, cramped carriage that did nothing to help with my already oversized condition.

"Really? When did the door become so small?"

"Here, let me take you to school." Dad offered.

I tossed him the keys, he pulled the soft top off in record time, pushed the seat back as far as it would go, put his bike on the back of the jeep and off we went. The West Bunker was decorated with Victorian stuff and we waved to the guys dressed as Victorian cops. Dad dropped me off, kissed me goodbye and I ran off knowing he would put the jeep back together for me. I filtered in with the rest of the people dressed in their costumes and came upon Brooke in her steampunk version in the hall.

"Nice. Way to put your own twist on things." I congratulated her.

"I'm not the only one." She said. "Wait till you see Dr. Daugherty."

When the day finally came to an end, my drive home didn't come without some difficulties. Exasperated, the hoop dress came off, and the somewhat embarrassing drive home in my pantaloons took over. The day's difficulties were washed away as Gabe came into view sitting on the porch swing talking to my Dad. Completely oblivious to my somewhat naked appearance, I exited my jeep catching my pantaloons on the panel, which caught my shoe and dumped me on my face on the driveway.

"Graceful." I grumbled.

Strong hands picked me up and put me on my feet. "May I escort the lady?" Gabe smiled.

With my face red, I nodded. When we approached the porch, my Dad had his hands up like a director sizing up a camera shot.

"That has a nice look." He said.

"Funny, Dad." I stuck my tongue out at him.

"I know."

"I can take it from here, thank you Gabe."

"Of course. Well, thank you for the long talk, Mr. Ritter. I appreciate your advice." His smile couldn't have been more majestic.

"Wait. You aren't staying?" Fear leaped into my chest.

"I'll be around." He winked at me, which made me blush. "And I think you should maybe put something on."

"What?" Looking down at my pantaloons, my face burned brighter.

"Not the impression I think you were going for, sweetie. Don't screw this up. Prom's just around the corner." He hung his head and sighed, then pushed me indoors. "Don't hold this against her." He apologized.

"I'm not a child!" My protests ended with a closed door, locking Gabe out. Gifting my dad with an evil stare, I hurried up to my window, but he had disappeared. Noticing the sudden inrush of cool air that chilled my body it felt so good against my hot body, and I loved the way it made me tingle. *Just the way if feels when Gabe touches me.* I fell back on my bed in my underwear and laid there imagining what it would feel like to be with him. As my body warmed, Cooper came bounding into my room disturbing my daydream.

"Oh, yes, such a good boy." I fluffed his ears. He followed me over to the window to await my Romeo.

The rest of the evening was rather boring. Dad had work to do and a conference call with a game designer in Tokyo, which left me to fix dinner, finish my homework, despite having only three weeks of school left, and pretty much be on my own. I continued to look out the window for Gabe but couldn't see him. Around nine o'clock I decided to go to my room. Dad's office door was closed and I heard him talking, so I passed on by. Closing my door, I checked my phone, responded to some text messages, and stared at the ceiling. Cooper laid next to me and I absently stroked his fur.

Scratch.

It took me a moment to register the sound.

Scratch.

Fear froze me to my bed. Cooper didn't seem to have heard it.

Click.

My head slowly rolled to the side and I looked at the window, totally expecting to see red eyes staring back at me. None appeared.

"You hear anything boy?" I whispered.

Cooper didn't move. He appeared to be asleep. I tried to shake him wake him but he didn't respond.

"Cooper?!" Fearing he had died in his sleep, I placed my hand on his chest and it moved up and down with his breathing.

"Cooper." But he wouldn't wake up.

Click.

I stared at the window and still didn't see anything. Slowly and cautiously I crept over to the window to look out. The moon had set behind some trees to the west and its light barely shown upon the driveway below. Not seeing anything I walked over to the south window and suddenly a doppelganger came crashing through the window knocking me down to the ground. It stood over me with its tentacles waving menacingly. Green eyes glowed in the dark of my room and its shiny white teeth dripped saliva. Frozen in fear, my body wouldn't move nor could I utter any sounds at all. Cooper lay upon the bed in deep sleep.

Gabe! My mind screamed. *I don't want to die. Not like this. Where are you Gabe!*

The doppelganger drew back its head and lunged at my neck ripping my throat out as I bolted up right into the darkness.

Startled, Cooper rose with his hair standing up on his scruff. I breathed deep, with sweat running down my face. Another breath drew deep into my lungs, and I wiped my brow with my hand.

"Fell asleep." Reassuring Cooper with a pat on his head, he wouldn't calm down, and stared into a dark corner of the room. Deep growls rose in his chest. I pulled him closer to me and again my body was succumbing to fear and shutting down.

Movement made my eyes widen as Gabe's face moved into the light of the full moonlight.

"Bad dreams?" He smiled.

Cooper jumped off the bed and into his arms licking his face.

"Jesus, Gabe. How long you been there." I tried to relax while purposely fixing my messed hair and pulled my sweat bottom up and covered my flimsy shirt with a pillow.

"Just before you bolted up right." He said scratching Cooper's ears. "I tried to get your attention but you wouldn't come to the window. So I climbed up the side of the house and let myself in. I heard you moaning and whimpering, so I was worried. Then when I saw you were asleep, you were so adorable, I just had to wait and see what you were dreaming about."

"Uh. Adorable huh?" *Too bad you didn't cradle me in your arms, so I could wake up in them.*

He nodded. "Yep."

We sat in the dark in an awkward silence. So many conflicting thoughts were running through my head. Mostly about having sex with him and living with him for the rest of my life. Not sure they were conflicting, but these kind of feelings I've never had for anyone. So for me, they were conflicting.

"Any more news on that man or doppelgangers?" I asked.

He shook his head. "No. They are going to make their move soon, though. The egg will hatch on Saturday or Sunday."

"I hope it's Sunday. We're still going to prom, right?"

"Of course. I wouldn't miss it. Just know that we may have to leave early if something were to happen."

I shrugged. "I understand."

More awkward silence.

"Why did that man call you old? I know you have lived a long time, but what is old for you?" I asked trying to make conversation. As far as I was concerned I could just stare at him all night, but he seemed restless.

He smiled at that. "Well, among Dimidius I am old. I don't have much longer to live."

"What? You're not going to die this week?" Then realized how stupid my statement was.

He laughed which was musical and warmed my heart.

"No. But my time is coming to an end." He suddenly seemed sad.

"How much longer?" I wasn't sure if I wanted to know the answer.

"About, fifty or sixty years." He said.

I felt relieved. *Still plenty of time for us.*

"I know what you are thinking, JJ. I'm not the type of half man for you." He said.

"Really." Anger began to boil inside of me. "What makes you say that? Are you afraid to love me? Afraid that I don't love you?" Now I was pissed. "I love you, Gabe. I have never felt this way about anyone in my entire life. All I do is think about you day and night. Some might call that an obsession, but I don't. I feel good around you. You make my day so much better. To hear your voice, to smell your weird scent, to see your golden eyes reflect the sunlight. God. It all feels so right when you are around. Don't screw this up!"

He smiled. "I think I was supposed to say those things to you."

My anger quickly dissipated and we both laughed.

He got up and came and sat down on the bed. My pulse quickened. Cooper jumped up and settled between us.

"You deserve a man who can give you a family. You know I can't do that." The sadness in his eyes broke my heart.

I placed my hand upon his face. "I want a family. I want my Dad to have grandchildren, but I want someone I can love with all my heart. That's you. As for the children. I'm sure there are other Dimidius who need a family, we can be like Mr. and Mrs. Wasabi. That would be fine with me and I know my Dad would love any child we got. So don't worry. Just say you love me."

A golden tear formed in his perfect eye. "I do love you."

Warmth washed over my body to hear him say it. He bent in to give me a kiss when a knock came at the door.

"JJ?"

"Yes, Dad."

"Do you have someone in there?"

"Yes, Dad. A boy."

Silence, then. "Gabe?"

"Yes, Dad."

Silence, then. "Uhm, why?"

"We are making you a grandchild." Silently laughing.

The silence was longer this time. "Oh, ha, ha. I get it. Getting back at your old man. Funny. Well, please have him leave by midnight, okay?"

"Sure thing Dad. Love you."

"Love you to. I'm going to bed."

I looked at the clock and it read eleven fifty. Gabe got up.

"I'll be outside. Your kiss will have to wait until Saturday."

"You'd better make it a good one." I told him.

"It will be worth the wait. I've had lots of practice to perfect it for you." He winked. He went to the door and left it cracked.

"Night Mr. Ritter."

"Night, Gabe, and thank you." I heard Dad say.

"She's something special." Gabe told him.

"That she is." And the front door closed.

I fell back. *It's good to be in love.* And my night went by without any more bad dreams.

Thursday was uneventful and Gabe wasn't to be seen outside my window. I thought about parading myself in front of the window, but I didn't want to embarrass myself or have Dad explain to our neighbors that his daughter was crazy. Though knowing Dad he would have told them I was trying out for the porno industry.

Friday morning I was up early and felt very liberated. I couldn't characterize the feeling, but confidence and freedom made me want to push the boundaries of the dress code today and I went for it. The nice long white dress I had originally picked out with the gold trim just wasn't going to cut it. So I found a deep red dress that had a long slit up the side, low cut front and short fluffy sleeves. I don't even remember where I got this dress or for what occasions, but I found some of mom's nice jewelry with pearls and gold, put on some dark red lipstick, heavy eye shadow, and pulled my hair back and tied it with a gold chain. I checked myself in the mirror and winked.

"You are hot!" and my reflection agreed.

Dad was in his jammies eating cereal when I came around the corner, he stopped mid spoonful.

"Do you have a second pair of clothing ready that I can bring you when I get that phone call?" He laughed.

"Psh, they won't even notice." I purred, since I did have a second set of clothes ready.

"Okay. What brought this on?" He asked.

I shrugged. "I don't know. I just feel good." And drank some orange juice.

He got up and put his bowl in the sink. "I'll wait for the phone call." He snickered as he went upstairs.

"It won't happen!" But of course it did.

With the day over, I sat on the front porch swing and watched the sun go down. To my credit I did make it to lunch before I was called discreetly into the office, where Dad waited with his 'I told you' grin on his face and the bag of clothes I had laid out earlier. Mr. Resler explained that the slit up the leg was a little high and the cut in the front was a tad low. But to his credit he only made me put on a camisole to cover my chest and I used safety pins to close up the slit to the knee. He complimented me on my costume and the day progressed normally. I did get some looks that I normally wouldn't have gotten otherwise which made me feel really good about myself.

Cooper sat next to me with his head on my lap and Dad was cooking dinner. I always thought I would be feeling really giddy about prom. Certainly everyone at school today was in high spirits, but voicing my feelings to Gabe, I knew every day would feel like prom now. Even though I didn't see Gabe, I knew he was out there watching over me. I smiled.

Love. The Beatles' song, *All you need is love*, popped into my head. And it was true.

Chapter Eighteen

True Amore

There isn't much to tell about the morning of Prom. I had a great meal cooked by Dad, who couldn't keep his silly grin off his face, while making side comments about how I should marry Gabe. Not that I didn't agree with him, though Dad seemed to think we should elope to Vegas right after Prom.

Brooke came over around ten o'clock and we met Alexa, Kaylene, Kennah and Lindsay downtown at one of the spa places to get ourselves all pampered up. We got our hair done, ate lunch, and strutted around the Sixteenth Street mall to show off how good we all looked. We left downtown around four thirty and headed home. I was going over to Brooke's to get ready and then we would leave from there to go to dinner and then head to the academy for prom.

As I pulled my red dress from the closet and put it up next to me to look in the mirror, my heart was full of joy.

"You look so much like your mom." Dad stood in the doorway with a tear in his eye.

My face flushed, not carry that he saw the dress before Gabe. I put the dress down on the bed. "I wish she was here."

He came and sat with me. "I know baby. I do too. But you are your mother's daughter and I am the luckiest father alive to have you. I hope you know how proud I am of you and how much I love you."

I nodded. "I never get tired of hearing it."

He smiled and placed his hand on my chin. "I love you. Have fun tonight and I'll see you at the after prom. Sydney will be there too."

"You finally realized that you like her."

"I do." His face held the expectation of a child waiting for approval from a parent.

"Took you long enough. Just make sure I get invited to the wedding." My smile told him I approved of her.

His face grew into a big smile. "Make sure you return the favor."

My face grew a big smile. "I will."

I gathered up my stuff, making sure not to crumple my dress, got in the jeep and drove off to Brooke's.

The driveway was absent of any activity, which made me doubt that things were going to go as I planned. Mrs. Wasabi came out of the house to greet me.

"JJ. You look lovely. I'll take these from you. Brooke is upstairs. Go on in."

"Thank you, Mrs. Wasabi." Handing my dress and other things to her, I bounded up the stairs. Brooke was sitting on her bed, reading, and not dressed.

"What are you doing? We have to get ready to go and meet the others for dinner."

She shook her head. "We may have to miss prom." Her eyes looked very sad.

"Why?" I did not want to miss this.

"The egg. It's starting to hatch."

Whatever anger had been brewing inside died instantly. "No way. When?"

"Not sure." She didn't appear too pleased. "Dad's calling the others to let them know."

"Aren't you happy? It's a dragon!" My heart was full of joy at the thought of seeing a real live dragon.

She shrugged. "I'd be happier in Christian's arms…But whatever."

I found her callousness intruding on my happiness. "Fine. Sit up here. I'm going downstairs." and left.

I arrived down stairs with no one insight. Looking, Set was in the kitchen.

"Where is everyone?"

He munched on some dried jerky. "Around." And he left.

My evil stare should have melted him to the ground but I guess his dragon hide was too tough. *Fine I'll go find them without your help.*

Having a good feeling they were outside somewhere, I walked out back and found the trail that lead to the green house. The sun was just above the trees in the beautiful May evening. Birds were chirping, the young leaves rustled, and I found myself really noticing the enormity of nature. The cool mountain air brushed my hair back and felt cool upon my face. The doors of the green house came into view around a corner. The peaks of the mountains began to gather the sun behind them and shadows fell all around. The handle of the green house felt warm against my cold hand. The door squeaked as it opened and the aroma of the flowers and vegetables filtered through the air. My steps were deliberately slow walking the path, so to let the sensations of running my fingers over the flowers seep into my body and enjoying the wetness on the pedals. The waning light of the day brought out the shadows, reminding me of that night. Shivers raced over my spine and I found myself at the back of the greenhouse. The table where we had dinner was still there along with a few chairs. The windows were new, and I sat down making the chair creak. The long shadows of the trees began to cover the panels and then little lights began to wink to life up in the darkest corner of the greenhouse. Fascinated, they gathered and began to migrate with the shadows like wildebeests. Suddenly, a bright light winked into existence next to my eye blinding me and forcing me to jerk away. I struck out at it in reflex knocking it to the table. As my vision returned, a small winged creature lay still on the table. The lights gathered around my head, accompanied by a small buzzing sound.

 Each light was a tiny winged creature no bigger than a large bumble bee. Their features were lost to their small size and I couldn't tell if they were angry or concerned.

 "Just blow on it." Gabe's soft voice said next to my ear.

 I looked up at him. "Not fireflies, I presume."

 Gabe shook his head.

"I'm so sorry. I didn't mean to hurt it. It startled me and I just struck out. Don't let it die."

His smile said it wouldn't die. "Gremlins are a hardy breed of fairy. Blow."

I slowly breathed in deep and lightly blew on the gremlin. Its wings flittered a little. Gabe encouraged me to blow harder. My breath must have felt like a hurricane to the little gremlin as it rolled away from under my blustery breath. It rolled off the table and suddenly popped up and flew around angrily. Its little wings giving off the light.

I laughed happily.

"Told you." He sat down at the table.

"How is the egg?" Not really caring as much as I should have. I just wanted to look at him.

He sighed. "It's really close."

"You look like an expectant father." I chided him.

He smiled. "I suppose I am, since it's a gold."

I reached across and grabbed his hand. "It will be okay."

Gabe was about to answer when the gremlins rushed around and then towards the entrance to the greenhouse.

"What is it?"

"Something is out there." He said watching the gremlins.

"That dog thing again?" Squeezing his hand. The hair on the back of my neck prickled.

"I don't know. We need to get to the house."

He grabbed my hand and we ran from the greenhouse. The moon was just coming up over the eastern trees casting its light upon the forest. A warm breeze rushed passed us. Along the path towards the house, odors were beginning to swarm around us.

The stench of rotten eggs began to randomly intrude upon my nose. The back door was open and Mrs. Wasabi was in the kitchen. She looked up, concerned at our abrupt arrival.

The stench grew.

"What do you sense?" she asked without hesitation.

He shook his head. "The gremlins became agitated."

Mrs. Wasabi's concern grew.

Voices filtered in from the front room. I coughed, the stench was much stronger now.

"Gabe." I started but he had already gone into the living room. The stench was beginning to become so strong that it was making me nauseous. Finding my way to the living room, I was surprised to see Christian and two other young men I'd never seen before, standing talking to Brooke.

Standing behind Gabe, I put my hand to my head.

"Didn't you get my message?" Brooke was explaining to Christian. "I am so sorry that you made the trip out here."

Christian's easy smile seemed a bit strained to me. The other two men were watching Set, who sat in a chair a few feet from Brooke's left side.

My eyes were starting to water.

"No problem. I just wanted to come and see the most beautiful girl in the world." His charm seemed contrived to me as well.

Brooke blushed, of course, as Set rolled his eyes.

Unable to keep my head up, I let it fall into Gabe's left shoulder.

"JJ?" Gabe asked concerned.

"It reeks in here, Gabe. I can hardly breathe." I rolled my head slightly to the right. Christian was staring hard at me as Brooke blabbered on about something. Strong hands grabbed my shoulder.

Mrs. Wasabi pulled me off of his shoulder. "Gabe." She whispered.

It happened so fast that I didn't even see Gabe move across the room and bury a knife into the chest of the young man on Christian's left. Then, Christian struck out at Gabe, knocking him across the room. Stunned, Brooke stood there and would have been stabbed in the heart if Set hadn't gotten his hand up in the way of the blade.

Brooke gathered herself and her face contorted in rage. "You bastard. You used me! Who are you?" She stepped back.

"Just an interested party in your dragon egg."

At the mention of the egg, Brooke involuntarily glanced upstairs, giving its location away.

"Dragons are stupid." Christian's eyes turned a sizzling bright red as his companion changed. He slowly began to hunch over and fur grew from every part of his skin.

"Werebeasts?" Set said disappointed. "How pathetic."

He grabbed the werebeast and threw it across the room.

"Upstairs, JJ." Mrs. Wasabi pushed me toward the stairs. I stumbled forward still nauseated from the stench. Scrambling up the stairs, I fell into Mr. Wasabi's waiting arms. He quickly walked me down the hallway and into Brooke's room.

"What happened?" His concern written on his face.

The whole situation was beginning to blur, but I must have rattled on enough to give him enough information to satisfy him. The sound of an all-out bar brawl came from downstairs.

"What about Mrs. Wasabi?" Fresh air coming inform the open window was clearing my head.

"Don't worry about her." He assured me.

He sat me on the bed. The egg had changed colors. The pulsating swirling color was replaced by a low steady pulse of gold light. Mr. Wasabi picked the egg up and shoved it into my chest.

"Hold it." Turning towards the door.

The sounds of struggle were intensifying.

The warmth of the egg felt really good. It felt like an arm full of clothes just out of the dryer.

"Don't drop it. Keep it safe." He walked over to the door. Mr. Wasabi placed his ear on the door. The door suddenly kicked open knocking Mr. Wasabi to the ground.

Christian smiled at me. "Just give it to me JJ. No need to die for it."

I scrambled backwards. "What are you!?"

He slowly walked in. "None of your concern."

"But you grew up with me. We went to Apollo Academy together since we were twelve?" My back bumped up against the wall.

He smirked. "After all you have seen, been told, is it so unbelievable? We've know that the Wasabi's were handlers for a long time. We knew they would get a dragon egg sooner or later. That Gray Mage is stupid. Incompetent. She is so absorbed with her war on the Gods, that she has forgotten those that hate her." He smiled. "You wanted to see magic, JJ, isn't that right? Now you've seen it. Give me the egg." He rushed forward.

I screamed while kicking out at him. But I never hit him because Mr. Wasabi had a hold of his leg.

"Run!' He pulled Christian down making enough room for me to run past.

Running downstairs, the living room was a war zone with Gabe and Brooke fighting and Set tangling with two Doppelgangers. Mrs. Wasabi laid on floor in a pool of blood.

Brooke saw me. "Run to the greenhouse!"

I froze.

"Go!" she yelled.

Free of my paralysis, I raced out into the night and stopped in front of a thing I'd never seen before.

Incredibly tall, its body burned a deep red that was outlined in black. Wings like those of a bat hung loosely by its side. Hoofed feet, which burned with its own flame, stamped impatiently. A howl went up, an all too familiar howl and as the creature turned its hideous red eyes towards me, I sprinted not towards the greenhouse but out into forest.

As my story fades from my vision, and my declaration of love dwindles into the night, the jaws of the doppelganger rip into my body. My only regret is leaving my Dad alone. I can die knowing that Gabe would have been with me, but the heart ache my death will bring my dad is crushing me.

The doppelganger flings me to the side and my body rolls through the dirt like a rag doll but I never let go of the egg. The sound of a helicopter appears nearer but with the blood in my eyes and the agonizing pain coming from my torn leg, I didn't really pay attention. I try and drag myself with my right arm away from the doppelganger.

Looking over my shoulder, the doppelganger's eyes pierce the night. Gabe's name rolls over my lips along with apologies to my dad. Pain erupts in my left calf and when I'm flipped over involuntarily, the doppelganger's tentacle has a grip on it. My blood soaked eyes catch a glimpse of the creature from the back of the house running through and then out of the trees in a fiery burst of hell. Its hatred burns fiercely into my mind. I can't understand it.

While it moves towards me, the egg pulses even faster now with golden light and deep sadness breaks through all the pain. *I'm sorry I couldn't save you. I wonder what kind of dragon you would have been. Kind, like your half-brothers? I'm sorry you won't get to find out.*

I pull the egg closer to my chest and lay my head down on it.

Suddenly, a huge thump sounds behind me and I am thrown up into the air. I land back down on the ground in a heap. The pain in my leg lessens and when I am able to force my body to see behind me, another creature I'd only seen in movies has crushed the doppelganger under foot.

The black dragon lifts its head into the night and roars. Turning its own hate filled red eyes towards the creature, it rushes the other, grabbing it with its mouth and leaping into the air. In utter astonishment, the dragon rises into the sky faster than a jet plane, and when it reaches a height far above the forest floor, it drops the burning creature, creating a falling star. Then flames light the night sky and the falling star vanishes.

With a heavy head, I lay it down on the ground when Brooke's voice echoes through the forest.

"JJ! Where are you!?"

Brooke's voice sounds so good to me but the next one that breaks the night's silence fills me with incredible joy.

"Over here!"

Footsteps rush towards me making me begin to cry. Rough, strong hands lift my head up and disappoint erupts in me at seeing Brooke's face first, but then Gabe's face is right behind her.

"Don't you die on me, you bitch!" Brooke's tears drop on my face.

"Hello to you too." Smiling hurts my face.

Laying on my back, the egg on my chest, my vision begins to blur. "Will you remember to take care of my dad for me, Brooke? I know he sees you as his daughter too. I don't want him to be alone." I'm having trouble breathing.

"You can take care of him." She says to me. "Help is coming."

"Sure. I'm scared, Brooke." Tears run down my face. "What's waiting for me?"

Gabe's hand caresses my forehead. "Your mother, Jennifer."

To hear him use my proper name is nice. My fear subsides.

"I hope so."

"JJ." Brooke's voice breaks with emotion.

"Hey, it's okay." I begin, but the sound of a cracking shell stops me.

Long slender cracks begin to run along the length of the gold egg. Golden ooze seeps from them and the liquid feels warm as it reaches my chest. Slowly, but firmly, the little creature pushes its way out of its prison and more of the ooze spills onto me. I smile so hard at the little golden eyes watching me that my face hurts.

"Hey, little guy." My sight is beginning to cloud. "I'm glad I got to see you before I die."

"You are not dying, JJ!" Brooke yells, but I see Gabe's look as he shakes his head.

As the darkness comes to claim me, I feel Gabe take my hand.

"I love you, Jennifer."

I try and tell him I love him too, but the darkness consumes me. The sudden squeeze of my hand lets me know I did.

Epilogue

Really, you let her die?

In the clear night sky the moon shined in full brightness. The dark, deserted street, absorbed the moon's light leaving only a faint afterglow of light. A black car pulled up to the curb in front of a warmly lit building. Cloaked shadows moved away from the car like they were afraid of what was lurking inside. Despite its black color, the car appeared bright and shiny, a beacon even in the dark.

Like a castle gate, the passenger back door opened with a slow deliberate movement that was neither hurried nor slow. When it was fully extended, a muscular leg stepped out onto the sidewalk but was quickly covered by the gray cloak that dropped to the top of the occupant's leather boots.

Rising up out of the car, the gray hooded person looked both ways down the empty sidewalk. Satisfied, the cloaked figure moved with steps of confidence and power that couldn't be masked by the outer garments of the cloak. As the person moved up to the lit double sliding doors, the figure's face was lost in the depths of the hood, despite the heavily lit doorway.

The doors silently opened with the slightest whoosh of air escaping into the night. The figure started to step forward but stopped and turned its head slightly to the left. In the shadows of the corner of the building, what appeared to be wispy white strands of spider silk, floated in space. The design could have been mistaken for the shape of a head, but nothing appeared in the middle of the white strands.

"This is your fault." The gray cloaked figure accused quietly. "You and he should have let me finish them."

"We were trying to protect your soul." The void between the strands answered in a raspy female voice. "It's not too late."

"That is for sure." The strong female voice inside the cloak chuckled. "Tell him, because of this, the Law has been violated. We finish this now. We'll see whose vision will prevail."

"We did not know they had acted. They did this on their own. The Law, for us, has not been violated." The concern of the void voice was readily apparent.

"They were allowed to act because you made me spare them. This makes them your responsibility. They violated the Law." The cloaked figure announced firmly. "After I destroy them for their transgressions, I'll be coming for you."

The void voice said nothing at the threat.

Satisfied the conversation was over, the gray cloaked figured walked steadily into the building while the double doors closed behind.

The gray cloaked figured strode through the white hallways unimpeded; individuals who came across the figure stepped back and bowed until they had passed. The elevator opened and several young women with brilliant white hair moved aside and bowed with deep respect. A quick incline of the cloaked figures head acknowledged their respect. The doors closed on the elevator and opened again several floors later. The cloaked figure moved down the hallway and came to a room, stuffed with people.

Mr. Wasabi was the first to notice the cloaked figure in the doorway. He immediately jumped to his feet and bowed. When the others noticed, they too rose to their feet and bowed.

"How is she?" The cloak figure asked a man in a white lab coat.

"Mistress, she is fine. Your quick action saved her life." His voice announced confidently.

Brooke rushed forward dropping to her knees and placed her head on the covered clasped hands of the cloaked figure.

"Mistress, my loyalty and life are yours. I cannot express my deepest love for you in saving my friend." Tears dropped to the floor.

"Brooke." Mr. Wasabi hissed but a shake of the cloaked figure's head silenced him.

"Very uncharacteristic for a blue to show such emotion." The cloaked figure stroked Brooke's blue hair with a pale hand. "It is a pleasure to see. Love of friends is important if we are to win. But I didn't save your friend, Brooke. That little dragon did."

The gold dragon that had hatched earlier, sat on JJ's chest. Her chest rose quietly up and down in a smooth rhythm.

"If he hadn't hatched on her chest and had some of his fluid spill onto her, she would certainly be dead. The fluids from a dragon's egg has special properties, Brooke. Save your gratitude for him."

"But without your portis to the hospital…" Brooke started, but the cloaked figure stopped her.

"We are family." She turned to Mr. Wasabi.

"My deepest condolences on your wife, Toyo. She was a premier protector." The cloaked figure dipped her head.

"She gave her life protecting others. That is all she ever wanted." He said stoically but he couldn't hide the tear that fell from his face.

"Who were those people, Mistress?" Gabe said from JJ's bedside. He had a hold of her hand.

"A mistake, Gabriel." The Mistress's voice reverberated around the room. "A mistake that will soon be remedied. Kerilink, time to go home."

The baby gold dragon took one long look at JJ's sleeping face, and then on wobbly wings flew from the bed to the Mistress's shoulder.

"What about JJ. Will she be willing to help?" The Mistress asked.

Brooke jumped right in. "Yes, Mistress. She has been told and pledged her loyalty to us."

The gold dragon squeaked with pleasure as the Mistress's head nodded in approval.

"Good." The Mistress turned to leave.

"Gray mage?" Gabe called out.

The Gray Mage stopped but didn't turn around. "Yes?"

"Will you give my deepest thanks to Set. I know how hard it was for him to return to his true form."

The Gray Mage's shoulders moved with mirth. "Think nothing of it Gabriel. He's already returned to Japan and began his hibernation to return to his human form. And in a hundred years, he'll be just as he was. As for you two; Brooke, I'll need you in Japan at the end of summer."

"Yes, Mistress." Brooke replied.

"Gabe, I'll be sending you and Mr. Wasabi a young Dimidius. A green. He's very special. Teach him."

"Yes, Mistress." Mr. Wasabi said.

"And JJ?" Gabe asked.

"Just love her."

With that, the Gray Mage left the room.

The End